KU-215-511

PENGUIN BOOKS
Running Away From Home

Rachel McAlpine was born in 1940 in Fairlie, South Canterbury. She is the third daughter of Celia and the Reverend David Taylor. Her grandparents were Christabel Wells, Roy Twyneham, Dorothy Warburton and Archdeacon Frederick Taylor, all of Christchurch. She has five sisters and four children.

Rachel McAlpine is a full-time writer. She is the author of a number of books of poetry: *Lament for Ariadne* (1975), *Stay at the Dinner Party* (1977), *Fancy Dress* (1979), *House Poems* (1980), *Recording Angel* (1983). Two plays have been published: *The Stationary Sixth Form Poetry Trip* (1980) and *Driftwood* (1985). Her first novel, *The Limits of Green*, was published by Penguin in 1986.

Running Away From Home

Rachel McAlpine

PENGUIN BOOKS

Penguin Books (N.Z.) Ltd, 182–190 Wairau Road,
Auckland 10, New Zealand
Penguin Books Ltd, Harmondsworth,
Middlesex, England
Penguin Books, 40 West 23rd Street,
New York, N.Y.10010, U.S.A.
Penguin Books Australia Ltd, Ringwood,
Victoria, Australia
Penguin Books Canada Limited, 2801 John Street,
Markham, Ontario, Canada L3R 1B4

First published 1987

Copyright © Rachel McAlpine 1987

Typeset in Compugraphic California
by Edsetera Book Productions Ltd
in association with Typocrafters Ltd, Auckland

Printed in Hong Kong

To my children,
Geoffrey, Kate, Ben and Diana

This is a work of fiction. However, in Chapters 10 and 11, the natural beach building techniques devised by Michael Smither are accurately described.

one

For the first white generations of immigrants to the Sleeping Islands, the name 'Rose' had power. It comforted people who remembered cottage gardens with delphiniums, larkspur, cornflowers: all the floppy pastels that softened the shock of lukewarm weather. By the time Fern was born, 'Rose' sounded dated and vulgar to her mother, who looked closer to home for a name.

Fern was aware that her name could shape her nature through the response of others. The word 'fern' had a furry, cobwebby feel in the mouth. People would hear the name and fill up with fine green wings, with fringes and probes from the ferns they knew. Unwillingly they stepped from dry sunlight into the dappled chill of native forest. They remembered mossy banks dripping with ferns, or treetrunks feathered with parasites or fallen logs grown glossy. Or they saw treefern, sprung like green blood from punctured arteries of the earth, poised and pouring overhead. They felt water dribbling or rippling, cicadas fizzing, or songbirds threading glass beads along their ribs. And in whatever form the fern entered their minds, it brought an expectation: the shape of the fern is so open and so dynamic, we expect it at any moment to be wounded or explode.

At thirty-five already, Fern had never felt her own personality. She would put a hand inside her head and fumble around for it. She would read novels and biographies, and admire the clear outlines of the characters: all had a heroine who was distinguished in

1

some way from other people. She looked at her friends and saw how crisp they were. But in herself she could feel only the pool of air held in the hollow of her greenery and never the fronds themselves, and certainly not that future frond, coiled tough and brown in her centre, waiting only for a push from within.

She would look for a long time in the mirror, and see a head, a body, two of most things, one mouth, one nose, the usual. She thought this was how her friends would describe her to a stranger: 'Oh, Fern is all right. She is the usual sort of person.' It was arrogance, because she conceived herself as the norm from which all other people deviated. It was blindness; and loneliness.

She couldn't imagine any other way to be, until she was forced to imagine being dead. She had accidentally married a man who always told her what to do; or perhaps she had done it on purpose. Perhaps they had both had a purpose. Every night for seventeen years he had rammed into her as if he were digging a posthole, and he had never looked at another woman. For that matter he had never really looked at her. He hadn't otherwise assaulted her, but she gradually became afraid for her life. His name was Alister Willmott. They lived on one of the old volcanoes of Northcity, in a fashionable suburb.

Her life had ominously grown nauseous to her husband and to their daughter Dorothy. She was shrinking in that area she sensed as vaguely associated with her personal behaviour. She would have blamed only herself, if she had noticed a self to blame.

Sometimes she and Dorothy used to picnic on a lonely west coast beach. The narrow gravel road was chiefly for the use of a farming family. If she hurried, impatient with dust and juddering, the car would skid on corrugations. After the last hill the track swooped down a straight stretch, turned right along cliff tops, and came close to the beach a few kilometres along. Fern favoured this wild, empty picnic spot, and Dorothy usually brought a friend.

Fern began to visit this beach alone. Six times on fine days she went for a solitary picnic, till it was accepted in their household as an unremarkable habit. Even this part of the plan used up almost all the courage she had preserved during seventeen years of marriage, and then, in a single day, she dipped heavily into her life supply.

That day, as Dorothy got ready for school, Fern packed herself a lunch she never intended to eat. Dry sandwiches; a piece of last Sunday's roast hogget, fridge-burned round the edges, something she'd normally have thrown away. She kissed Dorothy goodbye as usual, saying quite sincerely, 'Have a good day.' This was the day she was not going to turn right at the bottom of the hill.

Turning into the straight, Fern accelerated sharply. She knew the bottom of the cliffs off by heart: a vertical face of clay, fifteen metres high, dropped to a high tide smashing on black rocks. Her windows were wound open, her seat-belt tight, so that if the rocks failed to break her, the sea would swamp her lungs. At the crucial second, her hands of their own accord forced the steering wheel around and the car slewed wildly on two wheels, swinging on space. Then it swivelled into its own wave pattern from edge to edge of the road. Five times it hit one verge only to ricochet to the other, jumping out of her hands, skating on gravel. It took seconds which felt like minutes, and when it stopped at an acute angle on the crown of the road, Fern stopped too.

She undid her belt, opened the car door and fell out, and half crawled to the grass. There she sat with her head between grazed knees till blood was pumping at a nearly normal rate. So. Half an hour later she went back to the car for a barley sugar. At last she felt able to drive again, very very cautiously. The cows were shinier, the sky brighter, the earth shiftier than before.

'I've come this far. I might as well have my picnic,' she said to herself, and walked through a marshy paddock to the beach. Chewing the dry lunch and drinking her thermos of tea became a ceremony. It was a duty and a celebration of the gutsy body which had defied her. 'Perhaps I didn't need a personality,' thought Fern. 'The body may be enough.' Now her remaining option was a deliberate, accusing sort of suicide. Or was some other move possible?

She paddled her feet in the sea because she needed to. The tide was beginning to go out. As the waves thinned and slowed and sucked back from their high point, her feet made a sloppy spot and sank into it. Light was simmering in the water. Ripples twanged across the surface like notes running through a harp. A man with round edges and stained clothes and ears like old sandals walked towards her along the beach. She didn't feel ready for people, but he asked, 'Will you give me a lift back to town?'

It was time she left, so they got into her car. She said, 'I had an accident. My breast is hurting.' The metal enclosing them created intimacy. He held her left breast in his left hand for a while and the throbbing waned. Peace rinsed into her in shallow pulses; so easy, so fluent, so kind. He took his hand away and left the painlessness, and also a small new pain because of the lack of his hand.

As she drove away from the beach he said, 'I know you're not in a mood to talk. But my name is Orlando Proddleigh.' She dropped him in the city and on the way home she had a new idea: living. If she couldn't die without embarrassing her husband, very well, she would embarrass him and live.

At half past two she was back at her home. It looked like somebody else's home already, a solid, squared-off

4

mansion large enough for people to avoid one another inside, with a broad drive, plenty of lawns, and the oldest trees in a tree-green street. The kitchen was bossy, the dining room heavy, the bathroom too clean, the master bedroom a place of fright. Only Dorothy's territory seemed occupied by its rightful owner. Fern filled a suitcase with clothes. She took a heap of towels and sheets that would never be missed. She looked again at shelves and walls of ostentation. She gathered a favourite pair of saucepans, a photo album, a vegetable peeler and a whisk – and then she stopped. It seemed that no one on earth could require anything more, if they had freedom. Freedom! The word sizzled. Then as a greedy afterthought, she seized two pillows and eiderdowns. Enough – more than enough already; almost enough to clutter her up forever.

Her life had been lived like a dream in which the dreamer carelessly slops from one identity to another and another, is attacker and victim and bystander in turn, or all at once. Awake, Fern had never learned her lines. Today she said to herself, 'I have done something. I am both reckless and banal.' Her last glance round the house was nervous, but her going had barely dented this living-machine. She trembled as if committing a crime.

She drove to Dorothy's school and caught her attention as she walked out the gate. Dorothy got in the car and Fern declared, 'I'm leaving your father today. Do you want to come with me or stay with him?'

'You could have warned me, Mum!'

'No – I couldn't – I couldn't. I just couldn't.'

'That's just running away, Mum,' said Dorothy, horrified.

'That's right, dear. Do you want to come? Can't you decide?'

'Of course not,' snapped Dorothy.

Fern sighed, 'I'll drive you home anyway.' Still, she had enjoyed saying 'your father' in that very distant manner.

She wrote a note at the kitchen table: 'Alister. I have decided to live apart from you. My lawyer will be in touch. Fern.

'P.S. You are a rotten prick and you hated me so don't pretend you're sorry I've gone. You never were happy with me. Now's your chance to find out if you can be happy without me or whether you're just a man with a rotten temper. You seem to think I ruined your life somehow so really I'm just doing the decent thing.'

The letter surprised her. She was stamping her foot and going 'Ber ber ber!' Even so, it seemed too defensive so for good measure she added, 'Go poop yourself.' The spelling of 'poop' looked wrong. It was the rudest thing she could think of but perhaps he wouldn't understand. She crossed it out and wrote instead, 'Go poo your pants.'

Dorothy imagined the house without her mother. She rushed through her room gathering up posters and clothes and books, and stuffed them into the car.

'It never was you I was leaving,' said Fern, and a bone moved out of her heart where it had been paining. And Dorothy wrote at the bottom of her mother's note, 'I love you Dad and I will come and visit you often. But I think it's best to go with Mum. Love, Dot.'

Hilary was the friend that Fern automatically turned to. Hilary kept the key to her kitchen door under a rusty sardine tin full of cacti, and when she came home from work that night, there were Fern, and Dorothy, and a load of their worldly possessions.

There was a lot of raging and crying and comforting to be done, which Dorothy watched, half in, half out. Hilary was wild.

'You mean you actually planned to kill yourself without even telling me? You bitch!'

'I couldn't even tell myself, Hilary. It was supposed to be a surprise all round.'

'You do realise you've been completely off your head, don't you, Fern? Accident indeed!'

'It seemed quite reasonable at the time,' said Fern.

They were welcome to stay in Hilary's blunt, spartan house for as long as it took to establish themselves somewhere else. Fern had an early bath and saw that her left breast had been dramatically bruised by the steering wheel. It glowed blue and topaz and green and pink, patches of colour fluctuating in front of her eyes. It didn't hurt at all, and yet she had been sensing it all afternoon. She thought it was very beautiful, her warm marble breast, like a magic pumpkin. It was slightly swollen. She slept a long night.

Since Fern 'had to' get married at seventeen, she had been married exactly half her life. And since she 'had to' stay home and clean and cook for her husband and daughter and house, she had never had a paid job. Her lawyer said Alister was only too eager to sell the house and consummate their separation. On one level, he was sad that she was gone. On another, he was relieved, for what she wrote was true; he'd always wished he could have had the daughter without the trap from which she had sprung. Only a few weeks earlier he had bought a luxury town house, ostensibly as an investment but actually with divorce in mind. Puzzled by her premature defection, he nevertheless behaved fairly. Like her, he felt guilt and grief, which he alternately wallowed in and denied.

But we shall leave him to his quite satisfactory fate and attend to Fern, who now became caught up in the great property syndrome.

When she took two saucepans from the joint family home, Fern had felt like a thief. She wondered if Alister would send a policeman to reclaim them. Then she would

7

think bitterly of certain cushions she had embroidered. She deeply resented having left them behind. Fern would wake in the night, angry about those mauve cushions.

Hilary lost patience and said, 'For God's sake, Fern, go out and make yourself some more!' And so she set out to buy a house, and power, demolishing once and for all the role of silly woman which in the past she had condoned. It was like the dress her husband had chosen the Christmas after the baby was born. A red dress of watered silk, with a deep neckline. It stuck to her like burning, bubbling skin. When she wore it, men crowded round her, and Alister beamed. For the sake of peace she had tried to believe in this sort of Fern, but not with all her heart. Nowadays, she quoted 'reckless and banal' as her new, individual label. But if her breast was doing the thinking, it called her 'brave and practical'. She set out to buy a house with half the proceeds of the matrimonial mansion.

She became obsessed with house-buying, spending every Wednesday, Friday, Saturday and Monday reading the property pages, phoning agents, and peering at other people's houses. Hilary and Dorothy lived on the fringe of her obsession. It was a symbol of her independence and by definition temporary. She learned that sellers will always ask for more than they expect to receive but less than they think their house is worth. She learned about concrete piles, titles, plumbing, insulation, and the angle of the sun in winter. She found that the word 'cash' gave her an advantage over all other buyers.

Perhaps she was over-finicky, but remember, it was only the second major decision of her life. Each house represented a way of living. She couldn't visualise living anywhere but with Hilary, who was starting to crave for privacy by the time a short-tempered agent showed Fern an odd building that was coming up for auction. It was on a hill, in an expensive area. (Fern was used to expensive areas.) Fifty years old and very sound, it had been built as two flats for the use of reporters from the *Northcity Herald*. After a long rent freeze, the building was a liability. Inside it was shabby and dark with brown-stained wallpapers. Yet two rooms, at the ends of meaningless corridors, had huge windows with clear views of city and harbour. Access was by an overgrown track, parking would be tricky, there was no garage; Fern's now-educated nose smelt a bargain. She saw where a jumble of gimcrack walls divided the place into coarse, irrational shapes. The auction took place on a day of hailstones and high winds, when landlords were selling as fast as they could and mortgages were elusive. Fern's bid was accepted.

Hilary loathed the place and Dorothy refused to move. Fern employed a builder and acted as his labourer, carrying rubble down to his truck, endlessly up and down with timber and paint and tools and plasterboard. She had never been so tired or so pleased with herself. She could afford to knock down dividing walls, to spread paint and carpet around, and to put new vinyl flooring in her two kitchens and bathrooms (which remained, to put it politely, primitive). When she moved in, Dorothy and Hilary found her living in a place which still seemed very odd and not exactly convenient, but with a white, airy ease about it. Her obsession had paid off; she was smug, with a park, the sea and the city within reach. She had brought her share of the family furniture out of storage, and Dorothy was not too proud to move in.

two

Here we are at Chapter Two and I know what you're thinking: what do you care about the domestic arrangements of this person Fern? By her own admission she is a nobody, and her only advance after leaving her long-suffering husband is to have grown acquisitive and house-proud. Perhaps you feel like giving up on the book, although heaven knows I've tried to make it interesting for you. Only a vague memory of her encounter with the man on the beach has kept you involved this far.

It is possible that I'm projecting the irritation I felt with her at that period and that you, in all innocence and sympathy, have warmed to her by now. I'd better come clean: I'm Dorothy, usually known to my friends as Dot. I've been trying to write out of empathy for my mother as she was at the time, although you may have picked up a certain ambivalence. I must say I feel more relaxed now that I'm out in the open. I'd better backtrack for the record.

I was born 'prematurely' as they said in those days, and my father never forgave Fern. He was difficult, I admit. He was always very curt to her, or super-polite, straining ostentatiously to do the decent thing to a woman he considered stupid in every thought, word and deed. He wasn't like that to me; he was proud of me and I was the apple of his eye, or even the pineapple. But if it hadn't been for my girlfriend Maureen, I'd never have known that marriage could be OK.

As soon as I was old enough for the full horror of my

parents' marriage to sink in, I felt personally responsible. Can you blame me? I hated what Dad was doing to Fern: he had been chopping away at her for so long, there was almost nothing left. But to me he was generous, not just with money but with encouragement. At the same time he managed to transmit a certain amount of his own contempt to me, so that while I wished my mother could be happy, I believed she was not capable of looking after herself. For a long time I considered myself much more of a strong, interesting person than her. That was my father's dubious gift to me, something in my past I have to live with. I couldn't urge her to leave him because I had no faith in her. I loved her but she had never done anything in life except submit to bullying and run the household in a manner that fell far short of my father's expectations, so how could I imagine her coping with real life on her own? I removed myself from home as much as possible, by going to Maureen's and by taking up tramping.

It wasn't true that he was always internally sneering. There were some days when I could see he badly wished to be kind; but the patterns couldn't be broken. Why am I telling you all this again? It's like picking a scab, and it doesn't matter, it doesn't matter. I must learn to cut corners or this story will never begin.

Anyway, in my last year at school Fern had been degenerating, most probably at the prospect of my leaving home. But what could I do? I acquitted myself by judging Fern. I had very conventional ideas about marriage: people who get married, they know what they're in for. If they don't like it, they shouldn't have got married in the first place. I'd worked it all out you see, the way you can at seventeen. One thing about my home life, it made me determined to make a good marriage myself. I figured I could learn from their mistakes.

Well, when she turned up at school that afternoon, with her car full of clothes and two saucepans, I was impressed. She was like a dandelion forcing its way through the asphalt, and never mind if the traffic was bound to squash her again. She half assumed I'd come and live with her, which was by no means my first impulse. I didn't want to sacrifice my Big Daddy's affection and support. Everybody has to look after number one. Also, I liked my room, my home – I'd lived there all my life, and it was mine! But I thought I could easily enough bring Dad round to approve of me again; meanwhile, without my support I imagined Fern would collapse. In view of later events I blush to write that. But think of the events beforehand! You make decisions as best you can. When everything impels you to an overwhelming decision, it is usually true that one vital fact is being withheld from you. To compensate, a few strong facts and feelings tramp round your head, crowding the others out. You decide, and that's the essential thing.

My altruism had its limits and I was not prepared to live in a grotty old flat, no matter what the location.

Well, brace yourself: there is still more to come about house and garden. Skip it if you like, I wouldn't blame you. But first take note that it is, I promise, relevant. This story is really about the ownership of land in a big way: who owns the planet? What are the limits of possession and responsibility? It's all reproduced on a global scale, so if you lack the urge to read about the neighbours' wandering willy, think of it as a metaphor for the acid rain that crosses borders, killing foreign forests – just to give you one example.

Oh, look what I did! Truly, that was worthy of the General. You were quite justifiably bored, and what did I do? I tried to bully you into regarding my mother's fussiness as a glorious concern for the environment. How pompous! I beg your pardon. I haven't written a story before, and I find there are certain problems, like where to begin. You see, Fern began as a boring person and that's the fact of the matter; but she does turn into somebody far from boring. If I don't show her being boring, how will you appreciate the change? I should warn you, she doesn't get to ride on the mangrove till Chapter Five. But then I think that the rhythm of life is not so much 'badorm . . . badorm . . . badorm . . . ' as 'Slow. Slow. Quick quick slow' and that's the rhythm of this story. There are ice ages as well as earthquakes; and at the very times you are going backwards in the quickstep, you are the one who is out in front, even if you can't see where you're going.

I suppose I'm just impatient to get to the bits where I am the centre of attention. In my time I have written a lot of reports and essays, all supposedly objective. I had intended to tell this that way, with the glad eye of God and its perfect (though still one-eyed) vision. But now, I've put my cards on the table. At least I can say: 'This is real, this story, even though I've had to make some of it up. I'm a real person, I have a real mother, the Sleeping Islands is a real country, and our story is a matter of life and death to you.'

When we moved into the flats Fern's first preoccupation was the inside. She shifted furniture, bought plants and hangings, arranged and rearranged until the squalid parts were disguised (more or less) as quaint. After a few weeks things were roughly settled down, but I can't say it ever looked exactly right. I suppose she was straining for something that would feel familiar. Never mind, it was comfortable and pleasing to the eye, with a very deliberate mix of blues and greens and violets. Then Fern turned her attention to the grounds. Poor dear, she tried to reproduce the essence of our old garden. There, almost an acre of lawn clung tightly to the contours of our land, sealing it off from weeds and other intruders. We had lived in a personal park, English oaks and crew-cut grass inside a high white wall. Fern's attempt to make a serene retreat on a scrap of hilly suburb was a failure. What she achieved, with great effort, was tidiness. The lawn was tiny. Her trees were spindly. She planted agapanthus around the perimeter of her land till the house was trapped inside its own beard. Only the path looked pretty, always in a tangle of shiny taupata, looping and bending under the weight of its own grace.

In the course of her tidying, Fern compared her fence lines with an official map defining her boundaries. She was outraged to discover that the neighbours' driveway was partly on her property. She had some idea that this prevented her building a garage. She was a real pain at this time, because she had no money to build a garage anyway. And if she had, no doubt she and the neighbours could have come to some arrangement. Fern was beyond reason, possessive and mean-minded. It was a disease. Another symptom was her hysterical response to the wandering willy on the other side of her property. That house was rented to young people who didn't understand or care about rampaging weeds. Their wandering willy poked through the fence and trespassed under the agapanthus. She didn't feel safe. She was talking of getting her lawyer into action when thank heavens a distraction arose.

It was quite unfair of me to be so uppity about my mother, because at the time I could beat her hands down for cold-blooded materialism. If you call a man 'material'.

This was a year and a bit after my parents separated; I was in my second year at university. Work was top priority, but I kept a weather eye out for suitable guys. By suitable, I mean husband types. Unlike my friends I was not out for a good time: that could lead to accidents, like myself. I was willing to skip the good time, and while I wasn't frantic to get married, I knew what I wanted. Thus I began a Saturday-night-with-Charles habit. Quite often there was also Sunday dinner, a roast at one o'clock after church. His parents approved of me and I of them. All of us felt my relationship with Charles Menzies was progressing at the right pace.

Twice a year, Mr Menzies' law firm held a cocktail party. Charles generally attended, and he invited me. Mrs Menzies urged me to bring my mother. (It was an opportunity for them to evaluate her.) Surprisingly, Fern agreed to go. She had her hair set and sprayed, and dressed conscientiously in a frock with matching jacket. By now she had the assurance of a person who owns a house and has trouble with the neighbours. It rained softly, so her hair went frizzly. Her hair is rather nice when it goes fuzzy like that; it's like the brown fur on a new ponga frond. It showed that softness she had been trying to conquer.

At the cocktail party we met Jules Menzies, who was Charles's uncle. The family was proud of him but also embarrassed, because of his pale blue suit. Until recently he had been a partner in the law firm, working chiefly as a director of numerous companies. Now he had a full-time commitment as Director of the newly established Department of Philosophy, of which more later. He was not like Charles's father, not one bit. He held his whole body tight, like Mr Universe. He used his bright blue eyes like a knife and fork. His ears were small and tidy. He exuded influence and a calculated intimacy; his self-taught charisma had brought him a crackling power.

Introduced to Fern, he tipped his head forward when she spoke and his eyes tamped hers down and didn't let them up. At intervals he returned to fill her glass, although it was not his responsibility, standing just a trifle closer than was strictly comfortable. These were the gimmicks he generally used to bind a woman to himself. Fern was the type of woman he specialised in, although he did prefer them married. The world, he was very aware, was full of middle-class women at the peak of mature beauty, neglected by their boorish husbands. He did not know her story but he could guess it all bar the address. Well fed, well groomed, not yet too fat or too thin or wrinkled round the neck, such women were always cravenly grateful for his honest assessment of their potential.

'I'm very interested in you as a person, Fern,' he said. 'I'd like to know you.' So would I, she thought, frightened. 'Tell me about your childhood.' But it was time to go home. 'May I take you to dinner? No?' He looked sad. 'Are you booked for this evening? No? Don't you like me?'

'I don't know you,' said Fern.

'The very best reason for going out with me,' said Jules. 'Let's get to know each other, Fern.'

She didn't exactly want to but how could she knock back Charles's uncle? It was a new idea, going out with a man. He knew perfectly well that no one had told her she was beautiful and intelligent and capable and desirable for years and years and years, although it was all quite true. Over the coffee she had two conflicting impulses: 'Why not?' and 'But what would he think of my breast?' For her bruised breast had never healed. She had never gone to a doctor because it wasn't sore and she was rather proud of it. Whatever her self-image, it included this one very special attribute; but Jules might find it nasty.

Her mysterious reservations attracted him further, as is usual. He kissed her goodnight outside her front door, with a certain pressure on her pelvic bone. His arms around her were heavily muscled and he held her resolutely. After one kiss he released her without being asked and left, like an old-fashioned gentleman.

He was a busy man, and he conducted his affairs as efficiently as he did the Department of Philosophy. He brought to bear the same gifts for planning, timing, and cost-effectiveness. He gave her his prospectus, made a modest bid for her, and acquired her like a small subsidiary company that would more or less run itself.

When the time came to make love, the breast problem resolved itself. Jules liked kissing, deep and sloppy. He turned off the lights. His fingers played around Fern's hair and neck and he kissed her ears with breathy attention to detail. It gave her a slithery feeling, like swallowing too big a bite of hard-boiled egg. She would have liked to check them first for wax. In this fastidious relationship such things bothered her.

Clearly he wanted her to reciprocate; bravely she began to nibble and suck one of his ears, and it was squeaky clean. He went into controlled spasms, fluttering short of lift-off like a copulating butterfly. This encouraged her, and she licked the maze of his ear while it contracted under her tongue and thickened imperceptibly until she could not recognise its shape. It swelled to fill her mouth, pressing against the roof with tender flesh, humming; then a powerful juice spurted, like yoghurt flavoured with camphor. He sighed and nestled his swollen ear against her neck and she felt it slowly retract.

Fern was puzzled. She was ignorant and inexperienced as far as sex was concerned. The magazines I brought home told her, roughly, that all was normal, all was condoned in the search for pleasure. They were an effective antidote to anxiety.

She didn't undress for Jules beyond her slip, which amply covered her breasts. Sometimes his hand would stroke or pat the lace over her bosom, for it was in his interest to give her pleasure. Her left breast would nudge him off, but her right breast allowed it. As they grew more familiar, he would withdraw his ear from her mouth and worm it into her cunt for a more orthodox intercourse. At such a time she felt her first orgasm and thought, 'That's nice. That must be an orgasm.' On special nights he gave each ear a turn, democratically.

Naturally I knew nothing of this at the time. I simply found Jules Menzies at our house in the morning sometimes. Mostly he preferred to leave at midnight like Cinderella. Usually they ate out, but I began to feel that Fern's accommodation existed chiefly to accommodate him. Well, it was time I left, anyway. I joined two girlfriends in their flat, to gain experience in cooking and house management. Theoretically I could do this already, but living with a mother it can never be so.

This sexual business may sound very intimate but that's not really the case. You could never have said Fern and Jules were close to each other. He liked her to listen to him and she was an A-grade listener. But without her really noticing the pattern of it, every time it grew late and she felt it was her turn to talk, there she was with an ear in her mouth.

All the same she gained a good deal. While Jules only ever gave her the top layer of his thoughts, still she learned a lot about the way the world is run. Also, he sent her to an expensive hairdresser who emancipated her frothy hair, and banned the nervous matronly make-up that she used like a corset. For the first time you could feel the full force of her eyes, which looked as if they had been put in upside down. They had always looked queer to me, but now she simply let us see them, and I had to admit their flaring shape, twisting like flames, was special. They were still hesitating eyes. Jules bought her a few, key, high-fashion clothes to wear, and she was not Mrs Willmott any more, although she was not yet Fern.

Jules knew what he was doing, all right, when he picked up my insecure mother in her decent dress. Oh yes, indeed he did. I wasn't pleased when he made me perceive her as a stunning *ingénue*-sophisticate. I left home, grumbling that he was wrong for her. And so he was, but the worst imaginable man is sometimes the right man at the time and ultimately Jules was responsible for all the good things in her life, if you care to look at it that way.

He did let down his guard one night to reveal a few personal secrets. He felt his cock was sacred and so he used it only for procreation. He donated sperm to the Northcity Fertility Clinic for their *in vitro* fertilisation programme. They had also used his sperm successfully for artificial insemination by a donor, so that in fact he was the father of eleven children. This moved him as nothing else did. He had been immensely sad when he'd heard some years earlier about the unhappiness of couples unable to conceive. Although he had never married, he identified with their agony. He read of ingenious medical attempts to solve their problem, and reverently volunteered his sperm. Not many men pass the test, he said. Would-be donors are checked for physical health and must be normal in every detail (but nobody tickled his ears). No congenital illness or deformities or alcoholism or schizophrenia or tuberculosis, or any one of forty-three other problems in the family was acceptable. Smokers were out. Intelligence was a factor. Their spunk was minutely examined for the quality and quantity of sperm, which had to be nicely shaped, and swift wriggly swimmers. Jules was one of the elect: he had licence to procreate. Sex was his hobby, but fatherhood was a vocation. He made friends with a technician in the clinic who passed on secret information, so that he knew the names and addresses of his children. This was illicit knowledge, and it was supposed to be impossible for the children or their parents to discover his

19

identity. Also, no person was meant to beget more than three times by these methods, so that the chance of incest was limited somewhat. But Jules's friend knew how he loved to start babies, so she had manipulated the odds, even after one baby was born without genitals. Surgeons gave her a vagina, but no uterus, and blamed the mother.

Once Fern accompanied Jules to an auction of First People's artefacts where he had gone on behalf of a contact in RUSA. He bought a famous greenstone hand club. History dozed in its milky green body, for jade accepts the sweat, the self of all who handle it, so that when it is old and much travelled it is full of humanity, for better or for worse. Its shape was precisely, beautifully right; it was the fundamental shape that any club, and particularly this particular club, should be. It had been used by one great chief after another, stolen, buried, seized in battle, appropriated by a white land-grabber in the wars, presented to a Governor, inherited by first sons. The Sleeping Islands Museum offered a price that was substantial. The auctioneer thought it was all over, but Jules raised the bid too high for anyone to follow. After the sale two other aspirants added their funds to the Museum's, and the Sleeping Islands Art Gallery doubled the combined figure; with this consolidated fund the Museum offered to buy the treasure from Jules, who smiled and declined. The next week he carried it personally to his client in Washington, and returned as if he had been to the dairy for a paper.

Their affair lasted two years. It was meticulously controlled by Jules. As a rule they met once a week and did not telephone in between, except briefly to make arrangements. Jules never took a holiday as such, but a Cabinet Minister invited him to his beach house for two days at Easter, suggesting he bring Fern along to keep his wife company while they were talking over policy for the all-important Department of Philosophy. It was Jules's wish to enlarge the Department and broaden its scope of operations; he spent the two days convincing the Minister of this and exploring with him ways and means and implications. He used immense confidence as his chief persuader: a barely concealed expectation that any sensible chap was bound to see things his way, once he'd heard the full story from Jules. His words came out like silver foil; they wrapped round and round his listeners till they were just wincing to carry out his wishes.

His was a chosen personality, adopted in his youth after a close scrutiny of world leaders. He was good-looking and broad shouldered, and used a sunlamp at home to make his teeth seem whiter. He grafted on to his naturally humourless nature one eccentricity: he never wore grey, but kept a wardrobe of flamboyance. It was an outrageous risk, since he had to overcome all the laws of power dressing. But it worked. In any assembly of the influential, his cream silk suits and pastel ties at first aroused disdain. But now that his accomplishments had earned respect, his pert appearance diverted those same people, who treated him like a mascot or a pot plant or a woman. They let down their guard, they revealed everything to him, they wooed him, they indulged him. And so with a curious blend of assumed aggressiveness and assumed naivety, Jules Menzies had acquired power.

They arrived at the beach house on Friday afternoon. By Saturday afternoon, although the men were largely involved in exclusive discussion, Jules and Fern had spent more time together than on any previous occasion and he was getting on her nerves. By evening she loathed him with a wild irrational loathing. By the time they left on Sunday afternoon she had identified the source of her revulsion: Jules had an immense contempt for all women, including herself, and once the penny dropped, all his words and deeds confirmed this. Just as Alister had required her to be housekeeper, mother, suction pump and silly woman, so Jules's only use for her was as a sexual housekeeper and a non-controversial, decorative escort for occasions like this. To Jules, all social occasions were political opportunities, even a restaurant tête-à-tête, and she had been groomed to enhance his image. He was so much subtler than Alister in his contempt that it might have escaped her indefinitely if not for this prolonged exposure. I won't bother you with the details of her analysis, except to say that he patronised the Minister's brilliant wife.

She concealed her feelings with difficulty and on their next outing made a prepared speech. She stressed the pleasure she had got out of their affair and confessed she had found herself yearning for a stronger bond with him. To spend a whole weekend with him, as if she were his wife, had been traumatic, and she felt unable to go back to their weekly arrangements. Her feelings had reached the point of no return: it was all or nothing now. He looked impatient and irritated. She hastened to add that she knew this was inappropriate and unfair to him, and therefore suggested they end the liaison. She spoke formally as if proposing a vote of thanks. He agreed with her solution and expressed regrets.

Then she said she felt the need of some new interest to fill up the emptiness in her life created by their separation. As his Department was now expanding, did he think there might be a job for her there? One which would not necessitate the pain of continued close contact with him, naturally. She felt that over the past two years he had grown to know her qualities, which were not so obvious as to make her highly employable on the open market.

She had learned this diabolical manipulation from him, and it succeeded. There were situations vacant, it was true, and one of them was hers within a week. Without explanation, she changed her name to Willnott.

three

Fern turned up for work the next Monday as arranged. The Department of Philosophy used the top six floors of a Darth Vader building, all grilles and black vertical facings. The wide front steps led off in three directions, to Northcity's main shopping street and a couple of trendy lanes. There were six lifts, including a slow one for goods only and an express for the top floor exclusively. There were two stairways; the broader one was used for fire-drills and toilets and the other was a design error. Its outlets had been misjudged; rather than redesign every floor to accommodate exits to the rogue stairwell, the engineers had cut their losses. The top floor had a door to the stair, but it was superfluous.

In the commuter rush along Queen Street Fern felt she was the only person in the city with a destination that confused and excited her. Inside the Department's building the huge foyer went up three storeys; she felt spied on. The overwhelming mass of people passing seemed at once knowing, and cruelly indifferent. She asked a stranger, 'Where do I find the Minor Provincial Division, please?' She was half regretting that she hadn't arranged to arrive with Hilary, who now worked in the Department herself, along with five hundred other people. But it was the first paid job she had ever had in her life, and she wanted to give Hilary a surprise.

She met her supervisor at the reception desk and he led her into her work area. The whole floor was one open room, apart from the stem full of lifts, stairs, toilets and foyers that ran through the centre of the building, like a bolt around which the fourteen office floors were screwed. Wherever she looked there were white plastic cells, each with a working body at a white plastic desk, each hooked into the next cell and the next. It was like an acre of gleaming dentures. The same modular desks could be re-arranged to crowd more people in, or to give more space to the privileged. As a new staff member Fern was placed at the back of a row, furthest from the windows and nearest the draughts of the constantly opening door.

She was shown the instruction manual, the tea room, the toilets, and the last year's staff magazine. She spent hours trying to come to grips with the manual, which supposedly explained how to do the job. At morning tea she hoped to find Hilary but discovered that different divisions had different tea-drinking slots, with the timetable further complicated by Interdivisional Meetings. A bell rang bossily when her allotted ten minutes were over. Moreover, as an occasional smoker, Hilary would be ostracised in a separate small room with open windows. Fern tried telephoning Hilary on the internal phone, but she was not at her desk at the time, the phones were in constant demand for serious business and at least twenty people would have heard her conversation anyway. She went back to the incomprehensible manual.

After the second tea break she asked her neighbour, Ailsa, for a little help. Ailsa frowned and said, 'But you should have had the beginners' manual! How do they expect you to understand that old thing?' She called out across the field of white cavities: 'Anyone got a beginners' manual for Fern?' 'No!' the cry came back. Ailsa asked the supervisor; it seemed the manual was being revised and reprinted and all earlier models had been recalled and destroyed. 'Learn by doing, that's the best policy,' he said. 'Tomorrow we'll start you off on a real job.'

Disoriented in the extreme, Fern visited Hilary that evening and complained. Hilary calmed her down.

'The job isn't hard. Look around tomorrow. Most of those people aren't brilliant: they are roughly as competent as you are. They all had to learn from scratch, because there is no precedent for this job or for this Department. My only advantage over you is that I've been there four months longer.' She wrote down a few brief, practical guidelines for Fern, told her to ask lots of questions, and arranged to meet her for lunch.

The next day Fern plugged into her socket feeling already a little at home, although she still didn't know what to do. Her supervisor, a toothy, stupid man, had to be reminded periodically of her existence, but the women who worked around her passed on small jobs and answered her laborious queries until she knew what to do and did it. She began to perform her tasks a little faster and occasionally glimpsed their relationship to other jobs. Within six weeks she could do what was required. She walked ten centimetres above the footpath, or so it felt, just from the pleasure of having a job and a pay slip. At last she was important, like other people. She loved everything about the job, except that she wished she understood what it was fundamentally for.

When the Department of Philosophy was set up it attracted idealists. By the time Fern enlisted, most of the visionaries had either left or changed into civil servants, more mindful of tea breaks than of ethics or logic and fully transferable to any other government department. Yet this radical new institution had been designed to overrule benignly all others, to solve all problems by referring to first principles; a case of back to basics in government. It was agreed that such a department would be more dynamic and influential than a constitution, which might lie inert in a drawer. In those days the Government was able, even eager, to dignify as law many petty directives to individuals who happened to get on the Prime Minister's nerves. It was not in the habit of contemplating any possible higher obligations. The Department of Philosophy was designed to act as national angel on the shoulder.

Of course, to put it mildly, this wasn't easy. Each problem had many facets. The human beings presenting their cases varied in eloquence, in needs, in cunning and in power. Few variables could be measured accurately in advance. Community spirit, the number of knots in blue gum, the future price of liquid petroleum gas on the international market – oh, thousands, millions of factors had to be taken into account and advice given on a huge variety of decisions. The basic principle was that the good of the Sleeping Islands as a whole should be the first consideration, balanced against the rights of the individual. By 'the good', the Department of Philosophy meant economic, physical and spiritual good, in that order. There was an elaborate taxonomy which subdivided these broad categories almost infinitely, made cross references and identified exceptions. Fern didn't have to be a computer expert herself, but was expected to clarify factors that a succession of computer technicians would then consider.

How to do it, though; that was the problem. Eventually, overcome by the unbudgeable inertia of a massive organisation, most employees simply functioned like machinery.

So Fern didn't have everything. She didn't have a job that she knew for sure was intrinsically worthwhile, like making baskets, but she had a whole lot more than before. She saw it that way, as a miser would. When she came home at nights, her home closed around her firmly, encouragingly. Its right angles were more upright since

26

she had rationalised the tangle of internal walls, drain-pipes and wiring. She was overwhelmed, still, with the knowledge that she owned a portion of the earth's surface. It was hers to plant in cabbages or lawn, hers to litigate over. She enjoyed the firmness of its front steps, the symmetry of its uprising. She overlooked the jumble of doubled-up, fiddly kitchens and makeshift bathrooms. She had bought even the views out her windows – but not, maddeningly, the right to prevent them changing, because people chopped trees or planted them, painted houses and even built one without consulting her. She felt more normal but no less ordinary. But then that was the contradiction of the century, the urge to be special, but imperceptibly so.

When Fern had been a working woman for a couple of months, there was a social evening put on by the Department's Social Club. Charles was up from Middlecity for a few days; he was already working at the Department of External Affairs. His uncle Jules invited us to the social since he wanted to talk shop with Charles; he also thought it was his duty to attend such functions as a friendly gesture towards his staff. We dragged Fern along and Jules brought his new lady, Jessie. I suppose that was asking for trouble. Drinks, a buffet dinner and dancing were on the agenda. Quite a casual atmosphere prevailed in the eleventh floor cafeteria; people came and went, and when we arrived at about nine there were a couple of hundred there.

Fern was wearing one of the dresses Jules had bought her, with a carefree air. It was obvious she was flourishing alone; in fact she was irrepressible. She was giggling with Hilary and a crowd of women friends when she caught sight of Orlando Proddleigh, dancing like a seal swimming in and out of waves of his own making. He wore roman sandals and corduroy trousers much too short, with an open-necked denim shirt. He was dancing with Ailsa, who had a silly smile on her face. To be certain, Fern asked, 'Who's that?' and when Hilary said, 'That's Orlando Puddleigh,' Fern could tell that Hilary, like other women watching him, would like to lie down with Orlando. He was the only person at the social who had made no attempt to dress up; he was round in the shoulders, big in the belly, a thoroughly unfashionable body type. But most of the women and some of the men could picture settling down into him as if he were a sand-hill, hot with sunshine; could imagine taking a handful of him and feeling it slip away grain by grain, leaving a warm hollow.

'Does he work with us?' said Fern. 'Since when?'

'Oh, I don't know, several years,' said Hilary. 'Why?'

'I met him once,' said Fern.

'Once seen, never forgotten,' said Hilary, dedicated to chastity.

Ailsa dropped out and another woman moved up to take her place in Orlando's orbit, swinging in an oval round his dance. Sooner or later he joined the women at the edge and noticed Fern. They both said, 'Hello – remember?'

Fern felt a very gentle wave of sap lapping and overlapping in her trunk; she wanted to hold green branches over his head. He felt nothing special. His face was grown into a warm, confident, reliable face; it made you want to believe that everything would be all right. The cost to him of this face was that he held behind his eyes a lot of pain. He was very tired.

Fern came back to eat with us. She looked at Jessie. 'We should have a talk, get together,' she said. Jessie's eyes glittered with complicity over her round red Irish cheeks.

'Later,' she said. In twenty seconds they drew closer together than either would ever be to Jules.

'You know Puddleigh, do you Fern?' asked Jules.

'I thought his name was Proddleigh,' she said. Jules snorted.

'He changed it, from one silly name to another silly name. Don't ask me why,' said Jules.

'I expect he had his reasons,' Fern replied.

Jules gave her a warning, fatherly sort of a look. 'Not a very sound fellow, I'm afraid. He has great potential, nobody could question that. But he will not capitalise on it. If you knew the opportunities he has frittered away! Believe me, I've bent over backwards to help that man. He has no sense of career.'

Here Charles and I looked suitably disapproving, for we felt it, but not so Jessie and Fern.

Jules continued, 'I have my reasons for suggesting you steer clear of Puddleigh, Fern.'

'He might undermine my career?'

'I hate to say this, but Puddleigh is a notorious womaniser. He is the Departmental scandal.'

Fern and Jessie found this vastly amusing from his mouth, and Charles, rehearsing for diplomacy, changed the subject.

Fern and Jessie were both ready to go at the same moment and pressed towards the lift Orlando was entering. Then Jessie (mistakenly) thought she'd left her purse in the cafeteria and we all went to look for it, except Fern. In the lift she said to Orlando, 'Can we have lunch together soon?' and he thought, 'Oh no, no, not again!' and said, 'I've given it up.'

Fern said, 'You can have a glass of water while I tell you what has happened since I saw you last, and first.' Then she thought, 'But I can't tell him about my blue and gold breast, the way it still shimmers, like sun whisking over the waves,' and he thought, 'Oh no no no,' and said as usual, 'Yes.'

29

'I won't bite, you know,' said Fern flirtatiously.

'I've heard that before,' he groaned. Fern did hear the groan. She said in a flat voice with the bubbles ironed out, 'Could we be friends?'

'We'll see.'

For once, there were a few stars visible over the city, very pale and high. Fern said, 'Look, Orion's Belt!'

'Where's Orion's Belt? I don't see any Orion's Belt,' Orlando said aggressively. Fern pointed, waved her arms, explained.

He said, 'Orion who? I think it's very peculiar if you can see a belt up there.'

'Some people call it the Pot,' she said hopefully.

'But it's not a pot, is it? It's stars, saying, "Here we are again, we're stars."'

'Don't you think it's quaint, though, this ancient way of seeing things?'

'Ancient, is it? Ancient? There's a lot of it around.'

'A lot of what?' asked Fern.

'Oh, you know. Hammering stars till they're flat. Look at them! Out there it's rolling, it's churning, it's foaming, collapsing, imploding! But all you see is dot to dot through someone else's brain!' His whole body flashed in explanation and conviction.

Fern had quick defences ready. She surprised herself by laying these aside and taking his words at face value.

'And when you've joined up the dots, you know what you've done to the stars, don't you? You've drawn up the ownership papers. You've made a map, you've got your name on it, you've tied up the stars with ink. Rope in a few more dots, and then you've got star wars.'

Jules and Charles and Jessie and I came out of the lift and down the stairs and took Fern away from Orlando's raving. She didn't talk on the way home.

This marked the start of a syncopated friendship

between Fern and Orlando. At first they would lunch together once or twice a week until eventually it was more or less a daily habit. They had a standing (but provisional) arrangement for fine days in a small park, and for wet days in a cheap café. Fern never expected him to be there; he never expected to go and yet he usually did. What looked like a Darby and Joan predictability to their friends was a matter of daily surprise for them.

Although he consistently sought her out, he was not an appropriate companion for Fern. They would look out at the same scene, and she would enjoy the impeccable symmetry of the window frame, he the adaptable curves of clouds. She saw the city essentially as a hardboard map with street outlines and boundaries drawn criss-cross over it. Each rectangle or triangle was owned by a person like her; for her the multi-storey buildings were natural, righteous growths, like fingernails. He saw only a portion of the world's curve, distorted by rigid outcrops and underground parking lots.

He said she had flat eyeballs like everyone else in the Department. Their viewpoints were so far apart that they could hardly find common ground from which to argue. She was on a plane, he on a planet.

She soon found out why Jules was so incensed by Orlando.

For men, it was a simple thing to clamber up the pyramid of power. Indeed, eager hands would pull them up. Men were rapidly made supervisors, in charge of mostly women, many of whom were more capable. It was the same old story, except that here there was always a decision-making folder to show the world (should the world inquire) why such-and-such a man, thick as a brick, should be promoted.

From the ranks, a man of Orlando's abilities should naturally rise to the top floor in a matter of a year or so. But he was perpetually arguing with his superiors. And every time he differed he insisted on reducing the issue to matters of philosophy, at which their patience would run out. Among other things he was known for his aversion to straight lines. The Department's policy was that all graphs should be bar graphs or straight-line graphs, but Orlando persistently produced curving graphs, or three-dimensional models of spirals, globes, heaps, or waves – this was his view of the world and he went on representing it as best he could. Three times Jules had tried to promote him and three times he had nonchalantly refused. He was shunted from one division to another, each taking its turn with the recalcitrant Puddleigh.

'Why do you spend time with me?' asked Fern one day. 'We're a laughing stock with our squabbles. I don't agree with you ever. I don't understand what there is to agree with.'

'I like looking at your tits,' said Orlando. 'If only you knew what a lovely shape you've got! That skin over those bones with those juicy things inside you . . . then you'd understand me too. At least I can see what you could be. I can see it with my eyeballs.'

Fern thought she would change the subject. 'What are you doing in this job, then? Don't tell me you're hoping to convert the hierarchy to your point of view. You'll wait a long, long time.'

'It's a curiosity; I'm hopeful,' he said, rather unconvincingly.

Fern pressed him. 'You've made no headway with this institution. It's worse than ever, in your terms. And not only is it monolithic and inert, but in my opinion it is on the right track.'

'I'm getting to know the lay of the land.'

'But you must hate it! You don't belong here,' said Fern. 'You belong by the sea.' And indeed he had the shape of

32

a dune or a dolphin; she expected him to drop pipi shells out of his pockets.

'I won't stay here forever. I've decided to stay as long as you need me.'

Sometimes after an insult like this she was more than faintly annoyed with him and pointedly lunched with her women friends, talking of government valuations. He didn't seem to mind, but sat pacifically alone or with another group.

His feelings seemed unhurtable; he was politically angry often enough, but on the surface, personally serene. She couldn't describe his nature and yet it was certainly there. He was the least ordinary, the most outlandish person she had ever known, and she did find him almost knowable. He was wrong in all his ideas, but right in himself, like a cloud. Relentlessly spectacular, he was only doing what came naturally. She bickered and fended him off yet she grew less wary with him, and like other women, she loved him. Because she could hide this even from herself, he let himself get used to her.

Eventually she absorbed one thing: people (meaning Orlando) could challenge and disobey the men in charge, and although they became unpopular they were never given the sack: it was a government department. Jules Menzies and his executives objected strenuously to Orlando Puddleigh. They would sigh and change buttocks when he raised a point in a meeting. But this did not make him unhappy. Fern had spent many years with popularity as one of her goals, a taken-for-granted ideal. When she let it go, she felt five kilos lighter.

Well, the months went by and went by, and just the comfort of a friend like Orlando gradually helped Fern to relax and relent. That first night under the stars she had simply opened her ears and let him speak, responding to his churning moonlit image on the steps of Queen Street,

33

letting his words paint themselves as they would. But then, when Jules butted in from behind, I think she was reminded how two men already had tried to make her into their model woman, and so she brought all her resistance to bear against Orlando, all the familiar sieves to strain his words.

At least after her other experiences, Fern was alert to the processes of this relationship. She was only defending herself until she could safely gauge her own response. She was testing herself as much as him. Eventually she trusted him. As some people feel real for the first time when they see themselves on video, so Fern sensed herself materialising, atom by atom, as Orlando continued to attend to her.

She found she could talk and listen with him in a new way. When a subject was abstract or theoretical, she usually had an ever-ready 'but' on her tongue; a little bit of the other person's thought was quite enough before she interfered with it. But when Orlando talked, she plunged in; if it was a good day, she might catch a breaker and roar on the crest of it right into shallow water. And then she could choose whether to paddle out again into the surf, or spit and shake the salt water out of herself and rub herself down and go home. There was no undertow in his talk. Or to put it another way, when he began to talk, he painted a whole picture, big or little, and it was ridiculous to stand over his shoulder and say, 'A bit more red over there, don't you think?' especially when he might at any time give up on a piece and scrape off all the wet paint and start again.

On the other hand, he rarely finished talking an idea out in a single go, so before taking issue it was reasonable to wait till it looked whole. Then she accepted, rejected, or rejoiced. Sometimes she was appalled. But he had no wish to put his paint on her.

People had always come to Fern with their problems, not because she could solve them but because she listened. Now Fern was able to give them something special: an eye and an ear for the person as she was, then and there, whole. She responded to them with more of herself than before, because she had two centres of alertness now, her head and her wonderful breast. Also, she listened with benevolence and concentration as a late atonement for leaving her husband.

four

And then there was a change of government. Believe me, it was not perfect, and I'm ashamed to say I didn't even vote for it myself. But the new Government had one unshakeable policy which made the world look at us with new eyes: the Sleeping Islands would not from henceforth permit any nuclear powered or nuclear armed vessels into our ports. The new Prime Minister said this loud and clear and eloquently and repeatedly all over the world. RUSA, our friend and ally, shook its fist and beat us with economic sticks and moral sticks until we thought we might be bombed ourselves for being naughty children. The Sleeping Islands were so insignificant strategically that RUSA had never yet installed nuclear missiles on our soil, although Europe, for instance, was studded with red-hot dots. Our Prime Minister said, essentially, 'Nuclear warships are dangerous. Nuclear missiles are dangerous. Please stop talking gobbledegook, please stop making more when the earth is already full up, please dismantle what you have so that our grandchildren may live out the full term of their lives.'

The fury of RUSA was like a global tantrum; it was plain that they were furious not because we were wrong but because we were right. It was like in *A Midsummer Night's Dream*: chaos in the fairy court spread to international chaos and chaos in the lives of ordinary citizens. The world hierarchy was challenged without aggression, and people everywhere started to wake up. The Prime Minister made us most unpopular with the Fairy King and

Queen, only to find we had new friends by the million among people who hated sleeping with death in the bed.

I know this seems trivial by comparison but I'm sure it is connected: Fern began a little prodding of her own in the Department of Philosophy, a little challenging. The Prime Minister had set the example and made her proud to be a Sleeping Islander. 'Whatever else I may be, I am a Sleeping Islander,' she thought, along with a whole nation.

Once a month there was a staff meeting in the lunch hour. Attendance was voluntary, so only a small proportion of the staff would be there. The rest poured out the front door of the building with wallets and handbags, thronging down Queen Street in search of something to buy. Often the speaker at the meeting was an expert in one field who could give them background information that would help them make decisions which would be to his or her advantage. Fern practised asking questions at these meetings. When a point bothered her, her mind would throb, her ears mist out the rest of the speech while she clarified her query and rehearsed it silently. When she raised her hand at question time, her heart banged; when she stood, her knees trembled. It required the same amount of courage each time. Every question she asked was also a statement: 'I am here, I am thinking, I am discovering new levels of bravery.' And so she generated in herself an all-embracing curiosity about the world, including forestry, law, seismology, childcare centres, and the shellfish reserves of the Sleeping Islands. Like a mandala, her curiosity moved in all directions from its centre, herself. More and more she found herself thinking about a question that lay behind all her questions, although she could not articulate it.

Middlecity was where I spent my fourth year at University, specially to be near Charles. I got First Class

Honours, which had always been expected of me. My father was very pleased, as if he had done it himself.

Charles had been expecting for some time to receive his first overseas appointment. Usually the first posting is to a consulate or trade mission in some comparatively minor country, although you might well say that none was more minor than ours. But due to a combination of circumstances, Charles was told that in a few months he would be on his way to Washington. His responsibilities would be harmless; he'd be junior to the most junior secretary as far as we could tell. It would be more a matter of getting further training on location. Still, it was thrilling to be off to the headquarters of New RUSA, especially at a time when 'Sleeping Islands' was a dirty word there. Charles believed that the Prime Minister had raised the anti-nuclear flag expressly to make his own task more difficult. But I was his greatest fan, and longing to go.

We had plenty of time for a traditional wedding with all the trimmings. I organised it, Dad paid with every sign of enthusiasm, and Fern attended as a special front row guest. I decided on French champagne, silk pintucks and covered buttons, bridesmaids galore – why not?

It was a wonderful party, although Fern seemed to have some misgivings. She was not at her best; looking chic, yes, but vaguely embarrassed about the whole thing. When I had told her we were getting married, she'd said, 'Must you?' I wanted her just to have a good time, for my sake. There were plenty of suitable men hovering around, eager to provide it. And some unsuitable ones too – perfectly nice, but much too young. We did ask Orlando but to our relief he refused. He would have looked so out of place. For a little while Fern did warm up and giggle; that was when Jessie detached herself from Jules, and they shared – I dread to imagine what they shared. When glamorous Jules returned from baby-kissing, he smiled benignly, slipped Jessie into his elbow and firmly led her away to mix with Charles's superiors from the Department of External Affairs. Superiors.

That's the sort of thing Fern did these days. Pick a normal word like 'superiors' out of context and repeat it thoughtfully, her eyes following a little arc in the sky, half tangled in her hair. 'Superiors,' she said. Or 'career', and it was a rabid donkey bolting through the city to the rubbish dump. Or 'capitalise'. She'd changed all right. I couldn't blame Orlando any more; these were her own ideas, blossoming like ragwort under my very nose.

But all in all it was a great wedding, a grand social razzamatazz, a glorious binge, a last fling before we left the country in a month or so. We said goodbye to Fern then and there, as we would spend the last few weeks in Middlecity.

After a couple of years or so in the Department, Fern had had professional contact with Jules only very occasionally, though a few social occasions brought them together. He chose to remain isolated in his penthouse office, sending men in shiny grey trousers to do his internal messages. He preserved his charisma by remaining out of touch with most of his staff, who by now occupied half the armoured office block. He was a star whose influence was strongly felt, though his light was years away from most of the workers. His clothing was legendary, and he said his gorgeous dressing was intended to enhance the well-being of the people economically, physically, and spiritually.

One Friday morning his secretary telephoned Fern and said that Mr Menzies would like to see her. She had been expecting this, because she had been pitting herself against him. She was being squashed by the institution; she had a house, she had a job, she had a special friend, but she had no say. Her pretext was trivial in itself but symbolic.

It didn't really matter on what ground she fought, as long as she stood there firmly.

She made a detour to Orlando's desk. She whispered, 'I'm going to see Jules Menzies.'

'What for?'

'Insubordination.'

She walked up one flight of stairs and then on second thoughts took the lift the rest of the way. She didn't want to arrive breathless. She knocked on his door. His secretary, Rosemary, opened it, ushered her to another door and knocked. A pause. A continuing pause. Then, 'Come in.'

Fern walked in, quite perky. She saw his luxury office, but her eyes were drawn to the man himself. His brilliant colours tickled her eyes: silk shirt in salmon pink, silk tie in sea green, grey crocodile skin belt and shoes to match – shoes to match! He was like a puppet in a British TV space adventure. He stepped forward and warmly offered his hand.

'Fern! I don't think you've ever been in my office, have you? Do sit down.' She settled in a red woollen armchair and he crossed his perfect twill trousers perfectly. 'Now your Head of Division tells me you're having a little trouble with the new DPWL8. I'm sure we can sort it out. Tell me, you are happy here, aren't you, Fern? You like your job?'

'Yes. No.' She covered the field.

'Are you interested in promotion, Fern? The Department is committed to promoting a few women. We are initiating a positive discrimination policy. As you know I have a deep admiration for women, and you've proved yourself very capable. I am pleased to say you have more than justified my faith in you.'

'My foot,' thought Fern.

'Now about the DPWL8. We pride ourselves here on

having ninety-seven percent efficiency in our internal records, and we expect to improve even that. Your Head of Division tells me that you haven't managed to return your DPWL8 accurately once since it was introduced. And because we are almost family, I'd like to help you if I can.'

He sat back, raised prominent eyebrows under his satiny hair, and waited, quizzical, enticing. Fern let him work a little harder.

'Do you not understand the new version, Fern?' he asked kindly. 'We've been trying to make it more comprehensive, that's all.'

'It doesn't work,' said Fern. 'Everyone just makes up their answers because it would look too silly to put all the week's work under *Miscellaneous*. I'm the only one who's telling the truth.'

He picked up a handful of forms from his desk and read, '"Go stuff your stats up your toenails." You've developed a nice sense of humour, Fern. Would you like some coffee?' He buzzed an order through to his secretary. 'Now if this opinion were a common one, we would have to initiate some PR work. But I haven't heard a murmur of complaint from any others of my eight hundred and twenty-eight staff members, so I must assume that the form itself is perfectly clear and adequate, and that you personally have some kind of resistance to it, which I'm going to try and understand. Shall we go through bit by bit? In column A, we want you to break down the number of hours you spent dealing with questions originating from Members of Parliament, councils, catchment boards, harbour boards, individuals, or miscellaneous. In column B, the number of hours you spent on defence problems, legal, social, economic, environmental, or miscellaneous. That's not too hard surely?'

Now she had coffee in her hands.

'Thank you Rosemary. Then in column C, we want you to record the number of problems you have partially resolved, fully resolved, decisions confirmed, decisions reversed, passed on to another authority, or miscellaneous. When the forms are all returned at the end of the week, the computer can give us an instant summary of the quantity of work achieved during the week, and its nature.'

'That's what you think. But what's the point?'

He fixed his bright blue eyes on hers. Clear whites. They nailed her to the chair through her own eyes, without jiggling. He would grind to the edges of her brain, if she let him. He leaned forwards, intensifying the intimacy and the domination.

'My dear Fern,' he said ever so gently. 'This kind of analysis is precisely the type of work we are doing all day long. How consistent, philosophically, that we should apply it to our own weekly workload! How appropriate, how positive, how confirming!'

'That might be all very well if the form ever fitted the factors. But every neat square overlaps with every other one. There are no edges, not really!'

'Give me an example. What have you been working on this week, for instance?'

'Whether to allow water rights to the company which wants to export water to RUSA from the Black Fiord.'

'An important problem but not a difficult one. You have the taxonomy as a guideline. If in doubt, move it to the top of the ladder.'

'I hate it! I don't agree with it!'

'My dear Fern! How can you disagree with a mere formality? It's always been done that way.'

'The ladder is upside down and anyway a ladder is wrong here. You've got economic considerations first, defence second, legal third, then environmental, then social, see? Surely people should come first, or better, second after the environment, if we're going to show a bit of humility.'

'You must know the order is not a hierarchy of values, but of convenience, of reality. Of course people have the highest value! They are the nation's capital. But pragmatically, each category concerns people anyway. People are the common factor, not a separate entity. "Social", in this context, is simply a way of saying, "when other considerations are not relevant". In purely practical terms, you will always find it possible to solve a problem if you regard it as either an economic problem or a defence problem. That's a useful little tip. Otherwise you could dither all day and never decide. And decisions are required! Moreover, even if you choose not to regard it in this light, it will be considered that way at some later stage. The event will occur or not occur according to these criteria. These are just the facts of life, Fern.'

'Precisely. We don't make decisions at all. We make bits of decisions. I produce one dot, fifteen other people produce their dots, they go into a computer which rearranges the dots in some way which I don't believe and I don't condone.'

Jules gleamed. 'This is the democratic process. But I find you are, after all, ambitious.'

'I thought we were supposed to bring idealism to the way people make decisions in this country. But we don't. We merely cover up the cynicism of the people with the power. That's all we do. We prematurely justify obscene decisions.'

'That was never the intention, Fern. The idealism was always there, is still there in high places. Our job is partly to ensure that the left hand knows what the right hand is up to, that the country is ruled justly: that's the idealism. We don't alter things so much as insure them; we support

43

what was already strong but not altogether reliable.'

'But then what's the point of me and all the others? This is a bullshit job, and we're just going through the motions.'

Fern stood up, bound to leave. Jules Menzies stood too and she saw he was about to approach her, to put his arm around her shoulder and ease her out the door, saying 'Fern' all the way. She wanted intensely to stop him from confirming her as weak and himself as fatherly and seductive.

He took one step forward with his left arm out, ready to pat her into submission. He was only three metres away, in this huge office of his. He took another step and said, 'My dear –'

She had nothing but her body; her words had pattered off without making the littlest dent.

He took one more step and said, '– Fern', and she felt a surge of power around her heart and unzipped her jumpsuit, pulling it back from her left breast.

He stepped back aghast. She felt the weight of it, the slightly damp skin on skin at the base, the ducts tubing from the edges, the tug of muscles at the side and from her shoulder, the air swirling over the hollow between her breasts, the solid mass of it from ribs to tip, the cool point which turned rubbery as she stood there, the nipple which contracted and gathered itself to a hard knob aimed at him, condemning not as gun but as breast, its globular shape contradicting everything he promoted. And as he watched, its colours eclipsed his finery, oscillating blue and yellow and rose and silver and turquoise. The light pulsed out in wavering rims contoured like her breast and she was flying out in every wave. A belch of sharp hot air, and Jules Menzies fell to the floor. His spine arched, his heels hammered, his teeth clenched.

The colours faded and Fern zipped up. All her humiliation and frustration had gone out of her, blown a raspberry, and evaporated. It was a fitting end to her first job. She walked out the door and through the foyer, shutting doors behind her. She heard the drumming sound stop and a chair fall over, and then Menzies buzzing for Rosemary. It was time to leave.

There was a narrow door with a sign, 'No Exit'. Fern passed through to a staircase that was too steep, and stiff with concrete silence. Down and down she went, always on the verge of tripping; there were never any doors to let her out. There was no way of knowing how far down she had gone, no way of finding her way back to her desk or to Orlando's floor, no way of escape should anyone hostile chase her or confront her.

The stairs were unfinished, with rough boards and careless concrete. A few shafts of light came in from occasional tiny windows; loose wires hung where light switches should have been. As she hurried, the lines of the stairs turning and turning and the light needling from those random windows flickered in and out in jagged lines, a migraine pattern flashing in a dark mind. At a point where she felt sure she must have descended at least twenty-three floors she tripped and fell to the next landing. No harm was done, but sprawled with her legs cockeyed she found that left and right and gravity had lost their meaning. She took off her sandal and let it go. That must be down, so down she went, and down.

At last a doorway. A door frame, containing a door. But no handle! Fern blindly pushed and banged at the door which was unnervingly cold to the touch. She wanted to shout and sob, but refused herself permission. She leaned against the door-jamb giving herself a pep talk.

'Naturally it's locked. Naturally it's locked. It has to be sealed or the whole building would be open to burglars, wouldn't it? You'll have to rest, and climb those gritty stairs again, walk humbly through the thirteenth floor and use the lift like everyone else. You could climb at night. No, it's Friday. You'd be shut in for the weekend. Just keep calm. There are cleaners, they can let you out. It's not going to be complicated, see?'

Thus she kept hysterics at bay, only to find with horror that her hands had stuck to the door with cold. If she pulled them loose, she'd lose patches of skin. And yet her feet were wet and warm: her marvellous breast had melted a hole in the door and was peering through to the other side. She pulled her breast back inside and used it to warm her frozen fingers and ease them from the imprisoning ice. Her eyes could see nothing but darkness through the hole. With remarkable flair, her breast dissolved a large enough section of ice-logged door for her to gingerly clamber through.

The ground was slippery and uneven. With her hands scraping along a wall, she worked towards a glimmer of light. The air was cold and damp and greenish. As her eyes adjusted, she found she was in a huge space, not a room, perhaps a cave that served as foyer to some other immeasurably larger area. Green cobwebby icicles hung from an invisibly high and dark roof. A filigree woman with ice hair carved into sinuous ringlets by some below-zero wind stalked by, leaning forward, without a glance at Fern; she was holding a champagne glass made of threaded green ice. Her tattered dress streamed rigidly behind, as if held out by a cold wind that Fern could not feel. The woman stared ahead and passed around a corner. Fern could hear cocktail chatter somewhere, tinkling among the stalactites. She went in the opposite direction and came to the rim of an underground waterway.

five

At her feet was a muddy, slow-moving stream. And at its edge, wagging like a dog tail, was a barely recognisable mangrove plant. In shape it was a baby plant, still using up its water-wings of baby food, the two plates full of green colostrum. At this stage of development, with only two new leaves at the top of the stalk, it should have been hand high at most, but it was as tall as a man and not yet rooted, bobbing on the water in front of her, silently insisting that she get on board.

Fern stepped on to the fleshy pads of the mangrove and held its stalk with both hands. Immediately it wriggled away from the shallow edge into the channel and set off downstream. Behind them the water folded and followed them, pushing them along and winding itself up at the same time. It was like a first try on roller skates. The vegetable platform trembled beneath her sandals; her feet were wet to the ankle but they didn't slip off. She was proceeding at about ten kilometres an hour at this point, the speed you go in a car over control humps, she figured. That was in the few lucid seconds when she thought anything at all beyond, 'What do I do to stay on board?'

Before very long the tunnel opened and she was outside – but not in Queen Street, of course. There was no wind, only a soft drizzle which blotted out the edges of retreating water, so she couldn't see the shops and flats and houses and motorway which ought to have been there beyond the rain.

Then she was in open water. She recognised Mangrove

47

Harbour as the wind picked up. It caught the two leaves of the mangrove, sprouting at the level of her neck. They flapped and her craft wobbled. With one hand still gripping the stem, she used the other to seize the end of a leaf and instinctively held it to catch the wind.

Then they raced away, but the outgoing tide threatened to tear them to the northern exit from the harbour. The mangrove struggled and Fern knew this must be the wrong way. She changed hands, and leaves, precariously, and the mangrove tacked out to sea. They worked together: both passive, both active. The mangrove used its small root system as a rudder, retracting it when the sea got rough. The wind swept both along. When Fern absorbed anxiety through her hands and feet, she experimented until she had the plant going in what seemed the right direction. If she pulled the corner of a leaf towards her, it caught more wind and went faster: sometimes too fast, jumping out of her hand, unless she leaned heavily on her back leg. By moving the trunk of the mangrove forwards or sideways, she helped change direction. In choppy seas, Fern noticed the weight of her special breast would alter, hinting and helping her to balance.

Basically the mangrove was heading south, along the west coast of the Sleeping Islands' Main Island, which is not the larger island, you understand, but the one with most of the action. It was a hot day and Fern held on till she was sunburnt, hungry and deeply fatigued. She was using almost every muscle in her body, constantly making minor adjustments in her balance, leaning this way and that, holding her mast forward, sideways, clinging to one leaf or the other, responding to the wind's every change in force and direction. The exhilaration of the breeze in her face and self-propulsion lifted her heart, for she did feel self-propelled, being in friendly harmony with the mangrove.

They passed wide river mouths, steering well out to sea to avoid the turbulence of sandbars. They went past cliffs, some with beaches at the foot. They skirted big surf, skimmed over white-caps, avoided rocky reefs. They came close to the shore at a point where expensive new houses trembled visibly on neat lawns chewed to rags by the sea; the houses hovered a couple of metres above a raw stony shore, and the sea scraped at pebbles and cobbles and boulders in a row at the foot of the impromptu cliff. More stones, a long pipe on stilts over the sea, a stone groyne, another stony beach, another long pipe, more boulders, a long stone wall, more cliffs and boulders and stone walls, a breakwater; and past the breakwater, the mangrove implied that Fern must help them enter this port.

The sight of all this concrete and heavy stone in straight lines made Fern tired and reminded her of the Department of Philosophy, in spite of the perfect grace and symmetry of a single mountain standing behind the house-hills. She saw the remnants of a sandy beach; there she landed the mangrove and lay shaking on the sand. She wanted so much to sleep then and there, but the mangrove was anxious. It was twilight, and a few cars passed on a road behind them. The mangrove must be protected from dryness and prying.

Beyond the road was a long row of baches, tiny fibrolite shacks, most of them with signs of habitation and neglect. They were backed and overshadowed by clumps of pohutukawa, billowing out to form a single cumulous grey-green wall. Each bach held out its narrow edge towards the sea, and elbowed its neighbour in the dustbin. They were separated from the road by a single lawn and a single low fence, making a wavering line that was virtually organic, as if the houses were vertebrae of one spine.

There was a flat-topped yellow bach sinking into the ground or rising out of it at an alarming angle. The lawn was hairy with plantain and dandelion, which added to the camouflage. An old dinghy was propped up against a short length of tin fence. Fern took a chance and lifted the mangrove across her shoulders and carried it over the road, tucking it under the dinghy. The salty leaves were tattered where she had clutched them for so many hours of the day. The stalk hunched and wrinkled. She had no power to spare, but she did pull handfuls of grass and heap them over the plant, especially its roots. She rested in the grass in front of the bach.

To her left the sun was flamboyantly setting. The sky was violet, and clouds of red and green glowed around the tall chimney of a power station in front of a gaunt, cone-shaped hill. Other islands hunched in the background behind wharves, ships, cranes, big lamp-posts, and massive tanks of petrol and liquid petroleum gas. Obviously she had arrived at Pipetown, the city at the foot of the Moving Mountain. She knew the province well. Her Uncle Elliot lived right here in Pipetown, and she had spent holidays here as a child. Yet until she was right in the port and caught sight of the mountain, she had failed to recognise the coastline, thinking it must be a dream city. The original Pipetown was almost paralysed under asphalt and concrete.

She thought of sleeping under the dinghy with the mangrove, but they had been too close. Neither had energy left for the other. She set off in her wet, sticky jump-suit to find her uncle. She looked up and saw that the clouds had regrouped into fine shrimp-pink and mauve streaks, all radiating from the hill by the power station, the Wizard's Hat. Once, for the First People, it had been a teaching hill. Now the winds had combed their hair to glorify the hill, or the hill had sucked clouds to its tip and was wearing them as a crown. For some reason this lightened the mood of Fern.

As she walked, she wondered what story to tell her uncle, if not the truth. For the first time she felt some surprise at the day's events, seeing them through the eyes of an elderly uncle. What surprised her most was that she didn't feel personally surprised. She felt younger and more abstract than before. All she required of her uncle was food and a bed, not his admiration or approval.

The walk seemed as long as her sea journey on those burning feet, but at least by the time she reached his place the wind had stiffened her jump-suit into a half-dry condition. His modest house was dwarfed by a kauri which had been missed by the axe seventy years earlier, so she had this landmark to follow in the dusk. This was the house he had lived in all his life; it was also the house where her mother had lived until she married. Answering her knock, he let her in without fussing. He was brown and wrinkly, and his nose cast a shadow over his chin. She sort of told the truth.

'Uncle Elliot, a friend brought me here on a weekend jaunt. But now she is too tired to go on with the journey, so I have to stop in Pipetown till she recovers. May I stay with you a few days?'

Uncle Elliot tended not to talk to people since his wife had died. This made things easier. She asked for some night-clothes; he found one of her aunt's old night-dresses and a dressing-gown and slippers. She also chose a dress of her aunt's to wear while her jump-suit was washed and dried. Elliot showed her hats as well, and to please him she took to her room a pale turquoise cloche, draped for the mother of the bride. After sardines on toast and a cup of tea, Fern had a deep hot bath which stung her chafed skin but softened the knotted meat of her. She slid into the spare bed with a hottie. All night the bed rocked and galloped.

When she woke up the next day it was lunch-time. Into

51

her bedroom window stared the Moving Mountain. She felt stiff all over, legs, arms, shoulders, neck, back; even her right breast was aching. She went to bed again after a snack and a cuppa and lay there until breakfast the next day, as if the mountain itself was pinning her down. This was Sunday, a day of hobbling; on Monday, though with muscles still raw and twanging, she felt herself again. She greatly appreciated the loyalty of these tendons and muscles and nerve endings which had functioned satisfactorily all her life, and this skin which had held them all together and hardly ever leaked or worn through. She said goodbye to her uncle and set off after lunch to see how the mangrove was: dead, alive, or disappeared.

This time she followed a route through the town centre. Women were striving for a certain look, the Pipetown look. All around her there were long, loose beige skirts, cedilla heels plugging into the warmed pavements, layers of cream and fawn swinging over economical busts, and fine shiny hair lifting away in the breeze from necks. Faces were pointed and carefully made up. There was a solemn communal striving after fashion, a commitment to standards and to harsh lipsticks. When Fern caught sight of her reflection in a shop window (and she started compulsively seeking it) she was deeply embarrassed by her oddness. Purple cars with magwheels spun round corners, full of teenage boys.

Once at the port she hurried to the old dinghy and saw her mangrove with heaps of wet grass over and around it. A spoonful of tinned cats' meat and wet breadcrumbs lay on a piece of newspaper beside its roots. 'Somebody's been caring for you,' she whispered. 'Mangrove!' She felt it whimper. No sound, but a feeling like a rusty wire being pulled through her head. 'What do you need, mangrove?' Sadness dampened her, and two tears fell on its stalk. The flesh swelled a little and glistened.

She stood up and looked through the lopsided window into the bach. A huge young man returned her gaze and she jumped. Parts of him were utterly familiar, though she had never seen anyone with such broad shoulders. His features were delicate except for a wide, tall forehead. He had long eyelashes, brilliant blue eyes, a long jaw not yet developed in manhood, enormous wrists and hands and feet. 'Is this your mangrove?' he asked, emerging.

'It's rather a case of me being its,' she answered. 'And thank you for keeping it damp.' He took a dented aluminium bucket over the road and filled it with sea water, which he sloshed under the dinghy.

'We have to get it into the sea,' he said.

'That's why I'm here. I can't understand why it came right into Pipetown, can you? If I could travel around the coast, even three or four kilometres, it could rest privately in shallow water.' She looked at the harbour and added with disappointment, 'But I see we can't set out just now.'

'Set out?' he asked.

She tried to explain their method of travelling while she looked at the scene in front of them. It was a holiday Monday in the Moving Mountain province and the harbour was white with sails. A hundred yachts had just set off on a race which began with two figures of eight around buoys within the breakwaters. Little P-Class lolly-yachts followed behind them. The breeze was brisk and the yachts whisked whitely along into the waist of the course and out to the loops, like a field of cricketers changing position between overs, breathed in and out by an unseen lung. A dozen windsurfers with sails in hyper-active hues kept falling over in the wake of the yachts. Then the wind dipped out for a few minutes while it swivelled to a new angle, freezing the white sails. The windsurfers picked themselves up and made jazzy progress. Then the wind came back and windsurfers all fell over in

53

the wake of a hundred moving yachts.

No. Half of Pipetown was playing here at their last shred of a beach, watching from the verge, sunbathing on the sand, swimming or canoeing at the brim, or riding on the deep water. The mangrove was far too shy to make such a public appearance.

They went into the bach to have a cup of tea and to think it through. The electric jug was old and fat. It puffed up folds of steam which glowed in the sunlight. Brightness shone through green parsley and water in a milk bottle on the window ledge. A spider's web, a nacreous thicket, filled in one side of the window and caught the sun in occasional coloured wisps. The steam reappeared in random twirls above the parsley. Everything used the sunshine and transformed it. 'Tonight?' thought Fern aloud. 'Yes, when everyone's gone home, we'll go then.'

'I don't think that would be wise, sailing in the dark,' said the boy. 'Have you got lights?'

Fern sat on the couch, trying to get used to the way it subsided at one end. The springs made mysterious noises as she moved. The boy put tea on a gatelegged table, painted green over orange long ago and held together with masking tape. He moved gently, scarcely disturbing the air around him, which rested calmly in the hollows between his muscles.

On one side the neighbours were piling furniture into a van; on the other they were drinking beer and barbecuing chops.

'Their last barbecue,' said the boy. 'Tomorrow the bulldozers come. This was my friend's house. He's gone away.' His face was sad. The chair he sat on was frog-legged and might just last till morning. 'I came back for a last weekend. I don't live here.'

'Why are the bulldozers coming?'

'That's murky. They're supposed to be making a car-park, which people can use while they look at the sea.'

Fern frowned; obviously there was plenty of parking space.

'It's rather complicated,' the boy went on. 'This lane is legally a motor camp, due to some ancient anomaly. There are seventy baches. Some people have lived here forever, some people are new. But they're lived in, the baches. The City Council says the lane is too good for the likes of us: it's prime land, we shouldn't be allowed to squat. And then again, they say it isn't good enough. We ought to all have a bathroom and a kitchen and a garage.'

Fern registered the single cold tap over a red plastic basin on a home-made wooden bench.

'It's élite, but also it's squalid. So more in sorrow than in anger, they are going to knock the baches down.'

Fern knew this was a one-sided version of the situation, but her sympathy was hot all the same.

The boy continued, 'It's really rather a pity. But it all comes back to Greenpipe Limited, that's my private opinion.'

'Greenpipe?' Fern was genuinely startled because Jules used to be a director of that company, which was closely or loosely allied to about twenty others in related industries. When he took up his appointment as Director of the Department of Philosophy he had renounced all business interests, as was right and proper. But doing this was as easy as squeezing a briefcase through the eye of a herring. He had put the impressive proceeds into the hands of a lawyer, who spread it around a variety of respectable and conservative government-endorsed insti-tutions. Even so, virtually every week a decision was made by his own Department which caused him to grow richer, for that is in the very nature of the rich. Fern had a hunch that he was still advising the board of Greenpipe

Limited for rewards untraceable, because Greenpipe was his special favourite among companies.

The boy was looking out the window, warming his hands with his cup of tea. 'It's not even the City Council that owns the land,' he murmured.

'Whose is it then?'

'The City Council leases it from the Railways. The Railways requisitioned it a hundred years ago from the Church of the Second People, "in the national interest". Now they want to use the land for a branch line and sidings so they can load bulk LPG. The Church of the Second People was given the land by a white whaler, to be used in trust on behalf of the First People. I would say it still belongs to the First People, four times over. Once because they lived here first. Once because the price was three horses, three saddles, a hundred and twenty red blankets and some fish hooks. Once because it was sold by a chief who didn't even belong here. And once because the Church of the Second People was supposed to look after the hundred acres on behalf of the true owners for their moral and spiritual education. I can't think of anything more likely to lead the people out, morally and spiritually, than getting their own land back again. I should think it would leave Sunday School for dead. But you'll see. In a few months, the whole car-park will be occupied by Greenpipe Limited.'

After two cups of tea, Fern had a pressing problem. The giant boy gave her a key and some toilet paper and she went down the lane to another fibrolite shack with four high louvred windows all wound around with spiders' webs. Inside the ladies' half she found one shower, two toilets, a locked booth and a basin. Easing herself, she admired the lemon and blue paint on the borer-riddled wood. The floor was cracked concrete, running with spontaneous streams of water and spattered with working bee paint drips. After pressing the lever, it was necessary to fish inside the cistern and adjust a wire, or else it would flush forever. The whole place was roughly clean except for the spidered roof. She passed another tiny building with leaking wash-tubs, an old agitator washing machine, and a fly-specked notice saying, 'This area not for ablutions'.

When she got back, Fern said to the boy, 'Who are your parents?'

He was startled. He looked at her intently, and said, 'Why did you ask that?'

'You remind me very sharply of one other person and no other. I wondered if you were related.'

The boy was agitated and went for a walk on the beach. When he came back he said, 'I should just say my parents are Mr and Mrs Wal Winchester, and my name is Doug. But there is a mystery in my own mind. I wouldn't even mention it to my parents. They're not very bright, you see.' He said this with a certain kindness, innocently.

'And you are,' said Fern.

'You won't talk about this, because of the mangrove.'

She nodded. He paused frequently because it was hard to know what direction to approach the subject from, with a new friend. His voice looped itself around her gracefully.

'My Dad is very macho. He takes all the credit for my everything. (Except my gentleness or fear.) The bigger I grow, the more he puffs up. If I'd been a girl, it would have been as bad as having no children at all. He believes in all seriousness that getting it up is the same thing as being fertile. When I was younger, I used to try and explain the difference. Foolish, wasn't I? Because now I see that he has to believe this, or disembowel himself. Anyway, we don't talk of such things in our household . . . I'm their only child . . .

57

'I have to deduce all this from a very few clues. I over-heard my mother hinting about it darkly to a neighbour once. They went to Northcity to see a special doctor, before I was born. My mother had never conceived. They believed it was a failing of hers. My hunch is that I was one of the first children in the Sleeping Islands to be conceived by artificial insemination by an unknown donor . . .

'Dad used to nag Mum about having more sons. She'd done it once, all she had to do was try a bit harder, that's the way he looked at it.' This was one of his longest pauses. 'I've only told this to one other person, the friend who owns this bach. What's the point of raising the issue? The doctors cover all traces, in the interests of tidiness I suppose. When it comes to knowing who I am, I'm worse off than any adopted child.

'My life is based on a lie. They lied to each other and they lied to themselves and they lied to me. The doctors at the very least allowed them to believe that lie. It's a lie they want to believe, you see. And it's all for the pride of the men: the false father, the sperm father, and the doctor. I can tell you, it hasn't made me feel proud of being a man.'

Another silence. 'But then it's so common to daydream about adoption if you think you've got an inferior brand of parents. The idea, the sperm theory, it makes me miserable. But then I wonder if I'm making up this story just to avoid my own boring misery. I bore myself. The world's so interesting and I'm so dreary and ponderous. And maybe that's hereditary. I know it's connected with this birth business. But is it the cause, or is it just a clever excuse?'

His voice was not bitter; he spoke steadily. 'I don't know where to turn. I imagine my sperm father is a nasty piece of work. I can't help assuming that, since I've been deep in his mind for years: a man who extended his territory in such a sneaky way. And yet who knows? he may have had the motivation of a saint.' Pause.

'I keep away from girls. If he did it once, he could do it again and again. I don't want to fall in love with my sister. And I feel very strongly that I'm not going to be the one to give that man his grandchildren. I do let him dominate me, don't I?'

Although his story was full of turmoil, his sadness made him very still. You could see he would not want to harm as he had been harmed. Fern spent a long time telling him all she knew about Jules Menzies. Finally she said, 'And when he dreams, he doesn't dream in pictures.'

'What can you mean?' asked the boy nervously.

'Tell me what you dreamed last night and I'll translate.'

Doug fished in his mind for his dream. 'Last night I dreamed an old woman sitting on the top rail of a fence. She laid three eggs, plop plop plop into a heap of silage.'

'And you saw her?'

'Of course I saw her, except I didn't see her face. Her dress was nothing colour, the silage was emerald green, the eggs were violet.'

'OK. If Jules had dreamed this dream, he wouldn't have seen the woman. He'd see the word "woman". He'd see the story on a page, typed or printed. Do you get it? He dreams silently, in words and diagrams.'

The boy rinsed their cups in the red basin. The ceiling reflected the water's movement in surges of sunlight. 'And you say he might, must be my sperm father?'

'I think you would recognise each other at once. You could say it's a case of the family Jules.'

It was getting dark. Up and down the lane cars pulled away, laden with last possessions in the exodus. The boy said, 'I'd better go. I'll be back in the morning early with my transport to collect you and the mangrove. There's a nice beach by our farm. I'll take you there.'

She bathed the mangrove again before she lay down for the night with a ragged blanket on the couch. She slept lightly, with her head downhill, and the wind sped up and whooshed around the bach, dropping bits of branches on the roof. She heard a mouse in the walls and thought she could hear a spider coughing. At first light she woke to a throbbing in the port: it was a working day again. Cranes and pumps and engines banged at the western end of the harbour where the wharves were. A yellow dredge mouthed out sand from the sea floor and spat it into a barge. Two monstrous ships had queued up outside the breakwater, waiting for a berth. An orange tug and a pilot ship helped another vessel, all black paint and square cranes, into the port. Trucks went loudly past her front lawn, laden with gross akmons, rusty pipes, drums, and old wooden piles. It was true that if they wanted to get the mangrove out of Pipetown without attracting attention they would do best to go by land for a little way.

She heard rumbles and shouts from behind the bach and found that demolition was about to begin. Where was Doug? She wrapped the mangrove in the blanket and dragged it across the road towards the sea. A man in an official yellow raincoat told her to move along to the end of the road, because she was still in a danger area. He was angry with her, as if he had told her a thousand times already.

'But this is my thing!' she cried. 'Someone's coming to pick us up!'

'Not here they aren't,' he threatened. 'Now move!'

She knotted the blanket as well as she could and dragged it very cautiously along the grass verge, but it hit a rock and she felt the mangrove wincing. So she hoisted it on to her head and walked a few hundred metres to a safe spot, the car park at the other end of the beach.

Obviously the City Council wanted the whole embarrassing operation over and done with as fast as possible, and the bleeding mopped up and bandaged right away. They had all their men and machines on the job. Their biggest earthmover lumbered up to the first bach and easily pushed it over. Walls crumpled, the roof twisted at all angles and the machine pushed steadily on, over bushes and rubbish bins and abandoned garden furniture, and bach after bach lay down beneath its weight. Behind it, two more machines rolled in and shovelled the coarse debris into truck after truck, which dumped it into the sea not very far away, extending the reclaimed land that would shortly become a new wharf area. The homes were being mashed up and recycled. Fern had been watching for an hour already when she saw a procession of a different order moving down the hill towards her.

It consisted of three very large grey horses. The first one was walking backwards, picking her feet up high and backing daintily. It was an efficient process, granted that she had not been built with this in mind, but no one could call it fast. No amount of horn-tooting could speed her up, let alone unsettle her or turn her around. The next horse had no bridle or saddle either, but walked serenely behind, nose to nose with his sister. The last horse had a rider, the big boy, placid. This was his idea of an inconspicuous evacuation.

Close up she saw that the horses were very alike. They had delicate heads, fluted necks, and deep, heavy bodies. Their skin was smooth and flecked like polished stone. She stroked them, wondering, and he introduced them.

'Horses, this is Fern. Fern, this is First Horse, Second Horse, and Third Horse.' They looked at her. 'Are you ready? There's no time like the present.'

How could she climb such a big animal? 'I'm not going to ride the one that goes backwards,' she said.

He laughed. 'She wouldn't have you aboard, don't worry. She's our pilot. You get up here with me.'

Fern slung the blanket with the mangrove inside it over Third Horse's shoulders. The boy pulled her aboard easily enough with his left hand and she settled cautiously on the bare grey back. She thought of Orlando.

As they set off she looked over her shoulder and saw the first pohutukawa tree topple, springing its ripped roots out of the earth as a heavy chain and a bulldozer strained against it. They moved off through the city streets, First Horse going backwards, Second Horse keeping pace behind, and Third Horse with her three passengers bringing up the rear. The pace was slow. She realised they must have left in the dark to arrive at the port as early as they did.

Doug said his father approved of his using three Horses all at once: he thought it was manly, the boy who outrode the strength of three Horses and all that. But his real reason was that the Horses, as brother and sisters, were very close; they felt lonely when separated.

Wherever they could they followed tracks through farms, for the main road was hard and noisy. She travelled not uncomfortably, swaying in the same rhythm as the boy behind her, and feeling like a baby in his womb. It was well past noon when they turned along a dirt road that led towards the sea, over the boy's home farm.

When they reached the beach it was beautiful. The sea face of the hills was an orchestra of growth, flax clapping and karo squeaking in the wind. The tide was out. Deep grey sand swung from the green bank to an expanse of rocks. The boy turned the horses to the right and they walked to a large pool among the rocks. There they unwrapped the mangrove, which seemed calm enough now, though painfully desiccated. They laid it in the pool and it twitched its roots experimentally like a fish that can't believe its luck. Juice moved through the stalk, relaxing the kinks formed by that long journey on horseback. Then the mangrove wriggled eel-style round and round the pool and raced its tail, flicking its pads and leaves in a crazy display.

Doug had something special to show her. The tide was going out and the mangrove would be bound to stay in the pool until early next morning, he said. He walked her down to the very end of the bay. They could easily see the power station and the islands off Pipetown. It was also the end of the farm, and the limit of an old sub-tribe's territory before it was taken by the Second People. Here Fern saw a group of granite rocks about half the size of her own body. They had long ago toppled off some higher land, now eroded. But she could still see the body of a froggy goddess in one, and another was a sturdy phallic shape with an eye at the peak. On one side of the long rock there were two carvings, crumbling away grain by grain as the sea met them twice a day.

One carving was a crude copy of the other, a perfect double spiral with a radius as long as her hand. A third boulder was shaped to accommodate her bottom, but when she sat down it wouldn't let her stay. She stepped back. Following the lines of the spiral was compulsive. It sucked her eyes to the centre, arrested them and flung them out again. The two tails of the circular channels were at opposite sides, but not immediately opposite: the spiral hung from them as if the lines were strings and like a yo-yo it could roll to either side.

'What does it say to you?' asked the boy after an hour or so.

'At first it said revolution, cyclone and anticyclone, the fern of course, embryo and placenta; it said, "Go away, go home stranger!" Now it says nothing but rocks me too high, almost off the earth.'

'It's full of information,' said Doug. 'It was made by the First People, and yet they didn't know the wheel. It makes me think their ignorance was chosen.'

Fern thought of something. 'If Jules was here, he would take it away and sell it for a million dollars. A genuine stone age carving, don't you know? He'd want you too. How old are you?'

'Sixteen.'

'Are you still at school?'

'In theory.'

Fern said, 'Your sperm father will never have any interest in his ten daughters. But he'll want you for his very own. I think he'll wait till you're legally an adult and then he'll approach you. He knows your name and where you live.'

'Approach me?'

'Well obviously you'll be his heir. That is generally a meaningless term. But Jules is rich and influential. When he sees you, he'll shape a life for you. I can't picture what it might be. It would be a life of wealth and privilege, I think. Or is it responsibility? Do you want to travel?'

'Only with my Horses,' said the boy.

'I must be fair about this: all you have to do is stay right here on the farm and wait. And your sperm father will come, I think, and give you whatever you ask for. On the other hand, he'd be a hard man to run away from.'

Doug looked out to sea. 'I'll work it out,' he said. He showed her a haybarn on the hill, and some horse blankets. The Horses grazed and the boy went home, returning with some food and drink.

She asked him then, 'Why is she like that, First Horse, always backing into life? It's most impressive, but . . . Is it because she wants to be in the lead and also one of the gang? It's no fun being out in front, I suppose, if you're not sure if anyone's following.'

'I always assumed she was keeping an eye on her past,' said Doug, 'and on her siblings.'

'I see; like you,' said Fern. He left her then, and she slept deeply.

six

First thing in the morning she hurried to
the rock pool. The mangrove was standing upright now,
and impatient. Waves lipped over the rocks and it could
leave at any moment but was waiting for her.

As the mangrove signalled her to climb on board, Fern
found she was also ready to go, although rather inappro-
priately dressed for the trip. She had left her jump-suit in
the bach, in a brown paper parcel. The abrupt awakening
meant it was now buried in a heap of debris dumped in
the Pipetown Harbour. So here she was in clothes she had
slept in, her aunt's old dress and sandshoes, and the
turquoise mother-of-the-bride hat she had used for a
pillow, stepping on board the mangrove full of excitement
once again.

It bounded over the rocks and wave tops, leaping like
a flying fish. The knack of riding it came back at once,
though it felt like a year since her last trip. She sur-
rendered some of her will, cheerfully.

Once in deep sea, again they turned to the left and
followed the coastline south-west. They rounded the long
sweep of farmland, the green skirt that spread at the base
of the Moving Mountain, the one that ran away. The
perfect pyramid was their centre and they arced like a
compass pencil around its fixed point. They were the
moving ones, the Mountain was constant. There was
always the tip of the Mountain, bitten away in the centre,
source of a lava flow that had once rushed steeply down
its sides and slowed to make the gentle, even circle of

grasslands swinging around its base, like the skirt of a whirling dervish.

The landscape was also continuously changing. A minor range of bushclad hills swung into view and twisted back, was passed and left behind. They came to lahar country, studded with many small marble-shaped hills that were gobs of gathered stone dropped and isolated as the unstoppable stream of lava pushed down and out and entered the sea. Fern was glad to pass these bubbles of earth, for they had an old and holy look that made her weary.

The sea was calm now and the mountain clear of clouds. She was experiencing the journey as a pleasure jaunt, as if she had booked with a tourist office and was getting her money's worth. Then without warning the mangrove swerved to the right and headed away from the coast, which until now they had paralleled closely. Fern felt terribly insecure at this change of policy. The sight of land within swimming distance to a strong swimmer like herself had been immensely reassuring.

'Perhaps we are avoiding a current,' she thought. 'Or an undersea volcano.' She gave the mangrove the benefit of the doubt, but the comforting land receded further and further behind her. They were an exceedingly small craft to be so far out to sea. Urgently she tried to argue with the mangrove's intentions and found herself tipped into the water which was not by any means warm. The plant rushed off in its chosen direction and she screamed.

'Just joking! but don't do that again,' the mangrove seemed to imply as it backtracked and hovered while she clambered up again, saturated and chilled. She adjusted her chiffon cloche; it fitted snugly and she pulled out the edge to drain the trapped sea water. She tried with one hand to wring out her dress but the mangrove wouldn't wait for such fiddliness. It sped ahead. Before too long the wind dried off the worst of the water, though salt remained and the dress was sticky.

They rode high waves now, some head on, some obliquely, and Fern felt seasick. She was on the verge of fear but there was nothing to do but co-operate. The mangrove might have had its reasons for stopping off at Pipetown; she might as well assume it had another valid destination.

The wind stepped up, grey processions of cloud filled in the sky above, and it rained a little. The journey was a struggle for them both. Faster and faster rushed the mangrove as if there were real urgency, and so there was, for Fern was so cold her fingers were clumsy, although it was early summer. She felt her oval soul billow out ahead, pulling her along like a spinnaker and flapping when she changed tack. The rain flew away and she could still faintly see the coast far behind her, a white haze. A new outline of hills appeared in front. Nearer and nearer they rode until she realised there was a long, low finger of land ahead to her right, with a clump of pines at the end. The mangrove made a right-angled turn and headed for the lee side of this spit of sand, passing a lighthouse on the tip and following shallow water the length of the sand finger.

At this stage Fern felt great relief in herself and in her mangrove. They travelled calmly in the crook of the spit past fifty kilometres of sandhills. The new blue range loomed closer and larger, then gently slid away again, easing to the left as they came into the wide, calm bay. The mangrove was a kilometre out from the dunes and yet the water was almost too shallow to negotiate. The breeze was lighter and the sea was as flat as a puddle, with tiny wrinkles. They seemed to be coasting with the last of their momentum. At the base of the spit they passed a tall scoured-out peninsula. Up the channel they ducked low under a causeway and reached a muddy estuary. Cold and bedraggled and hungry in the dusk, Fern tumbled off into the mud as the mangrove settled behind a clump of manuka and reeds, burrowing its root into comfortable slime.

Fern scrambled through reeds and gorse and over a dirt road. The nearest house was a kitset house with a deck and doors upstairs and down. It stood above the other modest cottages; in a city it might have been despised but here it looked pretentious. Fern was beyond selecting her refuge; more tired and sore than after her previous day's sailing because of the stress she had generated, she collapsed at the gate like a Brontë.

She woke confused in an upstairs room and called out something incoherent; an elderly woman appeared at the door, staring at her. The woman's colour was bluish grey, like blue gum leaves. Her moko was an intensification of the grey: inky arabesque tattooed symmetrically over her chin and lower lip. Fern thought her very strangely coloured, and barely real, as if she were tattooed on the air.

The woman sighed. 'I suppose it's because I'm a ghost,' she said. 'Still, you can't talk.' She waved at a mirror and Fern saw herself burnt red over brown by wind and sun, pale grey from feet to knees with dried mud, and the top of her breast throbbing yellow and green where her aunty's dress had lost some buttons. The dress, once navy blue with tiny white posies, was sticky and splotched with mud. She was still wearing her hat, dented and droopy; she had started to feel rather attached to it.

'I don't think I'm a ghost,' said Fern. 'It's hard to be sure, when you put it like that.'

The old woman said, 'Of course you're a ghost. But you've got a body inside you.'

'I thought it was the other way round.'

'More fool you,' said the old woman. 'I recognise your

body. Pinch yourself.' Fern did, and felt nothing except alarm. 'I think you might be cold. I've run you a bath. Come along. You can call me Kehua, I suppose.'

Fern followed Kehua into a bathroom with an excellent hot bath ready. She noticed a gaping split in the back of Kehua's skull. Inside the head there was blue and brown smoke swirling.

She lay for a long time in the bath, topping it up with hot water now and then. Her aunt's dress lay on the floor, wet and filthy. Fern washed her hair and rinsed it. Then she found dry towels in a cupboard and after a rub emerged wrapped in two of them.

'Could I please borrow something to wear?' she asked. (This was getting to be a habit.)

Kehua herself was draped in a blanket. But she indicated a wardrobe and from a generous store Fern chose the roughest pair of trousers, and old T-shirt and a baggy woollen sweater. Now she would like some food. But Kehua said, 'I told you, I'm a ghost. That means I'm always hungry but I never get to eat. So don't expect me to cook for you.'

Fern found this interesting, because Kehua spoke English as if she had her mouth full. 'Well why do you need a house?' she asked. 'And all this clothing? Do you pay rent? Don't tell me a ghost can own property!'

Kehua looked at her coldly. Shortly she said, 'Own? Property?' several times, as if these words amazed her and as if Fern was offensively ignorant. She did explain that the house belonged to a city couple, the Ewers, who occupied it only in the holidays and the occasional weekend.

Fern took this in, then she found bread in a freezer, opened a tin of creamed corn and ate it on toast. A cup of tea and bed, again, to regenerate. As she drifted off she thought how much more natural she was feeling already.

She hadn't realised what a strain it had been, living a normal life.

In the morning she asked Kehua the name of the place.

'It was robbed of its name,' said Kehua. 'You are allowed to ask questions. But not all of them will receive an answer.'

'Wouldn't you like to be with your own people again, your own generation I mean?' asked Fern compassionately.

'I have a job to do,' said Kehua. She looked out the big window over the estuary to the Old Woman Bluff. Fern looked too, for the limestone landscape compelled her to do so. It loomed up between the estuary and the sea. A smooth profile at its left, sloping down to a wide marsh; then dog teeth on the horizon; then a mounting bracket to the monstrous cliff straight ahead, and another cliff, and another – corrugated carvings, vertical slices cut from two hundred metres in the air almost down to sea level. On the top was a long lip of green, sliding downwards to the right.

A jumble of tumbled rocks made an apron at the base of the cliffs, giving a clue as to how they were formed: a squeezing of tectonic plates deep below the earth and sea, when part of the earth had sprung high into the air with no other way to go. The Moving Mountain had rumbled, and melted rocks in its womb, and bled them out red-hot in a circle to the sea; Old Woman Bluff had risen intact like Aphrodite from the ocean, losing only a hillside of boulders in the process. And millions of years earlier, before volcano boiling over or bluff going up like a lift, the Moving Mountain province had been somehow neatly gripped by the northern hook of this Other Island. For there was once no Other Island, but only one. If it was fundamentally two, they were locked so firmly together that they felt like one. When pressure had been exerted,

71

this island had so easily let the other one go, let it drift to the north out of reach and out of understanding.

Downwards and outwards from the bluff were gaunt channels and ribs of earth, bruised here and there with a dull green where scrub had begun to colour in the dead valleys. Fern distinguished grey patches of burnt kanuka from the grey of exposed rock. Black patches signalled the worst ravages of the last bush fire. As the bluff softened into hills on the right, there was densely growing kanuka forest, adapted to the prevailing winds, bending intently up and over the hills, leaning for its very life. Fern was very conscious that beyond the bluff and the kanuka hills was the open sea: not the mudflats of Gorse Bay, which lay behind the Ewers' house, but the ocean, along the edge of which she and the mangrove had travelled. She could hear the hush of the surf, though it couldn't be seen.

While they watched, a misty rain travelled over the estuary like smoke, with one blue window open to the sky. The bluff was blurred, almost erased before her eyes. Kehua kept staring past the rain which was suddenly heavy and sharp on the glass. Beyond it the blue patch stretched, the clouds grew fluffy and bright, the cliffs returned, the green glowed, and a patch of sun illuminated the cap of an odd boulder shaped like a toad-stool. The water in the estuary, sitting in its low-tide channels like a torn puddle, was white, grey, silver, dun, white, patchy . . . Fern was awed by what she recognised now as Kehua's task. It was to hold the Old Woman Bluff, to hold it in place.

That day and every day Fern went over the road and through the gorse to visit the mangrove. There was no remaining trace of animal empathy. It was concentrating on resettling after its emigration, and on growth. It was already a giant, considering the stage of its development. How tall, how broad would it be in twenty-five years, she wondered. Would its offspring be typical, or a new strain? Irrationally, Fern couldn't help feeling responsible. She looked around at the stripped and scraped hills surrounding her. Once they had rippled with kanuka shapes, and further into the valley forests of totara and kahikatea had grown for hundreds and thousands of years. Now the ruling plant was the colonial gorse, imported by well-meaning people to fence the squares of land they'd hoped to convert into English pasture.

In the township area, every original plant had been eliminated, except for bracken whose thick elastic roots interlaced under the surface of the sand. The only trees were a few pines, grown unmanageably tall and straggly, with limbs cracked and dangling, or maimed by chain-saws. Most of the inhabitants in their small cottages lived on strips of bare land. She saw an old man bending down to weed a dry strip of earth. The wind lifted his hair and flicked it. There was no bush or flower or vegetable on his section, only rough pasture grass, and baldness.

Next door the gorse was taller than her head. Great bunchy chunks of green thorn beaded with yellow flowers bounced in the wind as she looked out the bedroom window. This was the plant which bristled over more visible acres than any other now, witness to the Second People's presumptions. Its seeds remained active in the soil for at least a hundred years. With a packet of matches in one hand and a spraygun in the other, the Second People terrorised the land, and the smell was acrid. The purpose of terrorising gorse was largely to re-terrorise it the next year. Yet gorse had every reason to believe it was legitimately occupying the territory.

Now the gorse was sheltering a new cycle of growth, kanuka huddling among protective thorns. In the end, gorse was in sympathy with bush, and in opposition to farmers who took on more land than they could handle.

Fern was bound to wonder whether the mangrove, like the gorse, might take over more than its share of the Other Island. She found it hard to believe that even her extra-ordinary moving mangrove could survive a winter in Gorse Bay. It was surely far colder than the mangrove's normal environment. But then the mild and fertile land of the Sleeping Islands was not the natural habitat of gorse: it proved instead to be its paradise. This could be true of the mangrove. If it blocked the port and smothered the mud flats, that might be bad, and she could be held responsible. But then she thought of the times she had tried to steer the mangrove off its chosen course and decided she'd simply been used by the plant as a bird is used by a seed. Plants do spread over the earth. That wasn't good, it wasn't bad; it was part of the earth's turning.

Fern spent her days placidly now, and they became weeks. She swam in the tiny port where the water was always warm after skimming the sunny shallows of Gorse Bay. Old fishing boats had settled gently by the wrecked wharf, one on top of the other, making a platform that served as a new wharf for the two remaining boats, and for Fern when she fished for herrings. She wandered round the base of Whale Peninsula, sometimes surprising a seal. Often when the tide was out (far, far out) she walked the damp mud to the best cockle patches on the low tide mark, through convolutions of snail tracks, and eel grass, and gesticulating crabs. When the tide turned, it bolted and bubbled back over the sand at a brisk pace.

Other days, she crossed a causeway to the west coast of the spit, to wild breakers and rocks, and endless heaped-up curls of golden sand. Sometimes she jogged on wet sand and reflected clouds jogged with her, keeping pace. She was now awake in her feet, which were usually bare. Mostly she avoided the valley of burnt scrub and the abandoned coal mine. She ate well and read well from the stores of Mr and Mrs Ewer. She asked Kehua questions when she was particularly visible, but Kehua had little conversation. She talked sometimes to the oldish, vigorous people who lived in the area.

Fern found out that the people of the Other Island knew their island as the Main Island, and called the Main Island the Other Island. They were both really Main Islands, being large and peopled, or then again, in spirit they were each only half of a single island. For that matter, there were other Other Islands in the Sleeping Islands, small hearts and sugar buns off the coast in all directions. Fern began to refer to them by their correct names, which dated from a more generous age. The north main island was in fact Stingray Island, and the south main island was Nephrite Island, because it was the source of jade, its waters were jade-green, and the land was shaped like a kidney.

Kehua was far from being one of the first of the First People here. Thirty-seven generations before her birth, her ancestors had sailed their long canoes to this tweak of land rich in soil, trees and fish, and they made it home. In their carved canoes were packed kumara and voices and genealogies. The land and sea made new stories of special fish and crops and storms. From each new generation came heroes and heroines and marriages and poets and children, and insults and raids and revenges, binding them ever more closely to the land. Centuries went by, and it was simple and exciting for Kehua's tribe to go on living where they lived.

Their area was used in a friendly way by other tribes. First People from the north would beach their canoes at the place with no name, after a journey far south to gather greenstone. They would squat for a while and roughly carve the jade, doing what was necessary and leaving the

75

chips at the base of the spit that curved like a giant fern frond around the flat waters of Gorse Bay. And if a mistake was made in ritual or in craftmanship, they left the artefact behind in its home island. They took the bones of whales beached on the spit in their canoes as well, to carve in the north into kidney-shaped hand clubs and ornaments.

Then the Second People came. On Stingray Island they spread out their farms like picnics on a tablecloth laced with bullets. In the north, the First People found that their spoken laws, complex and subtle, were muddied and ignorantly abused as the invaders acted out their strange beliefs about possession: they possessed the land as demons possess a body. Patterns of small wars, conventions of cruelty and chivalry, were exploded by muskets. Starving for clarity, the First People fled in a ferocious refugee flock and slashed at Kehua's tribe, overrunning the south.

Since then, the place with no name had seen a hectic sequence of residents taking whales, coal, gold, timber and scallops. And whales, coal, fish, trees and grass gave way to gorse. For a hundred and fifty years, no one people had stayed in the place with no name for long enough for a name to stick and be remembered; only individuals who thought of it with a private name. And all secretly regarded themselves as First People. The Old Woman Bluff was never owned or claimed, but oversaw the changes. One day, Fern saw a helicopter land on top, and three men walking around, pointing.

Another day, there was more traffic than usual. Holidaymakers and birdwatchers drove past their house. Fern was drinking a cup of tea when she discovered there was a station-wagon pulling into the drive below. The Ewers! They pulled up the roller door and drove into the garage under the house. Fern's only instinct was to avoid them. She slipped out on to the back deck and slid down the metal pole which supported it, leaving the house reeking of occupation. Kehua had simply vanished (it was easy for her), slipped over to Whale Peninsula, site of her village before she died.

Fern's problems were only beginning. She forced her way into the gorse on the section next door, and hid in a makeshift goat shelter consisting of two sheets of corrugated iron and some concrete blocks. Luckily the goats had trodden and eaten the gorse down well inside the lean-to. Nevertheless, Fern was very, very uncomfortable as she crouched on dry, broken gorse and listened to shouts of indignation (and curiosity) issuing from the house next door.

Then a shower of raindrops rattled on the tin roof of her hideaway, and the three goats trotted to their shelter. One hairy black-and-white muzzle after another pushed into the opening. Finding her, they bounced back, frantically bleating. There was heavier rain. Reaching consensus, the three nervous goats forced their way into their own house and after much twisting and stamping settled in a heap almost on top of her. Their smell was noticeable, and Fern wondered whether they were equally offended by her own. They stared at her tolerantly through slits in stripy golden onyx eyes.

She was in the most exposed position, pressed against a jumble of concrete blocks with the rain aiming directly at her. Tall gorse strained much of it before it filmed into the shelter. Stalks old and coarse, as if a potential gorse tree had been chained to a stake, forced to wring every centimetre of growth through a rusty puzzle. Rigid spikes as long as fingers pointed at her from every angle. Gobbets of dead gold flowers drooped with the weight of the rain. It was a thicket of energy, ready to burst into fire when the time was ripe.

Huddled with three rancid, restless, hairy, hoofy beasts

between rain, corrugated iron, and gorse, Fern asked herself for the first time since leaving the Department, 'What am I doing here?' She had squatted in the property of a respectable family without permission, sleeping in their bed, looking out their window at their spectacular view. She had no excuse, except that a ghost was already in residence and didn't mind sharing – a likely tale in an almost new house which had seen no deaths. Naturally when they turned up, guilt evicted her instantly. To evade their righteous anger and possible legal repercussions she had scurried straight to another piece of land with a fence around it, indicating that it too belonged to someone. She was now crouched in the sleepout of three goats, still without being invited: she was certainly still trespassing.

Yet she had a perfectly good house of her own up in Northcity, which was probably being burgled, vandalised or squatted in at this very moment. The lawns would be knee high, the mail all over the footpath. Furthermore, her last mortgage payment was overdue. She was jolted out of her mangrove mentality and began to regard herself as a person with a problem.

It occurred to her that she was more attached to the mangrove than to her car. (Whatever had happened to her car?) She had hinted to one or two residents of the nameless place that she was living in the tall house with the blessing of the owners, and shortly her lies would be exposed. Not lies, exactly; just unsuccessful guesses. She could run away, but only in one direction, and not without advertising her departure. Then, by definition, she'd be leaving Gorse Bay, and she wasn't ready to go. Or else she could brazen it out. She imagined the worst possible consequences: police, judgment, paying the penalty, clean slate. She practised in her head receiving the owners' abuse; it wouldn't be any worse than Menzies' unctuous manipulation, and anyway, she had her secret

78

weapon. She would be neither senselessly stubborn but just tell the truth and try to make a deal.

She waited till the rain stopped, pushed the goats out with some difficulty, and scrambled through the gorse, over the fence, and up the steps to the main room of the house. Through the glass doors Mr and Mrs Ewer saw a middle-aged woman in an old-fashioned navy crêpe dress torn ragged, barefoot, bleeding copiously from fine scratches and deeper ones, and quite damp. However, she spoke to them as if she were wearing stockings.

'May I come in and discuss a business arrangement with you please?' Reluctantly they let her in and showed her where she might sit – she, who had been living there for weeks! 'I am the person who has been living in your house. I am very grateful to you for your unwitting hospitality.'

'Unwitting hospitality!' cried Mr Ewer.

'I hope you have found everything in order.'

'Everything in order!' Mr Ewer expectorated the words.

'I have been using some of your supplies, you will notice,' said Fern.

'Our supplies!' Mr Ewer compensated for a lack of originality with plentiful indignation.

'That was very remiss of me, and I apologise,' said Fern. 'I intend to replace them very shortly. I should explain that the house was open when I arrived, and I couldn't find any key to lock it up. Did you realise that?' she continued, putting them gently in the wrong. That was another trick she had learned from Jules.

They looked at each other accusingly, diverted from their common enemy.

'Did you realise that?' cried Mr Ewer to Mrs Ewer.

'You're the one who locks up!' cried Mrs Ewer in despair.

'In any case, I was glad of a place to shelter when I happened to be stranded here, and I do thank you. I took the attitude that I was protecting your house. As you know, you get all sorts coming here in the summer. Surfies, druggies, birdwatchers – all sorts.'

It wasn't very convincing and Mr Ewer said sarcastically, 'All sorts!'

'I have a proposition to make,' continued Fern, maintaining the initiative. 'I've decided to spend some time in this area. Would you permit me to pay you rent, including retrospectively of course, until I find my own place? And if you know of anywhere suitable in the long term, I'd be grateful to you.'

Mr Ewer said, 'She'd be grateful to us!' and named a figure which was double what he should have asked, and half a city rent.

'I accept,' said Fern graciously. 'And naturally I shall pay my share of electricity.'

'But we don't want a stranger with us while we're on holiday,' objected Mrs Ewer. 'That is hardly what we built this place for!'

With dignity, Fern explained that of course she would remove herself until the family had finished their holiday. No problem. They were there for the rest of the week; she would take over on the morning of their departure. They shook hands and Fern walked down the steps, head high, and along the dirt road to civilisation. It was not an amiable arrangement, but she had done the best she could.

Almost at once she got a lift from a crowd of holiday-makers. She squashed with two teenagers in the back seat and half an hour later was in the nearest townlet, the settlement of Oystercatcher. She walked down its main street, past the general store, the pub, and the county offices. It looked like a very placid Wild West town. She found the post office and pushed a brass handle into a tall-ceilinged, wooden interior.

From a cubby-hole she telephoned Hilary at the Department of Philosophy in Northcity, transferring the charges to Hilary's home phone. Thank goodness, the Department was not on holiday. She fended off most of Hilary's protests and queries. Did Hilary know anyone who would want to rent her house? Hilary left the phone to look at the staff noticeboard. Five staff members were in need of accommodation, she reported. Fern asked Hilary to lease her house, first helping herself to any of the contents that she fancied. She asked her to clear out her drawers of clothes and papers, and toss them into a cupboard somewhere. She said to sell the car and to forward the mail, especially her post office savings book, to the Oystercatcher post office. She promised to write as soon as she had some money for paper and pen.

When she said goodbye to Hilary, she asked to be transferred to Jules Menzies' phone. His secretary answered; Jules was absent for the day. Fern gave her resignation to Rosemary, overcoming the temptation to plead sickness, or otherwise soften the act.

All she had done was stall for time. Some day she would make a more convincing decision, but this would do for now. She went to the boarding house at the end of the street and asked for a room for three or four nights. The owner looked dubious and asked for a deposit. Fern explained in her ladylike voice that she was waiting for some money to be transferred, and would otherwise have to sleep in a ditch. The owner gave her a small room; such things were not rare in Gorse Bay.

On the fourth day a big heap of letters and bills arrived in the post office, together with her handbag and bankbook. She took some money out and sat on the beach to read her mail.

There were letters from her daughter Dorothy, which is me, of course, and shortly I will show you those. But first, I will mention that the only other significant personal mail which had been stacking up in her letterbox was a series of notes from Orlando Puddleigh.

'Dear Fern, surely Menzies wasn't that bad? What happened? Your friend Orlando.'

'Dear Fern, just tell me where you are, OK? I'm worried about you. Your friend Orlando.'

'Dear Fern, are you sick? Can I help you? Your friend Orlando.'

'Dear Fern, this place is awful without you. I miss you. Your friend Orlando.'

And so on.

seven

And here is the first of my letters to Fern:
'Dear Mum, I'm writing this on the plane because I know
you'll be looking for a letter straight away. We've been
stuffed with food and drink three times already, but now
they leave us in peace apart from the movie up front. We
have technically arrived in New RUSA already, having
gone through customs in Honolulu. It is strange in the
Northern Hemisphere: whatever direction you go, sooner
or later you arrive in RUSA. We can only admire the – oh
no, that doesn't sound like me. I think I might be trying
too hard to be the diplomat's wife.

'Well, please don't worry about me day and night,
though I doubt if I can stop you. It must seem like a big
adventure to you, my setting off to a foreign country. But
if anyone is safe here, it is Charles and me, with the full
force of diplomatic immunity behind us.

'All the same, I feel, I think, like one of the early white
immigrants to the Sleeping Islands. Terrified; thrilled. I
wonder if I shall want to civilise the RUSAns, or go
native? All my love, Dot.'

Next letter: 'Dear Mum, I imagine you've been sending
letters to an insufficient address and that's why I haven't
heard from you yet. I can't believe you haven't written
because it's a law of nature that mothers write to their
absent children once a week. Anyway please take note of
the full address: Sleeping Islands Embassy, PO Box
9492910, Washington DC 21197403, New RUSA. If you
didn't get the district number the letters might wait

forever. I did go to the Chief Post Office, but it was like a city, and I got lost.

'Some of the habits of the New RUSAns still shock me although I have been here three weeks now. Did you know, everyone lives in apartments instead of houses, rich or poor? There's always a security guard in the lobby, with a GUN, I might add, behind bullet-proof glass. Bullet-proof glass! (I suppose it does prove there are bullets.) To let you into your own home! Very bad manners, eh? And the apartments are not smaller than houses, but larger! The ones I've been to (these are not poor people) are twice the size they need to be. And listen to this: they all have more bathrooms than bedrooms!! Maybe three bedrooms and four bathrooms. This is true, no kidding. They are all obsessed with cleanliness and privacy. Everyone does their own private poos in their own private territory. (But it all gets mixed together in the end.) And every place I've seen has been like a high class hotel: new furniture, all matching – classy, but it doesn't feel homey. Sometimes I think about dunnies I have used up in the mountains, where an outhouse with a long drop is luxury, compared with downing trou in the bush and getting slashed by garnia or hooked by bush-lawyer spines in the bum – oh boy! The best ones are the ones that haven't got doors, and are built to the view. OK, I'm acquainted with real bathrooms in real houses too; yours are grisly but they have those nice asparagus ferns . . . But I'm afraid these people must be soft, like the last of the Romans. I hope I don't get soft. But I can tell you already, it's going to be hard organising a real tramp from here. I've started going to the Breathless Gym, for goodness sakes, but it's not the same at all.

'Oh dear. I sound like a whinging import, don't I, grizzling because it's not like it was back home? Slap. I repent. And by the way, this horrified fascination of mine is reciprocated. The RUSAns are very interested in the Sleeping Islands, very interested indeed. And mostly, they don't approve of us one bit.

'Charles is busy and sends his love. He is quite at home already here, believe me. He would like to smack every Sleeping Island bottom for the nuisance he has here in Washington. He himself is so sublimely reasonable: why can't we all be like him, and especially why can't our Prime Minister? That's his attitude. When I overheard him at a cocktail party talking about our antinuclear stand, he was so soothing and compromising that I felt downright scatological. He sees impudence where I see courage. And he's supposed (in a small way) to represent you and me over here! I suppose he is still insecure in this new job. That's my charitable view. But then again . . . I know RUSA is very very scary and enormous – that's the whole point, isn't it? But after all, we have right on our side!

'Much love, and don't give up on the writing. Love from Dot.'

Not surprisingly, Fern was amused by these letters, and my other ones. The only thing which distressed her was that her asparagus ferns would be dead by now. Back she went to the guest-house and answered my letter with a minimum of detail. She more or less implied — well, I'll include her letter here.

'Dear Dot, I am very interested in your news of life in New RUSA. It seems a long way from my old life, and even further from the new.

'The reason why I didn't write before was that I have moved to Gorse Bay. I have had enough of working in that silly place. Now that you're married and away, there's no need for me to keep on the house in Northcity. So I'm renting it out while I see a different bit of the world. It is staggeringly beautiful here, and one hundred percent peaceful. They seem to go together. It is literally one of the ends of the earth, and it must be the opposite of Washington. It's so quiet that in the evening when the birds have stopped singing, even a dripping tap can give me a fright.

'Meantime I don't exactly have an address, but the post office at Oystercatcher will hold mail till I can pick it up. So we are both starting a new life and a new landscape at the same time. Keep in touch. Love, Fern.'

'Keep in touch'! My own mother! What she said was true: there was no need at all for her to keep on working at the Department or to stay in the City. But – I didn't have any way of following that 'But – '. I just felt insecure. Me with three bathrooms and her without an address! I pictured her pausing fastidiously at various hotels and hoped she wasn't using up her savings rashly. Nothing in her letter, you'll notice, about mangroves or ghosts.

Well, after dealing with further business, she did some shopping. There was a tiny op shop and she bought two woollen jerseys, a pair of trousers, and a jacket. At the store she bought a box of groceries and a pair of gumboots. Then she paid off the guest house and joined a tourist party travelling in a four-wheel-drive bus to the spit. They dropped her off at the Ewers' house: it was the day before the owners were due to leave.

They stood on the deck united in disapproval as she brought up the groceries. Then Mr Ewer spoke before her well-bred manner could confuse them.

'We've changed our minds. We don't want you here. You can thank your lucky stars we're not getting the law on to you. We've told the neighbours; they'll get the police if they see any funny business.'

'You want me to go, now?' asked Fern. She'd been expecting this, more or less.

'We want you to go, now,' said Mr Ewer. His wife

looked defensive, his daughter anxious, his son truculent.

'It's a long way to the grocery store,' said Fern. 'So I hope you don't mind if I have a drink of water and take one of these loaves of bread.'

The daughter rushed to get her a drink. Nobody asked where she was going.

'Thank you very much for your hospitality,' said Fern. 'I'll just be next door, if you need me for anything.'

'If we need you for anything!' said Mr Ewer.

She took her loaf of bread and bottle of water and bag of clothing down the steps and out the front gate. Then over the next fence, through the gorse to the goat shelter. With the Ewers watching from their upstairs deck, she crawled into the tiny hut. For all they knew, she would stay there forever. Because of this, their daughter became a feminist.

The Ewers left the settlement the next morning. In the evening, as soon as it was fully dark, Fern crept quietly to the house and tried the door. Kehua arranged for the door to open itself. They didn't turn on the lights (not that Kehua ever did) and they spoke quietly. Fern could move freely indoors but otherwise she was a prisoner tied by the neighbours' eyes. She couldn't walk over the wild hills, or on the beach to look at the blue mountains jagging down to the sea. She could watch black swans and godwits and seagulls through a crack in the curtains – but she couldn't go gathering mussels or cockles, not even at night, for the stars were furry with brightness. She might just as well be joining dots in the Department of Philosophy.

'Why are you here?' she asked Kehua. 'Instead of some-where else, I mean.'

Kehua hesitated, and then spoke. 'It's hard to say. There is no essence. You have to have all of it, all at once. There are symbols. Everything is what it is, and is for what it is for. You can borrow my head for looking.'

She swung her chair around so her back was to Fern. Fern averted her eyes from the cleavage in the skull, but good manners have nothing to do with visions. Kehua forced her to look into that smoky cavern, where the air smudged and swirled. Fern's gaze went deep in the hollow of the old woman's head and into her eyes of blue-black jelly, and once her breathing settled down, she began to see – things.

She saw her first sighting as if through the far end of a telescope. From infinite distance, down a long tight tunnel, she saw a hint of movement in a spot as large as a comma. It was hard for her to see it at all, because it was not related to anything in her experience. A mole of flame, perhaps, a mirror of wax, a mercury nailhead . . . fire chasing rock, rock breaking water. Fire stretching, water crumbling. Water waiting, rock rising, fire falling . . . The tiny lobe breathed in and swelled, and fire and steam wished for land and sea, and rock forced it. The bubble blew up and up and the surface warped, magnets melted, and a Sleeping Island slid into lonely waters as a continent split along its weakest joints. The Sleeping Island stretched like steam and raggedly tore through the middle. The globe breathed out and its petals cooled and locked together uneasily. It throbbed, every million years or so.

Hundreds of pulses passed while Fern's metabolism adjusted to this way of knowing. Her mind accepted hibernation for repairs. She was conscious only that the world was a world, it whirled like a hula hoop, and there were no straight lines in its components or its motion.

Then she was looking more closely at Nephrite Island. As the planet throbbed, east and west were squeezed together and the island narrowed and waisted, and rivers ran backwards and lakes turned upside down, and the centre buckled to form a spine of high land from north to south. In the same short millennium, the Old Woman Bluff rose out of the sea like a monstrous whale. The air roared and the earth spasmed, till the crest of the tallest land-wave burst, the sky plunged and the Old Woman Bluff was stranded, sea gushing off her back. And all the while, plants were working out their problems and inventing themselves. Tree ferns found themselves to be in all ways satisfactory.

Kehua closed her eyes and Fern rested for twenty beats of the earthly heart, twenty million years. Then she saw Stingray Island flower in fire, bud with popping volcanoes. The Moving Mountain built itself by bursting again and again into flame, its red core coming to the boil and overflowing continually for fifty thousand years. An andesite boulder of distinctive shape rolled down towards the sea: in this stone, the squatting haunches and the bulging brow of Hine-Mother-of-us-all could already be detected. Volcanic ash rained in a generous circle around the peak, isolating it in a sea of hot soil. And plants took advantage of every intermittent cooling.

Then ice, tall ice, crawled over the land, almost to the top of the mountains; Nephrite Island was buried up to its head in ice. Clamps of ice reshaped the side of the Moving Mountain. Ice scraped and gouged out valleys with relentless weight. Humps became mountains deeply chiselled by gravity locked in mobile ice.

Then Fern followed Kehua's eye-path to look straight down the valley outside their window, beyond the estuary. The end of an aging glacier retreated to the head of the valley. The ice was high and heavily scored; brown debris and green light were trapped in its travelled depths. Young tree ferns raised their ancient shapes at the edge of the ice once more, green fins of the world vibrating as it swam through space. A handful of penguins as tall as a woman waddled uncertainly along the ice-claw. Faced with a cosmic change of weather, they had to decide for posterity whether to withdraw with the ice or return to the sea.

The picture blurred for a beat of thirteen thousand years and Fern now had a new perspective, closer, at ground level. She was left on the shore as a huge canoe packed with people pushed off from the shore of a Pipetown which had no pipes and no white people – but people! People. Her mind simmered. She was a person, and here were people in the Sleeping Islands. She looked on, fizzy and fearful. The tribe had barely arrived on the slopes of the Moving Mountain and begun to settle when it belched and dribbled bits of metallic ash and white-hot lava. Not a major eruption, but one which Kehua's tribe (for there she was, hints of her face on many faces) interpreted as a fair warning. It was a thousand years too early to build houses on the Mountain, so they left for the empty south.

In this canoe were fifty people, and others followed. Also in this canoe was the old lump of granite which had been blessed in preparation for the time it would be carved into the shape of Hine-Mother-of-us-all. With proper ceremony, it was safer to carry the stone to the south with the tribe than to leave it in the path of lava. It would become their greatest treasure, their celebration of arrival in a new home, a source of ultimate comfort.

Now with scarcely a break, Fern's eyes moved over six or seven hundred years, into the eyes of Kehua as she was the day before she died. First thing in the morning, she had a leisurely look at the estuary from the hump of Whale Peninsula. As she watched, the water was first tight and shiny, reflecting perfectly the Old Woman Bluff beyond it. Little by little, channels of aluminium brightness appeared and spread as the tide came in. At last the water was all brightness and the bluff was no longer twinned. A small wind pinched the water, shading the colour to deepness by the headland. All over the bluff-tops and the hills and up the valley beyond there was forest: not only the familiar kanuka, clotted like cream on the most exposed slopes, but giant trees which did not cringe before the winds. They arched and towered, changing the very shape of the land, so that the winds found a different route around them. She turned slowly round to survey the almost empty water which was not yet Gorse Bay.

After this peaceful beginning, Kehua had a busy day. She was old. She moved about her village, taking her time; people deferred to her. She approved the flax-scraping of a group of younger women. She nodded and gossiped with their mothers, cooking fish and kumara in a steaming pit. She teased two old men who were reminiscing about their days of hunting those earthbound birds, tall as people but more solid; a heavy mass of muscle on tree-trunk legs. She said you could steam that meat from full moon to full moon, and it would stay as tough as whalebone. Still, it gave strength. She sat in front of her people-sized hut in the sun, leaning on her stick. A young woman brought her baby and Kehua patiently told her how to brew kawakawa leaves into medicine. She saved a few cockles for her favourite grandson, who was at Big Rock with the priest, learning (slowly) the genealogy of eighty generations. When the young man returned he was shining with sweat, well muscled, with brave eyes and lover's lips.

And she slept without fear, Fern's spirit in Kehua's old body.

There was barely a glimmer from the sun in the east when tiny noises outside started sounding wrong. Then there was a great roaring chant at the very threshold of the village and Kehua got up slowly, pulled a wrap around her and went outside to see a mess of fighters from the region of the Moving Mountain flaunting muskets, spears, clubs and axes. Nobody had had the slightest warning of this particular raid, but she knew at once why they had come.

She saw women behind the terrifying battalion, for their journey was an emigration as well as a war party. One young woman stepped forward among the men. She was a poet and the niece of a chief. With a jolt, Fern recognised her own ruffly brown hair (in a tangle of flying insects), and looked into her own upside-down brown eyes. The woman fixed her gaze on the young man who was Kehua's grandchild, shaking dawn dreams out of his head. She called to him and he accepted his life from her, and went with her as husband to an alien canoe at the base of Whale Peninsula.

The enemy women hurried after them. Then screams began to slice and writhe, and blood shot high into the karaka trees. Kehua saw her family dismembered, the old ones felled, the warriors speared; as for the babies, the family's future, their eyeballs were popped out, trailing threads of blood, and swallowed whole. The neighbouring village did not escape, and thus the entire wisdom of the group, all its history and density and sense, all its delicacy and power, all were eliminated in a single day.

Because she had run after her grandson, Kehua was last of her village to die. She watched too much, too much, and ran to the cliff to make her own death. She was caught by a warrior chief who split her skull with a single blow from a greenstone club like a slice of a glacier's kidney. Her soul rushed screeching out of the hole in her head, rushing north towards the northernmost cape of Stingray Island where all souls enter the underworld. But it was pulled back with a twitch like a bird in a snare; her spirit was hostage to Whale Peninsula, whose earth had been made rich and sacred over the centuries by the blood of all new mothers. Every placenta grown and shed for a baby here had been buried here, and every placenta fed a tree. The land claimed Kehua and gave her certain tasks: mourning the dead, touching the trees with her grey neon shimmer, and guarding the Old Woman Bluff. She was not exactly a person any more, but she was chosen as the token person of the land. All this Fern understood without words through the eyes of Kehua, who of course had not been known as Kehua while she was alive.

There were three vaults of strength in the tribe and the murderers stole from them all. Some important people were taken as slaves, and the involuntary bridegroom would be integrated into the adopting tribe. The conquerors lit a fire on the beach and roasted the most significant and tasty parts of their most significant victims. They ate, and scattered bones on purpose. They ate the strength of warriors, the authority of chiefs, the voice of poets and the sweetness of children, and they tore the bones apart and muddled them up. Then they loaded treasures into their canoes: old weapons full of conquests and cunning; ornaments of jade and whalebone; ornate boxes of valuable feathers; and the granite statue of the goddess Hine-Mother-of-us-all. Then they sailed away, for after this brief encounter they decided that Whale Peninsula was too wild a place to settle. They travelled east, out of sight, and south, with their pride well fed.

Fern was more than ready to stop looking, but Kehua forced her to continue, for her picture was far from finished. Massive logs now lay scattered all over the big valley and the hills. The land was torn into new holes. Young plants were crushed and parted. Heaps of debris smouldered and then the landscape was a towering blaze. Mountains of smoke arose and covered the whole of Gorse Bay, and in Australia the sun rose brackishly and smelled of burning.

Kehua thought, 'They call it breaking in the land. Why does the land need breaking? It would be better to leave it all in one piece.'

They watched it grow green, brilliant sunlit green. Rain fell, seed germinated, grass sprouted. There were neat golden hedges keeping fat white sheep in their paddocks. Each farmer had a certain block of land allotted. His own sheep had to stay on his own block of land, getting plump on his own grass. The gorse hedges were chubby, dividing the curvy hills and valleys into straight-edged sections.

'They call it grazing. But even a graze takes a while to heal,' thought Kehua. 'You can loosen the earth and plant your kumara and the ground is not broken; it's only moved around. And when you've finished, the bush comes back. It only takes a couple of hundred years.'

And then there were gorse bushes scattered through the paddocks and the farmland looked worn out. Fern saw a whole new layer of activity over the land and under the land. The valley was filled with cottages, a railway line came down to the sea; she saw a very long wharf driven into the shallows, with a dredge working, and coal-carrying ships lined up on either side. There were grocery shops and a butcher's shop with children swinging on the hooks, and a piano accordion playing; a tennis court that peeled up at the edges in the hot sun, and boarding houses; and a sly grog corner where men in black trousers drank behind the gorse bushes.

Fern heard Kehua thinking, 'They never did break the earth for the coal. They entered it. If you're brave enough for that, you deserve the coal.'

Then the cottages in the valley vanished and the mine props collapsed. Beside the mine, a small clump of trees had escaped slaughter. Water flooded the abandoned shafts and the cleft became a delicate glade. Fern looked closer and saw that the pool was used as a dump for bits of machinery and rusty corrugated iron and plastic bags.

Kehua's thought distracted her: 'You can take fish out of the sea, and you don't break the sea. It closes over behind your nets. But what are these things called breakwaters? There's something happening down the coast, over the Old Woman Bluff . . .'

Fern's eyes pulled back from the valley. Over the estuary a flock of black swans flapped to the east, holding their beaks and bodies steady in a single silent string. The air closed behind them. Then she looked far again, and saw the whole landscape golden with gorse; the sun blazed and the wind screamed down the valley and a power line cracked in the whipping of the wind. The gorse caught alight and burned and burned and burned. In three seconds fire exploded from the foot of the bluff to the top of the bluff, and the face of the Old Woman crackled red and then black.

'You silly child, stop crying,' said Kehua. 'It's only the lifetime of a moth, you know. I'm doing my best. Everything will change one, two, three more times before the world is finished.'

'What do you mean, finished?' asked Fern.

'How do I know?' said Kehua.

eight

The history of the world had been Kehua's parting gift. Fern prepared for a journey somewhere else. She decided to borrow a haversack from the Ewers' store cupboard. They had five, one for each of the family and one to spare. She packed up food and her bundle of clothes, a large lemonade bottle full of water, matches, a tin-opener, and a tin plate and mug. She took a sleeping bag as well, one that fitted neatly on the haversack.

She hardly slept that night. She lay in the bed, trying not to wear it out. Fat possums scrambled over the roof and the deck and hurled themselves at windows, scattering turds with the sound of machine-gun fire. The lining of the house cracked loudly as it cooled down. Rain threw itself on the roof and then stopped abruptly. A raping burglar rattled the garage door below, and advanced up the stairs with heavy steps which never reached the top floor, steps which thumped in perfect time to the blood surging in her temples. Moas with beaks like pliers snuffled under the bed as they changed position. Darkness nibbled her edges and chewed forty times. Shadowy faces shifted the curtains aside and poked at her with one eye. Multiple sclerosis and cancer fingered her heels and calves. The wind came in steady surges through the absolute night-time silence of the place with no name. She was huddled on the face of the earth, and the earth was snoring through its nostril, the estuary. She had gone too far, and the only solution was to go even further.

Next morning, far from fresh for her journey, she

wanted to kiss Kehua goodbye, but it was rather unsatisfactory. She aimed her nose at Kehua's nose but met no flesh of course; what there was of Kehua went right out of focus. She tried to say the sort of thing which is very difficult for a woman who used to wear navy blue court shoes with a burgundy trim.

'Kehua, if you ever need anything . . . I'll be thinking of you.'

It sounded like a gift card. Wearing her hat for good luck, Fern left the house and went to see her mangrove. It was fattening its stalk and had used its green reserves, sprouting five more branches. There were eleven other mangroves of varying sizes and stages established in the estuary. It was a migration of mangroves. She took her leave.

The water on the estuary was so tight and even, she felt she could walk on its surface. She planned to circle the water and climb the Old Woman Bluff from the east and south, and then turn south again along the coast. In the distance, burnt kanuka ghosted the slopes like grey peach bloom. She passed the straggle of houses in the nameless place and turned right along the gravel road towards the mine, the road she hated most and most avoided.

It was surely a scene from hell. For a couple of kilometres, a forest of rough grey stalks surrounded her. Each stalk was about as high as her head and topped by a knot of burnt brushwood that tangled into surrounding stalks like a neglected head of hair; unwashed, unbrushed, uncut until beyond all grooming. The dead gorse was without gradations of colour. Scars in the bark seemed to hold no shadow; hairy planes tilted to the north caught no light. Nothing moved. She walked and walked through dead combings from the animal, earth. Branches were petrified in acts of fending off, poking, elbowing, scratching. The gorse trunks seemed not to grow from the earth but to be suspended from the mesh of twigs above. Below, there was green, a red-green of small reeds and tight lumps of lichen. At almost regular intervals a revival of kanuka appeared, each plant with its spatter of brittle leaves like tiny exclamation marks, some pimpling into white buds, some starred with flowers already. In almost equal numbers, young gorse sent up soft new bristles. Light bounced back and forward between green reeds and red rushes, fresh after the night's rain, which ran swiftly over the surface of puggy grey soil and never penetrated. On the dry areas, a film of white sealed the sour pakihi.

Looking again, Fern thought she saw young pine trees, scattered haphazardly. On and on she walked, and all round the tiny Christmas trees were flourishing. She grasped one and tried to pull it out of the clay but it was baked in hard. Definitely not a pine tree: the spines of even this baby plant had pierced her skin. She sucked blood and flicked her hands. And now among the burnt gorse she saw what must be one of the parent trees, roasted rigid, all ankles and shin bones cocked and kicking, a petrified tree bent in and out of its own shadow with spikes on black alert. Here and there a gross shell, a twisted knot of hard wood split open by the heat, rocked heavily on a branch, either empty, or showing a kernel as tight as a stone. Some of these rocky seeds had exploded into new bushes; others were still locked tight in their iron cradles. Not knowing the bush, Fern called it Mean Spiky.

To the left, a bulldozer track led into the grey. Once she had followed that track and found a sweet surprise. It led to an unburnt hollow where a wavy opal pool was edged by reeds. From any other angle it was hidden by trees and hillocks. Rushes held the water, and were held by it. There was a rough red cottage at one end, and the day she'd found it, a single paradise duck honked in the silence, fatly suspended on the water. There were buttercups by the back door of the shack. As she watched, Fern acknowledged an ugly feeling inside her, the urge that leads to conflagrations: she wanted to own that cottage for herself. She did her best to extinguish her greed in the waters of the pond, and came away peaceful. It was good to know that a secret pool existed beyond the charcoal.

She walked past the last few cottages of the mining village and then struck into a patch of bush on her right. She clambered up a steep face, holding handfuls of long ferns. Spiny bush-lawyer creepers caught in her clothes. Young lancewoods and a mountain cedar sheltered under giant pongas. White pines dwarfed them all.

Now she climbed on to a bare, rounded hillface which stretched out to others. A stone way led from one rim of a hill to another. The surface was hard and dry and waterproof. All the plants were tiny, crouching on their hands and knees. Few were larger than Fern's little finger. They did not live in visible communities; each was isolated in a circle of bare stone or tight grey earth. Individual mountain daisies with furry grey leaves vibrated endlessly in the wind. Lichen clutched the earth. Heather locked tight into itself. Hebes as big as her thumbnail lay down flat. Crimson insect-catchers raised their wheels of sticky rosettes, each plant half the size of a blowfly. Miniature orchids buzzed dead blooms in the gale, independently.

The hills were shaped for easy walking; their colours were grey and grey-brown. The occasional flare of yellow-green that Fern had seen from Kehua's window proved to come from reeds regenerating. All over the hills there were stumps, small clumps of crumbling black, the remains of reeds burnt two years back. They disintegrated if she pulled at them. But here and there a sharp green needle pushed up from the cremation, and in damp gullies and pockets reeds were growing thickly.

On the dry, high spots, the earth was a natural cement. Her dress twanged like a sail as she hurried towards the coast. On the rim of the furthest hill she saw the ocean, ripped by the same wind that shook the plants and filled her dress. Although her path lay south, she turned right to climb to the top lip of the Old Woman Bluff, just for a last look around.

It was a broad, flat lookout. No wonder the men from the helicopter had been waving their arms! Far out to sea, Fern could faintly see the cone of the Moving Mountain, two hundred kilometres away. Behind her was the estuary, two hundred metres below. She could see the lavish sand and surf of the spit, the empty bulk of Whale Peninsula, the small port and insubstantial houses of the place with no name, miles and miles of intricate mauve mountains fingering their way down into the wide waters of Gorse Bay, the scrub and pakihi of the burnt country, the gaunt, tight hills she had just traversed, more limestone cliffs along the fault line to the south, green farmland, sheep, patches of regenerating bush, and spindly, listening kanuka forest. A flax swamp throbbed far below, citron green, as the wind moved through in shudders. The shallow waters of the estuary were patchy with brown shadows through their pale expanses. The crust of dirt on the bluff was very thin, exposed like icing on a slice of lime and iron birthday cake.

Fern started walking down the back slope of the bluff towards the ocean. She stumbled on what proved to be, improbably, a surveying peg. When she got to the bottom she was overtired, and not only from the walking. In the last few days she had changed her perspective many times; she had lived much more than her share, vicariously. She had almost lost her sense of what is ordinary.

I have given you the history and geography of Fern's sojourn in the place with no name as fully as possible, telling you some things twice even, because she insists it was something that changed her deeply. There she stayed still; she was a receiver and not a doer. She says that in her journey up the valley and over the bluff to the sea, she became 'jolly'. Strange word! Her jolliness arose from new conflicts which were far too hard to resolve: so she stopped trying. You could guess them no doubt but I'll spell them out.

I suppose a textbook might call it an identity crisis. She had never felt certain of herself, only of certain details: she came from the Main Island; she lived in Northcity; she was white, descended exclusively from Second People; and thus she was one of the rich and guilty, one of the ones who had almost destroyed the First People. Now she had discovered that all her wholenesses were merely half-healed offcuts. She had said to Kehua, 'It's hard for me to realise that you might be one of my hundred and twenty great-great-great-great-great-great-grandmothers. My parents always swore quite fiercely that they were lily-white Second People. And yet my mother called me Fern; it could have been her way of giving a hint. It was not the fashion to know the truth about such things in those days . . . I thought I was one of the robbers, and now I find I have only robbed part of myself!'

'It is always like that,' said Kehua. 'Always.'

Fern thought, if this was the pattern of the world, it didn't actually matter who she was. She didn't need a ticket, tickets being meaningless in the long run. You could call it a stress-management technique she had stumbled on: sure that she would die, she might as well stop worrying. So she played on the beach and paddled, and found mussels to cook on her campfire, and slept under a tree in a sleeping bag that was hers for the time being.

Kehua had talked of the way her bones were turning up

101

in the soil of Whale Peninsula; the Ewers had found her skull and brought it home to bleach on the window sill. Kehua's spirit was tied to the skull by a band of elastic invisible light and was bound to return to the skull after every oscillation or expansion. So Fern experienced herself now too, tied gently to both First and Second People. This freed her from some concerns. There was no going back, but some choice of ways to go forwards.

In the morning she made a plate of Weetbix, dried milk and water. She ate it with a piece of flax cut with a pocket knife (courtesy of the Ewers) and it tasted good. Then she packed up her things and set off along the coast southwards. She walked (very slowly) for half a day before she came to a place where people lived; along clifftops, past rocks and a stretch of gigantic silky sandhills, past wind-swept hills faced with nikau palms, past gravel beaches and scraps of sand. The shacks and cottages she reached marked the start of a rough metal road.

The road ran alongside a long narrow beach which curved inland at the far end. Fern studied the houses. They were all a little the worse for wear but one was cheerful in colour, with a roof still red and weatherboards still noticeably white. A huge rhododendron bush sheltered other flowering, rumbunctious species. A vegetable garden was laid out in rickety concentric circles, with cabbages as big as boulders and carrot tops as high as her shoulder. (Remember she wasn't very tall.) Well, a fertile place was a good place to ask for hospitality, she supposed. She knocked on the door. And again. No reply, so she called out 'Cooee!' It seemed the right sort of approach. A voice came from the right, rather wobbly, from inside another conglomeration of trees. She walked into an orchard and saw a pair of pink wrinkled stockings in an apple tree.

'Catch!' Fern caught an apple as big as a teapot in her

arms and fell flat on her back under the weight. By teapot, I mean one of those large aluminium ones that you use for parish teas. Picking herself up, Fern saw an old woman straightening her dress at the bottom of the tree. She peered at Fern and said, 'Excuse me, I'm certainly not dressed for visitors.' From the lower hook of the apple tree she took a fur cape and covered her shoulders. She smoothed her hair and pinched her cheeks, which were brightly rouged already. 'You'll just have to take me as you find me, that's all there is about it. That's if you've come to visit me. That's the last of my Orange Pippins.'

They went in the back door, Fern staggering under the weight of the apple till she put it on the kitchen bench, which was a narrow kauri block, the wood swollen and grooved by decades of cold water scrubbing. The kitchen was tiny, yet it took up a lot of the house.

'Sit down, sit down! We'll have a cup of tea and a piece of apple pudding. I'm still getting used to these luxuries here – see my new stove?'

Fern admired the black iron stove on its pert iron feet as her hostess threw in another log.

'Extravagance! No wonder I keep making apple puddings.'

The old woman giggled and poured boiling water from the iron kettle into an enamelled teapot. While it brewed she touched up her make-up, lavishly streaking a red lipstick well beyond the edges of her mouth. It was like crayonning over a very old apple. As they sipped tea and finished their apple pudding, she looked helpfully at Fern.

'Well now. What's your name? You're not Lily are you? Or Elsie? What am I saying, Elsie died of the whooping cough. Peggy? Isabel? Vera?'

'My name's Fern.'

'Stuff and nonsense! I never called any of mine Fern. Unless it's short for something?'

'My mother was in a rural phase.'

'Was I indeed – a rural phase! A pretty long phase, that's all I can say. I've been here for nearly ninety years I'll have you know. All my life I've lived here. Except for my little fling when I was fifteen. My godmother invited me to Southcity for a holiday, you know. She said if I didn't go then, I never would. And I got me a very fine dress – you wouldn't believe the shops they have there! One of those shops, it took up a whole street, you know. And very fine ladies selling you things. Nothing is too much trouble . . . But I never went back, she was right about that. Fern! You must have been in between Daisy and Dandy, that's it. Well well well. Welcome back, Fern.'

'Thank you.'

'You do speak lovely, Fern. I'm sorry I didn't recognise you at first.'

'I'm not your daughter. I came here quite by accident. I have a different mother entirely.'

'Are you the one I gave away? Well there were two really, but one was a boy. And then my third to last, I got the fever and I just couldn't manage that one. I'm sorry; I hope you didn't mind.'

'No no, I don't feel badly at all. You are not my mother, truly.' Fern had practised this thought; she was pretty certain she had not been an adopted child, but in the days when she was born, people sometimes pretended.

The old woman seemed to take this in. 'I'm sorry, my dear. We seem to have got off on the wrong foot. But you see I had so many children. I do lose track. And some of them I haven't seen for thirty years. It was not such a silly mistake. It was all such a long time ago.'

'Not at all!' Fern made that sort of comment now and then.

'I had one every year. Every year. Starting when I was

sixteen. Stopped when I was forty-six. Some of them died. But mostly they lived right here in this house.'

'It's not a big house for thirty children.'

'Don't be silly, they weren't here all at once. That's the good thing about children, they come out one at a time, or mostly they do. So you have a chance to get used to them.'

'I still say it's a lot of children,' said Fern.

'They all left home by the time they were twelve or thirteen. There were never more than about ten at a time. One or two that died, and two that were given away. Four in a bed, top and tail. It wasn't so bad. Never had a midwife. Usually got the eldest to catch the baby coming out . . . That last baby, he wasn't right in the head. He died before he grew up. But mostly good strong children. We made our own fun.'

'Are you living all alone here then, I mean now?' asked Fern hopefully.

'All alone. My husband died. Anyway that's what I tell people. Mind you, I don't know why I bother.'

'Aren't you lonely? After all those people?'

'Glory box the pox, lonely! It's been peace and quiet here for the last thirty years. Thirty years of babies. Then some years with just children. Then thirty years of peace and quiet. Oh no! I've got out of the habit of babies now. Doubt if I could have one if I tried. Haven't had one for forty years or more. But you need a man for babies, that's how it's done, you know. My old man – no – I don't want any more babies. I don't care what you say, they wear you out.'

'I'm sure they do. I only had one, and I felt quite tired,' said Fern.

The old woman shook her head in amazement.

'You see, I need somewhere to live, myself. If I helped you – '

'Helped! You wouldn't be much of a help. One baby and you felt quite tired, did you?'

'I could pay you, and buy food, and make your life comfortable perhaps – keep the fire going – do some gardening – '

'Don't you touch my garden! Have you got your own teeth?' Fern nodded and the old woman looked cunning. 'You can stay for the night. So long as you've got your own teeth. You might be useful. We'll see. You go for a nice long walk and I'll get the tea.'

Fern walked south along the beach and then up the river bank and found it opened deeply into a small harbour. The surrounding hills were lush with grass and sheep, with just a little bush in the gullies. It was like standing in a tight green basin. The river mouth was sheltered from the sea, and a well-used wharf stood at the end of a row of houses. There was the Teatown general store that doubled as the Teatown post office. A road led up the valley, maybe going to Gorse Bay. No sign of mangroves here. She returned to the cottage, not in a hurry, not intent on creating her own destiny, which was blossoming with oddments.

Her hostess had changed to evening dress: a black crêpe, with shoulder-pads and long fitting buttoned sleeves, a gored skirt cut on the cross, and sequins around the breast bone.

'Would you like to change for dinner?' she asked sincerely.

Fern spread her hands in apology: she was already wearing her only dress.

'I'm sure I can help you out.'

Fern followed into one of the two bedrooms. Two rails running the length of the room were laden with dresses. Fern was winded by the sight of frocks from every era for the last seventy-four years. A Ming blue miniskirt hung beside an ankle-length grey cotton with a high white lace collar. A cap-sleeved everglaze with a sweetheart neckline swung its circular skirt beside a blue beaded Charleston number. A strapless red satin bell-skirt hung beside swirly pink chiffon harem pants, a sack-dress in LSD squiggles by a navy lace sheath. Needlecord and gingham and tweed had their place, but the emphasis was on evening elegance, and grosgrain, crêpe de chine, shot silk, taffeta, polyester, velvet and georgette predominated. Just to walk into the room was to smell the rush of personal history.

'May I choose anything?' said Fern, overwhelmed.

The old woman frowned; she had something specific in mind. Off a separate stand she took a man's evening suit of black wool faintly tinged with green.

'If you would kindly be the man, I would be much obliged.'

So Fern put on a yellowed shirt with gaping neck, a bow tie which the old lady arranged for her, and a suit that dangled far below her wrists and ankles. They turned up the ends and sat down to stewed hare, roast potatoes, pumpkin and boiled cabbage. There was pudding too, a boiled apple pudding with custard. They sipped water out of peanut butter jars, and toasted each other across a candle. The kitchen was a little too cosy.

'My name is Hattie Taylor. Short for Harriet. All my lovely clothes are from my godmother. Every year she sent me a special dress for best. Every year. We had dances in the old days, you know. We'd all go on the old horse and cart and by the time we got back it would be time to make the fire and put on the porridge. There was the Spinsters' Ball and the Bachelors' Ball and the Hall Ball and the Whitebait Ball – oh, they were great times! I started going when I was just a girl – I helped with the supper, that's what. And I went with my husband till he – and then I just went by myself with some of my children. There was one old chap, he was great on the fiddle. When he played, you just had to get up and dance, you just had to.'

'But is your godmother still alive?' asked Fern.

'Oh, pox in my socks no she is not still alive!' cried Hattie. 'Dearie me, she would be a hundred, hundred and twenty years old if she was still alive!'

'But the dresses – ' began Fern.

'Well let me see, when she died, her daughter took over and sent me dresses and things, but she's dead now, and now it's her granddaughter sends me – sometimes it's hand-me-downs, sometimes it's the latest fashion right off the shelf. I've lost my bosom but I've still got my waist. And shoes, now and then I get a pair of shoes. These are my favourites, lovely to dance in.' She hiked up her dress a little and showed off her black patent leather pumps with buckles on the arch. 'Nice, aren't they?' Her head emerged from under the table. 'Dinner's over. Shall we have coffee now, or after we've danced?'

Fern looked round the kitchen. It was about two metres by three. The other rooms in the cottage were each larger, possibly as much as four metres long. But they were both crammed full of beds and clothing.

'Where can we dance?' she asked, not surprisingly.

'We go out to dance,' said Hattie, who pulled on her fur cape and led the way down the path, across a paddock, through long hairy grass to an elderly weatherboard hall. Hattie opened the front door with a big key and turned on a light switch. 'Here we are!' she said.

The rafters were dusty and cobwebbed; some pews were angled oddly at one end, but there was a large expanse of floor. 'That's where the boards are rotten,' said Hattie, waving at the pews. 'But otherwise it's a lovely floor.' She took a tin of powder and scattered some on the boards, humming and chirrupping. 'What do you do best – a waltz? Some people don't know how to waltz.'

'Well I do the woman's part best,' said Fern. 'I don't think I could manage the man's part.'

'You'll just have to try, that's all.' Hattie took a thick gramophone record and put it on the machine. She wound the handle up briskly and lowered the needle into the groove. 'Ask me! Ask me!' she said.

'May I have the pleasure of this dance?' asked Fern, as creaky violins got into the swing of things. She held the stringy body of Hattie on her right arm, and one hand in her left hand. Although she was no taller than Hattie, she was heavier. Hattie made decisions about direction, pace, and fancy bits, conveying instructions like a flight path through the muscles of contact. Fern's superior weight lent momentum. They were a good pair, after all. At the end of the record, which was startlingly soon, they both clapped.

'A foxtrot?' asked Hattie. And a foxtrot it was, and a quickstep, a rumba, a gypsy waltz, a military two-step, a tango, and then a waltz of the slow romantic type.

Fern became more and more excited and danced with more flourish as the evening wore on, although she couldn't help realising she had much to learn. Her worst problem was pain in her hands; every puncture from the little Christmas tree had generated pus and inflammation, and all of them hurt with every moment. At one stage she asked Hattie for instruction in a reverse turn – but Hattie frowned and hissed, 'Not here!' Then the evening was finished, with a bow and a curtsey, and the last record returned to its brown paper cover with a hole in the middle. Hattie took a cloth from the back of a pew and wiped up a puddle on the floor. She walked across the paddock with one hand holding the wet cloth and the other tucked pertly into Fern's arm.

Once back in the kitchen she rinsed the cloth and hung it over the stove where it steamed pungently. 'That's the only problem with physical jerks at my age. Do you want coffee now, or cocoa?'

The sophistication of the evening took a nosedive when they both chose cocoa, or so Fern thought, unaware that in Washington cocoa was the latest fashion in after-dinner drinks. 'You can stay with me, I've decided,' said Hattie. 'But I warn you, I can't stand people with false teeth.'

Fern slept in the second bedroom. With four small beds jammed edge to edge, it seemed underpopulated, but she was glad to have it to herself.

nine

I can leave Fern at this point because she stays there for, oh, weeks and weeks without a change. There was mail piling up for her at the Oystercatcher post office, which was rather more remote than it had been before. She never gave it a thought, but simply eased herself into a life with Hattie. Meanwhile I was writing to her but not getting any answers. Writing and writing, in fact, and becoming quite hysterical.

'Dear Mum, the more you don't write to me, the more I read the letter you did send and find it highly peculiar. What you say is fair enough, but what about all that hasn't been said? This is the seventh letter I have sent since I got your one. I might as well be writing to myself. So if my letters also start to seem a bit weird, blame yourself. Writing to a silent mother is inclined to make a person feel hurt, then self-righteous and cross, and finally (at least I hope there's no worse to come) reckless. I'll say anything and everything which might make you react!

'My last letter was much about parties, receptions, functions, etc. This one will be too, I suppose. I am not encouraged to seek a job. I don't have the right sort of visa, and besides, it's *infra dig*. And among all the women I have met so far, there is not one willing and capable person who is free to go tramping with me. In the summer vacation, maybe. So I waft and ponce around Washington, knowing its streets, shops, galleries and diplomatic apartments as I used to know the mountains at home. It makes me laugh when I think of that wedding of mine.

My feet hurt from high-heeled shoes and parquet floors and pavements. I can't shake off a slight cold, and I blame the greasy air that has sunk in the basin of the city and cannot fly out.

'I am growing used to the sound of sirens having tantrums on my doorstep every day. And yet in so many ways the New RUSAn has a natural sort of good manners which would positively alarm the average Sleeping Islander. There's a kind of innocence, a sweetness in the way they make friendly advances. I'm generalising, which is rash, but understand I am just trying to convey a flavour of life which is very unlike ours . . . They don't take their time about making friends. Granted that Charles and I come with our credentials on display, they immediately invite us to parties parties parties and other outings, even when they can safely bet they'll disagree with us (well, me) on most controversies. They hold nothing back, they set out to win at first eye contact. They are safe from irreparable misjudgments, because so few people in this circle stay here longer than a few years. No friendship here is an incarceration. Nor a reward for patience, nor a commitment with hooks. I like it and yet I feel invaded. I hate my own scepticism. I'd love to see a fantail, a cabbage tree, a fish swimming – oh no, I did see a live fish last night. If I tell you about last night's reception, it will tell you much about our lifestyle.

'I told you already (if only I knew you were listening!) how we met General Merit last week. Last night's party was at his apartment. The General is an awesome man. He plays the game of Washington sophisticate, but somewhat contemptuously. The General is a sort of dream of RUSA. I imagine RUSA imagining this particular General and wanting one, so they made one, and there he was. Is. He does not glitter; he has a grey-green, half-hidden glow. He's splendidly built and sternly handsome, with an

112

outstandingly straight nose. Looking the way he does, he simply had to be a general or a movie star. If he were selling shoes, for instance, he would make everybody miserable. He does not display emotion; his features barely move at all. But he looks at you – well, me – intently. I do not doubt that he notes, considers, and records in his head every word I say. He exploits silence. His concentration is always on a slow burn, a safety valve, the eternal flame taking care of the waste gas. I have never fancied uniforms before, but with the General I can see the point. His is very dense, thick yet fine, with layers of ribbons over his heart. I guess he needs the strongest of containers to insulate the fuel of him. He moves stiffly but with dignity, making his uniform work for him. He reminds me of a crayfish; not least for the possibility of great succulence inside the armour.

'What am I writing! Well it serves you right. What am I writing? It's only now, in writing this down, that I recognise that yes, there's an illicit, perverted craving in my response to the General. It may be because of this effete lifestyle. I don't know if that's an argument in favour of writing confessions, or against it. In any case, you can relax: this is a man with immense responsibility and total self-control. I'm more likely to fuck the Statue of Liberty than General Merit. There. I have altogether lapsed from my writing-to-mother mode. That proves I don't believe in you, I don't believe you are there in that nonsensical place, your mail is piling up and up behind some tiny counter and will never be collected.

'But if this has become a diary, I will still post it. I'm not sure I'd like Charles to read it, and he just might if I leave it in the waste-paper bin.

'The party. Gorgeous people, wit, warmth, alien chatter. I don't understand half their conversation. Florid trays of canapés served by uniformed stewards and maids, champagne cocktails always at the elbow. As usual, wealth is indicated mostly by space. The rooms stretch on and on around corners to tall windows with smudgy views of the city and a starless sky. Even rank can't buy a view of the stars here. The chairs and couches are twice the size I'm used to, and covered in peach suede; square, interchangeable, vastly expensive units. Any two would fill up your sitting room; at one glance I can count twenty-five, and there's another room round the corner. Money means overplaying space, underplaying colour and shape. The eye travels gently along pale greys and whites. The only works of art are a blue Picasso, four Renoirs and a handful of treasures from the Sleeping Islands.

'Truly. I asked the General to explain. I immediately suspected they had changed hands at the time of the great First People of the Sleeping Islands Exhibition, which had lent the private treasures of the race in one priceless shipment to New RUSA. Travelling at the time I did, I missed the exhibition both here and at home. But I doubted there could be two stone images in the world like the one that dominated the main room. It had to be the magical Hine-Mother-of-us-all, and all the kilometres of film that have taken her image have surely failed to diminish her stupendous energy level. Mum, she's not queenly or godly in a way I'd ever pictured! Her power is squat; she squats on your soul. Her brows overhang in folds, her shoulders flow out of her ears, her hips come out of her waist. She is a monstrous foetus with all knowledge of good and evil, she is ape-woman with eyeballs bulging full of secrets, she is a small star squashed as it fell to earth, she is organic and all the carving is like a tattoo on her one and only inevitable stone body. She is so very old, so crumbly at the chiselling. Look at a line of her mouth, a shouting oval, and you think it's a lip standing out thickly. But then there are other lips, or are they tongues? Each contour edges the

114

next one over: looking at her is like being slightly blind. Much more is held back than is given, and what is given can almost knock you over. Her nose, her hands, her mouth, her cunt – any part is a sort of chant, and a careless glance becomes a meditation exercise . . . When I saw her, I knew for sure I was only pulp and bone.

'What fabulous offer could have convinced the First People to part with her? Hypnotic, gutsy queen, she-god of a whole tribe's spirit – she is not something lightly to be stolen.

'The General named a sum so huge I could barely comprehend it. It was the equivalent of winning the national lottery every month for ten years. It was still robbery, though from a willing victim. I told him so.

'The other five items had been bought for him by an agent in the Sleeping Islands. The First People Exhibition had functioned for the General as a catalogue from which he had drawn up his shopping list. He's got a superb greenstone club, with lines as pure as the stone it's made of, rolling light inside itself like a scroll. A big, solid wooden canoe-bailer shaped in a sort of hollow W, with an eel-head on its handle. The prow of a war canoe with carving that made me choke up, because it's the sort of carving that I'm somehow used to. There's a whalebone ornament, simple. And a spear with the usual flat tongue-point, carved into and out of itself.

'I must say I was overcome with contempt, and I let fly. I said, "You greedy pig, how dare you raid our country like a pirate? These things don't belong here! Look at them on their wanky marble stands, and us drinking champagne all around them!"

'He raised an eyebrow and said, "They are not out of place. Aesthetically they would be universally admired. They are perfect of their kind and any person, of any time or place, is bound to recognise that." His eye tracked to a soft and sensuous pre-teen girl holding a kitten, a swirling, rounded Renoir.

'I said, "Oh it suits you does it to put this with your pet Renoir? Well there was passion in that painting once, and honesty – but you'll never see it here, not here. And you think you'll tame the First People treasures too, don't you, by choosing only what your supercivilised eye tells you is lovely or strong or quaint, and rejecting everything else, and putting it out on display like a department store! You've even got floor-walkers, haven't you? I don't think you realise how exceedingly silly you are." (By the way, I'm inflating my side of the conversation. It's not exactly what I said, but roughly what I wish I'd said.)

'He said, "It's the innocence that we need. We city cynics have a need and a right to seek refreshment."

'"Oh ho," I said, "if it's all so innocent, why do you put it in those voodoo lights?" It was true that he had underlit Hine-Mother-of-us-all, for example, so that her shadows and depths were exaggerated. "Are you scared to look her in the eye?" Got a bit carried away there.

'He was patient with me. "They are intrinsically inno-cent because they are primitive. They use basic media, stone and bone and wood. They symbolise unconscious needs that are quite simply fundamental to man."

'"Primitive! I never heard such value-saturated mission-eering in my life! It just so happens that you like this style. Maybe you were told to like it. So you pat the artists on the head, and you say 'More please!' although the need for this particular art has long ago been demolished. Look baby, this used to be ordinary everyday stuff! (I beg your pardon, Hine.) It seems we can't value anything until we have made it rare." When I'm at my most furious, I often find accidentally that I'm furious at myself. It does tend to weaken the argument. The General and I were part of a single syndrome.

'"Why are you cross?" he said. "This has nothing to do with you. These things are timeless and placeless; they belong to all mankind."

'"Then how come you had to pay a fortune for them? They all had a reason! The prow – where's it going, what's it doing here? It wasn't made for your apartment, it looks all wrong. Bailers are for bailing, prows are for leading, clubs and spears are for killing, gods are for – " I was going to say, for power, when I realised he might well be using Hine-Mother-of-us-all for just that purpose, though clumsily. "Gods are not to be trifled with." I was so frustrated in the face of his absolute certainty, the impenetrable security of the very very rich, that I kicked him, Mum, a good stab on the shin with my useless strappy emerald-green shoe, and then for good measure I stood on his foot with one high heel, putting all my weight on it and half-remembering some statistic about the death-dealing pressure that amounts to.

'Other people were standing close around us, so close that nobody noticed. They were trying not to hear our little talk. General Merit did not blink, he just opened his eyes a little wider and looked at me with a terrible intimacy. Oh, it was a bad moment, Mum. Then I remembered I was Charles's wife and said, "Oh, sorry. It's rather crowded, isn't it?" This amused him. I did not wish to amuse him! I tried again.

'"To put it another way, General, this is like holding a cocktail party in a cemetery. Don't you feel that?"

'He said, "I felt someone standing on my foot." I wanted to punch him and scream, but at the same time, I felt I was about to be swallowed up. Perhaps he was even a match for a holy spirit or two. (Explosive notion.) I went to the bathroom.

'One of the bathrooms, that is. It's larger than your sitting room, Mum. I sat on the toilet fuming, surrounded by acres of peach and grey tiles, and mirrors, and a tubbed avocado tree which reached the ceiling. I wondered what would become of me. I had childishly insulted a courteous and powerful host, and when lost for words I had stood on his foot. Although new to marriage, I certainly knew that it depended on a delicate ecology of conventions and self-control. Having deliberately selected a life of exquisite stability, why was I flailing around in this violent, meaningless manner? Perhaps I was ill; illness can make you angry. But then again, anger can make you ill. What do you reckon, Mum?

'When I at last relaxed enough to pee a cascade of champagne cocktail, the splashing below me did not sound quite right. I thought it was just that fancy RUSAn plumbing, but standing up, I realised there was a goldfish in the toilet bowl. Horrors! I was paralysed. What was it there for? An existential question of the first water. In the end I thought my own piss would do less harm to me than to the goldfish, so I took the gold-rimmed tooth-glass and after much dipping and diving, I caught the poor little thing and put it in a basin full of mostly fresh water, that is, as fresh as it comes out of the taps of New RUSA. Then I pulled the chain; at least that step was obvious enough. And washed my hands in the other handbasin. Then I dithered, and really, as you know, I am not a ditherer. I felt that I still had a problem of morality, hygiene, or local etiquette. Or maybe it was the goldfish who still had a problem.

'Then there was a knock on the door. I plopped the goldfish back in the toilet bowl, feeling distinctly guilty, and opened the door to a Nigerian lady in blue silk and a butler with a bucket full of goldfish, a soup scoop, and a slightly scornful face.

'Mum, I don't want to become like a New RUSAn. I'm just starting to find out what I'm like.

'Write to me. (That is a scream.) Love from Dot.'

Scream I might but Fern didn't hear me. The Oyster-catcher post office was far away from her now. Hattie was on rural delivery, so if Fern had got herself organised, she could have had mail at the gate. She had got used to my being away more quickly than I had. I suppose she thought about me sometimes; but she didn't crave for tokens.

She was growing accustomed to life with Hattie, and changing Hattie's life at the margins, as much as permitted. For instance, she made a routine of scrubbing floors, both in the cottage and the church hall. She was allowed to do washing, which meant getting used to boiling up the old copper, rubbing the clothes on a corrugated wooden washboard with yellow soap, wringing them out by hand, and all that very physical system. Hattie was not altogether fastidious, and had got used to the acrid stench associated with her little bladder problem. Fern was keen to ameliorate conditions in this respect.

For instance, Hattie hadn't bothered much about baths because it was a nuisance, boiling the copper and heaving buckets of hot water through the kitchen window till the hip bath was full. Fern streamlined the process with a garden hose and shortly baths were the regular thing, three times a week. Hattie muttered about pneumonia and said the tank would run dry, but she secretly liked sinking her scrappy old body into hot water. Fern persuaded her that complexion and hair were improved by soap. When the time was right she introduced her to shampoo, which was a great success.

They went dancing on Friday and Saturday nights. And during the week, at home, Hattie gave Fern instruction until she was a fitting partner. She lost all self-consciousness and adopted Hattie's style: stagy, buoyant, usually bouncing where any other couple would glide. Shoulders and elbows went up and down, in and out, hands were flung wide or burrowed in between bodies, thumbs followed and led. There were moments of grace, but many more of physical parody. They danced more like milkmaids than ladies-in-waiting. When they did the polka, sometimes Fern also was in danger of wetting her pants.

Perhaps the reason why Fern avoided contact with her past, and even with her daughter, was that her whole life at this point was in neutral, or in a swirl, like water at the moment the tide turns. It is not uncommon for people to withdraw from city life to Arden or Sherwood. We know the impulses that lure us there: but we tend to assume that retreat is a conscious, intellectual choice. Fern had been hurled into her quaint and secret life without explicit consultation with herself. She had barely taken responsibility for her change of address, apart from those half-hearted gestures to Hilary and me. She felt happy and slightly wicked. Her joints moved more easily. She was getting used to the notion that (within the law) she could do precisely what she fancied. When she thought about her separated life in Northcity, which had seemed like a paradise of freedom at the time, it now appeared heavily programmed and preordained. Life with Hattie was an appendix in the flow of life; she had been sucked into a lay-by, an aneurism where the spirit paused.

It's odd, when you think about it. She had worried so much and so long over what house to buy, as if the wrong choice would have made her unhappy forever. She'd tried to anticipate every consequence, and all of them seemed insurmountable. It seemed when she bought that house she was tying a knot which would never come undone, and yet that's a decision that could be cancelled with a single phone call. Seeing the history of the world had made her acknowledge the huge imponderables, like earthquakes. Even in personal terms, life or death could be determined by a sudden sexual flare between enemies. You'd think this insight might make a woman feel more weighted with responsibility, nervously debating every word and deed, wouldn't you? But instead, Fern was much relieved to recognise that personal decisions were not momentous after all.

She loved her liberation. She felt she was a better person away from her property. She could not have defended this feeling with conviction; the concepts were lacking. If she tried to articulate it among the apple trees, she thought she sounded half-witted. If she hid, it was not from herself, but from the judgment of her friends and former colleagues. But she was less ashamed than she had been at any time since she was four years old.

She was gathering strength. She walked freely for hours on the rough hills behind the village, which was known as Fish Beach, down the coast to the general store, up the river mouth beyond Teatown, over farms, through bush, along the beach. Closer to home there were a couple of dozen baches, cottages and holiday houses. These were quite frequently in use, as people from the city could drive to Oystercatcher, turn left across the limb of the island, circle the wide river mouth, pass Teatown and get to Fish Beach in three hours. Seven people there were fishermen, either quirky bachelors or middle-aged and married. There were no children at Fish Beach, but at Teatown there was a two-teacher school for the district.

Sometimes Fern would meet the fishing boats as they came in after a stint at sea. One windy afternoon she was standing by the wharf as the *Footloose* approached. The sea was high and the boat was tossing trickily as it drew near. She saw a figure working on board; heavily built, but streamlined, rather like the boat itself. The figure was foreign to Teatown, but familiar. Her skin began to itch. By the time the boat drew up to the wharf it was certainly Orlando.

When he stepped on shore her legs wanted to dance to him but she walked. Her arms went out of their own accord, as they do when they've been pressed to the sides of a doorway for one minute. They had never touched in the Department, nor needed to. She grasped his wet hands at arms' length. Then she felt like running away. 'Don't go,' he said, while he finished his share of carrying boxes of fish to the boss's truck, tying up ropes, and so forth. He gave her a schnapper and then walked with her to Hattie's place. On the way they had time for a few exclamations.

Like, 'What on earth are you doing here?' from Fern.

'I came looking for you,' said Orlando. 'I followed the trail from Oystercatcher. Hilary told me that much. I wrote to you. You should have expected me.'

'But your job – '

'I've got a new one, as you see. And your job?'

'You'll meet her. She's had thirty children.'

'And you're number thirty-one?'

'More of a home help. Except it's mutual,' said Fern as they went in the lopsided gate. 'I mean, we just live, you know.'

'I could mend that for her,' said Orlando. The gate was tied up with binder-twine. Fern considered the offer. Hattie had earned every bit of help she could get; that didn't mean she'd welcome it.

'Tread carefully,' said Fern. And they went in to Hattie, who had never shown any curiosity about Fern's earlier life but accepted her whole like a baby.

Orlando had arrived at Fish Beach four days before and had taken over a one-roomed shack. Within minutes he'd been asked to help on the trawler, because the man who owned the shack had been taken to hospital in the city.

Orlando had stepped straight into the life of a man he had never met, a seventy-year-old bachelor who liked deer shooting, gold fossicking and trout fishing, who had worked on the *Footloose* till he was as frayed and twisted as an old rope, who smoked an aged pipe badly in need of a decarb, and sat in front of the fire in a greasy moquette armchair with unsprung springs. The shack was made of corrugated iron, the fireplace out of boulders and mud cement. The bunk was narrow, and doubled as seating when Fern came to call. Orlando was at home here, because he could hear and see the ocean. The red shack reminded Fern of the hideaway beside the pond, near Kehua's house. It quickly seemed familiar, but perhaps that was because Orlando was in it.

Hattie was a great talker when she got a chance; living with Fern meant she had chances every day. On the other hand, she wasn't used to listening. That was fine as far as Fern was concerned, since she was working things out from the inside. When Orlando arrived, he made her talk. Then he summed up what she had said and not said: 'You're all right. But what about Dorothy?'

'What about Dorothy?'

'She's on the other side of the world. She also has had a journey, to a place even stranger than this. For some reason you assume she has reacted just like you. But maybe she's calling out to you.'

'She's grown-up,' said Fern uncertainly.

'So am I, but I badly needed to hear from you.'

So Orlando arranged for her mail to be forwarded from the Oystercatcher post office. It came in a carton, there was so much. Lots of it was from me.

'Dear Mum, All right then, don't write. Be like that. Why should I care? (Have I done something wrong? Hurt your feelings? Forgotten your birthday? Let you down? I'm sorry I said fuck in one of my letters if that's it.) The closing of the brackets is arbitrary. That's not really in parentheses, anyway. It's central. It's the main thing I want to say to you, along with WRITE TO ME! Please, please! Just tell me you're not dead or in hospital, OK? I know they'd have told me if that had happened. So I'm a fusspot. I learned that from you.

'I picture you in a small guesthouse by the sea, having morning tea with an ex-schoolteacher about the time I am in the theatre or partying again. I picture you renting a respectable bach on Sandy Beach, teeming with teenagers in the weekend and sleepily suburban during the week. Playing bridge again. Learning to crochet. What do people do in Gorse Bay? You are in the inhabited end, aren't you? I looked it up on the Embassy atlas and saw long wide blank spots, and dotted red lines where the tarseal runs out. No, that's not you. I just know you're at the east end. It looks surprisingly long and large, Gorse Bay.

'Hey: Jules is over here on a visit. It seems he knows the General very well. Small world! In fact he's here to do business with him. I am not in on the secret so I can't give you any details. Charles is pleased to see family, though Jules is not staying with us. I must say Jules seems quite at home in the General's company, though a little over-excited. Tell me one thing though: how can a salaried civil servant justify making a deal like this (whatever it is)? You won't answer so I'll have to. I guess he's using his annual leave, or else he's acting for the Government.

'Well, we don't have gorse here, anyway. Nature is utterly subdued. No, untrue; that's only true in the city. And we have been to the country! We had quite a lovely weekend, in fact. We all went to the country retreat of General Merit, up in Vermont. He says we must go again "in the fall". Imagine "the fall" occurring every single year, as if once wasn't enough. He says the area is famous, people come from far and wide to see the forest turn scarlet, and we must come too. This time, it was all green, a story-book illustration. Not like the real country, ours. They have all these soft hills, curvy: I can't think of anywhere at home the least bit like them. They look as if they have been softened by constant feeding and stroking. You could get the idea in Vermont that everything is hunky-dory in the world, till you go inside the so-called farmhouse of the General. There it's opulence again, not in the furniture this time, which is sort of rustic (naturally), but in the treasures.

'Mum, he's got his own art gallery there! He's had an old barn converted, and (as always) made secure. He has paintings on his walls that put the entire collection of the Sleeping Islands to shame. You know how we have a few crummy works from "overseas"; and you know how foreigners laugh when they look at our "permanent" collection, and wonder why we bother, and ask where we keep the work of local artists . . . Look, if the Director of the Sleeping Islands Art Gallery stepped into the General's barn, her eyes would haemorrhage with envy. I find it hard to believe that one private individual has the ability, let alone the right, to keep such things for his personal enjoyment, in a place where he only goes about twice a year. Is this what Picasso and Monet and Renoir and Rembrandt and Dali worked for?

'All his paintings were dead certs for capital gains; I think that's the main thing they've got in common. His collection is not exactly daring. I even suspect he doesn't exert a personal taste when he shops for art; it looks as if it's been chosen by a stockbroker, not a real person. Except that I do have a suspicion that his favourite is Renoir, and that he is slightly embarrassed about that. Getting off the track here. And by the way, that was not a rhetorical question. I would really like to know the answer. It might be "Yes" or "Who cares anyway? Certainly not the artist."

'They laugh at our "Welfare State" over here and they fear it too. They take it all so personally, as if my passport were imperilling my soul. If they knew the patient was on drip-feed they would doubtless be relieved, but I am too loyal to give them the bulletin. Still, we are different. We have a different set of assumptions and a different style of thinking. I feel so wrong here! And yet these people are so kind. They are like very clumsy, good-hearted spies. They try so hard to listen to me, but not in order to understand. They want to forgive me and cure me, they want to save me!

'To Charles's acute discomfort I continue to be a bit of a missionary myself. Which is funny. I'm the only person I've ever heard being rude to the General. Everyone else is too conscious that he is one of the most powerful men on earth. Well, I know that too. But I go on insulting him because I think he represents the appalling madness of RUSA. Ironically, it's for my sake, not Charles's, that he goes out of his way to see us. I can't prove this, I just sense it. I feel I'm being fiddled with somehow. I don't think I'll try to explain that at the moment.

'People have a bit of a thing here about the Sleeping Islands at the moment. It's partly to do with the First People Exhibition, which they were very taken with (and part of which was taken with them, as you know). And partly it's because of our refusal to have nuclear arms in our harbours or on the Islands. That seems to me a sane, gallant stance that could infect other nations with health, in a "Simon says" sequence. I deeply believe we could provide a way out of the nuclear nightmare by calling the bluff of RUSA and its theoretical enemies and giving them an exit from the trap they're in. If the world would only say with one voice, "The Emperor has no clothes!" then

RUSA and the others could accede to the will of the world without losing face, and little by little turn off their warheads, unsoldier themselves, and unlock their doors.

'There are some people here who approve of us; they understand the way we look at things. But the others think that nuclear disarmament amounts to adopting a victim's posture. Millions of people here bolt and double-magic-lock their doors, stand guards at the gate, and still keep a pistol under the pillow. You've no idea, Mum! This whole nation is founded on the strangest of all possible human rights: the right to carry a gun and shoot people you think are your enemies! Would you call that a human right? Democracy here has a demonic power which is almost out of control. They're still playing cowboys and Indians, and now the cowboys have nuclear weapons, and the Indians are you and me. Most New RUSAns feel outraged, wounded, that the Sleeping Islands should beg to differ with them over the safety and value of nuclear warheads. They all take it so very personally! They've all tried so hard to protect us, personally. Carried our burden and all that. Didn't ask for the burden of keeping "world peace" (some peace) but had it thrust upon them. All they ask is gratitude, and a little bit of rest and recreation. Hmm.

'Already, as you know, quite vicious reprisals are mooted on the trade front. I have heard whisper of plans to disrupt the Sleeping Islands by fostering rumours of bank failures, and even of an assassination plot against our Prime Minister! God forbid. And people who appear to be quite sane otherwise actually condone these suggestions, yes, quite solemnly. Strangely, the General is much milder in his response. I dare say he can have his war without consulting us.

'Now that I've started telling you about the mass insanity of these extremely nice and hospitable people, I may as well carry on. They pride themselves on being logical! Oh, I'll use up my lifetime's quota of exclamation marks at this rate. The President wanted twenty-one more intercontinental missiles, OK? You know why? Because RUSA is about to hold further disarmament talks (they go on more or less continuously) with their rather unconvincing enemies, the United African States. To have twenty-one more missiles will put them in a strong position when they approach the talks: that's their sort of logic. Now you know why the politicians have approved these missiles, despite their better judgment? (Let's overlook the fact that RUSAn military manufacturers contributed millions of dollars to their campaign costs.) The argument that won the day went like this: "It would be more dangerous to RUSA for the Government to oppose the President's will, on whatever grounds, than to do without twenty-one more intercontinental nuclear missiles." Nobody would dream of mentioning the danger of acquiring twenty-one more missiles, let alone suggesting that if they were serious about the disarmament talks they should deny themselves these little toys. When I talk on this subject to almost any New RUSAn, I talk in tongues through bullet-proof glass. I'm not making all this up, Mum. It's not my cynical interpretation of the facts, but the facts themselves as reported po-faced in the papers here. They do actually believe that nuclear weapons prevent nuclear war!

'If this isn't enough to convince you I'm in a madhouse here, let me tell you that half of New RUSA actually yearns for a nuclear holocaust. They long to show the rest of the world that they are an awfully strong nation. And they expect to be with Jesus when it's all over, because they fought to save the world and preserve world peace. The sooner we all die, the sooner they'll be with Jesus, having preserved world peace, mark you. And the rest of us cowards and traitors will be with Satan where we belong.

'I can't go on. I want to cry. Tell me one good reason why I shouldn't?

'The Sleeping Islands are waking; we've got our cowboys and our policemen are carrying guns. That makes me ashamed. We've lost our innocence and I don't know if it's once and for all, or if we fall a little lower every year, or if we're climbing out, perhaps to fall again another year. When I look at RUSA, when I look at the nuclear stockpile I fear the fall. In the Sleeping Islands we have erected our flimsy barrier, and we hang on with our teeth domestically – but I want doors to be open, trust, peace, impossible things like that! I worry that one drop of cynicism or fear is enough to poison the population of an entire nation, that it leaks through the ocean into our sunny waters, and yet that we cannot blame the RUSAns wholly. It's a function of being human: being greedy for power. Only now, the consequences threaten to wipe us off the face of the earth, and serve us jolly well right.

'Excuse the raving, Mum. You're copping all the frustration I feel when I'm arguing with the General. And why should it even be argued? Right is right: it should not require a lawyer to defend it. I'm a floundering vestal virgin, a lonely, fumbling advocate of a flaring truth, from which millions of people avert their eyes to squint at the goldfish in the lavatory bowl. Oh, they drive me crazy! Why can't they be like us? Why are we starting to be like them?

'I still didn't stop, did I? I should revert to the personal, for after all, these are very personal people. But even though they are so ready to leap into intimacy, I am starting to withdraw. I feel so odd, so different; I want to creep away. I don't feel right, although it's real enough, their warmth and interest. Even from Charles I am withdrawing. He is so tactful among "them". He's stopped thinking of them as them. So he's one of them, openly and

129

honestly open and honest; but he's not a blurter. Charles will never be a blurter.

'Land of excruciating ironies: it is only the General I am drawn to. I'm a hawk on his string. He lets me go; he tugs me back, even at the verge of the merciful clouds. But that image is upside down, because in any other society he would be nominated a god. He is interested in you. He knows quite a lot about the Sleeping Islands. Ridiculously, he was able to tell me things about Gorse Bay that I didn't know myself: about the terrain, climate, population patterns, prevailing winds and all that. He hasn't been to our country but he would like to. He probably will go, one day soon. I wish I could.

'Now Charles is back from work. Love. (Sigh.) Dot.'

ten

'What a strange world she lives in,' said Fern. 'Thank goodness it's so far away.' (It wasn't very far away at all.) Then she had the decency to sit down and write me a proper letter. Orlando vetted it, to make sure it was the type to reassure me this time, and not to freak me out completely.

'Dear Dot, I'm really sorry, I am sorry. I didn't realise you'd be so worried about me. But of course you would be; it's only natural. Please be calm now.

'I moved to a different place, another tiny town called Fish Beach. You have had trouble adjusting to a huge city after Northcity; I've had trouble getting used to life in the country, and I suppose other things just went out of my head, and other people, even my only daughter. I think it's because I had spent six years learning to stand on my own feet, and not to rely on anyone but me. I forgot it was possible to reach out a hand. I don't understand it. But that's over now.

'Strangely, it is thanks to Orlando Puddleigh, about whom you have always had such grave misgivings, and who has come to live here too, that I have at last received your letters and picked up my pencil to write to you. He's not living with me, you understand, but he lives nearby and is a good friend. My best friend, I think.

'I am living with Mrs Hattie Taylor, an old lady (but very vigorous) who accepts a bit of help in the house, in return for which I live here cheaply. The mail is going to come direct to this house from now on, so do keep writing.

I'm glad you didn't quite give up on me.

'Reading that through, I realise I am still holding back. It's because it is all so hard to explain! If I told you much more, all at once, you might be alarmed – but for no reason. I am well, sane, happy, relaxed. You could look on it as a holiday, rather a long holiday, but so pleasant. I am not in a hurry to return to the city. If you think this is bad, reflect on why. Is it puritanical, your disapproval? Or does it stem from envy? If only you could come and see me here! Then you'd just feel happy that I was having a good time, and doing nobody any harm in the process.

'Dot, how is Charles? You haven't said very much about him. Just enough to make me worry. (My turn this time.) He is not, is he, unbearable as a husband? You know I have tried to be a good mother-in-law, and not to interfere. But whatever my private opinion about Charles, this General sounds dangerous to me. Still, who am I to talk? You could say I have been living dangerously myself. Not now. Now I'm quite patterned and suburban once again. Just tell me.

'I think we're quits, don't you? We both leapt off the wharf, we both have been making somewhat odd new friendships, we both live on the same planet. Probably we can talk to each other now, as precarious adults.

'I love you, you are wonderfully brave, there is only one of you in the world although we do have some things in common. My new life may seem strange to you, but to me it is much less frightening than yours. As a mother I wish I could find some words to help you cope with RUSA. I can't, except I am listening now.

'Love from Mum.'

'Dear Dorothy, This is Orlando speaking. I just want to say please don't worry about your mother. She's fine and leading a life that would be the envy of half the civilised world, if ever they got to hear about it. Her financial situation is satisfactory. Her house is let to reliable tenants and under the care of a well-known land agent. Everything is in order. She has friends here, including me.

'Yours sincerely, Orlando Puddleigh.'

These letters did disturb me, although on one level I was reassured. But now that I know what sort of life they were leading, I can't see how, at the time, they could have been any more explicit or helpful. Moreover, Orlando's opinion was not one I particularly respected so that the less he said the better. At that time I still had only a vague and hostile impression of him, derived from what Fern had told me, and that one early encounter at the Department of Philosophy social. I felt he was unreliable, feckless, and sloppy in his habits. I was well aware of a fundamental attractiveness, too, which made me angry. By the way other women responded to him, I deduced quite reasonably that he was a ladies' man. In fact I sensed that Fern was holding something back, for she had always insisted that there was no sexual element in their relationship.

From the maturity of my twenty-fifth year, I remember that at eighteen I was staunchly on the side of authority and the known order of civilisation, institutions, Acts of Parliament and so forth. Until I hit RUSA, I was definitely a 'they know best' young lady. My resentment of Orlando was partly a recognition of the deep threat he represented to these values. I suppose I was still not free of that inevitable jealousy of my mother too, something that was a secret from myself until quite recently. I was then a pert university student. I knew it all, especially the brute facts of human relationships. Why did this sexless, sexy man pay attention to my mother, who by definition could not be in the man market, being my mother: why? I could hardly admit she was anything more than capable and smart (for which I gave her full credit). That would be to undermine the brave start I had made myself, and to concede that the current blurriness of her life was perhaps not a direct consequence of her own inadequacies. I could safely admire her for coping. I dared not imagine that in the future she might do more than simply cope; that she might make something better than a good married life without a man.

I had firmly attached myself to a man like my father in every respect except for viciousness. Charles wore a collar and tie when we went out at night, even as a student. He trimmed the edges of his parents' lawns. He was a bulwark, a rampart, a breakwater erected by me against such as Orlando. He was then studying law and political science with an average of A-minus in his grades. He always intended to join the Department of Foreign Affairs. The way was straightforward, straight forward thank you very much, and eyes front. No wonder Orlando gave me the willies when I met him at that time!

I think it is only fair to tell you more about Orlando at this point, since I did learn to know him later, when my life system was being jolted off its axle.

It was not so strange that he came to Fish Beach. He had been born and raised in Flat Valley, at the other end of Gorse Bay, about sixty kilometres away. His parents had a farm. His father was a dreamer, his mother a tough practical worker. You could say his mother farmed, and he and his father sometimes helped her.

It was not an easy proposition. Their old square house sat on the flat just beside the river. For the first few years of Orlando's life, everything went calmly enough in terms of the seasons. But as more and more timber was milled upstream the floods began; they've been taken for granted ever since, as if they were acts of God.

On nights when rain threatened they would go to bed in their clothes, having lifted everything off the floor to high shelves. Even so, they could be caught on the hop. Orlando woke one night to be hit in the face with one of his gumboots. It had floated up on the rising waters which were already level with his bed. He was ten years old. He waded waist high in swirling water to his parents' bedroom and screamed them awake. Then he did his flood job, struggling through the storm to the back paddock in bare feet to drive the bull to higher ground.

Each raindrop felt like a bucket of water dumped on his face, the willow trees whipped him, his feet floundered through a groundscape altered with mud-slides and swamp made sloshier. The bull was stupid as well as mean, and this time it had to be turned into the face of the rain before it could be driven out the gate and so to the nearest hill, where the cows were safely huddled.

It was not his first or last flood. They were flooded several times a year for seven years before his mother solved the problem. But this was the one which remained in his mind, leaving its mark as surely as a glacier. The gumboot in the face, the shock awakening from a dream in which he was winning a sword fight, the dark roaring waters, the parents losing their roles and sleeping instead of waking him up, the cold feet torn by stumps in the swamp, the water like a wall no axe could break, the monstrous immovable bull, the streaming horns lowered and twisting, the bellows washed away in the gale sucking part of his heart up and out and into the wet willow trees.

The bull was responsible for the flood. People had cleared the land above for livestock and so made way for water falling in seasful from the heights to crash on the ground without any braking on beech leaves. The young Orlando was thrilled as well as shocked by the drama of the storm. The bull was part of that, and yet perverted, trapped, a force domesticated until it formed a more phlegmatic danger in itself. He would have stabbed the high flank with a sword if only his stick had been a sword, even a blunt one; and expected not blood to flow but something more sluggish.

He saw defence operations, fortifications each time more ambitious and no less futile. Earthworks, sandbags, ditches, new watercourses, boulders – nothing, ultimately, could turn aside the force of water avalanching down bare hills and into its varicose veins, could rope the bulky waters and stop them overwashing.

Every autumn, winter and spring, they counteracted water with water. The whole house had to be hosed and scrubbed to whatever level the floods had reached. Mats and blankets were washed and left in the sun to dry. His mother burned manuka and cooked mutton and filled the house with honeysuckle, but nothing quite eliminated the smell of flood and mud. The dark house with the corridor straight down the middle smelt at first sniff like a barn, of cowshit and sweat. Familiarity bred recognition of a more primaeval scent, both more human and more vegetable: rotting leaf mould, genesis of organisms. Every November, their paddocks were bounding with buttercups, just as if the soil had been unsluiced, unsquashed, unsmothered.

Eventually his mother saved enough money to move the house to higher ground. For good measure she had it jacked up on tall piles. Even so, there were times the waters lapped at the front door, and some winters they lifted the mats to see damp floorboards, moisture spreading from nail holes in Rorschach blotches.

Their location made them a key household in the area. Whenever the rain was heavy, people from Oystercatcher and from Kehua's settlement and Fish Beach would telephone Orlando's parents to find out if the road was open. For the Ministry of Works had built a huge new bridge to fly over the floods, but since they had ignored local knowledge, there was still no end to flooding.

Orlando's father was a man of vague optimistic gestures. He was able to forget about floods. Every flood was a great surprise to him, a remarkable, majestic, once in a lifetime occurrence. In other words he got off on the floods. I suppose that was why his gestures (a couple of sandbags, another willow stake planted) were so paltry. He possibly hoped they would be futile, as he was essentially on the side of the water. The river was life to him, and humans and cattle only waterbugs skittering over the surface. His feathery, poetic nature was what attracted his wife to him in the first place, and drove her to despair, and then to strength and resignation.

So that was the smell, the feel of Orlando's childhood. He learned or inherited some of the best and the worst of both parents. From his father he learnt to see shapes and distances, and to be absent-minded about people. His parents were always watching the skies; his mother deciphering cloud changes, his father admiring them. Sometimes he glimpsed the height and the wetness of clouds. He was taken to the sea for fishing trips, and was awed whenever he came close to it. The sea helped him to comprehend the ellipses of the water cycle. He lifted his eyes to mountains unlike any others in the Sleeping Islands. He saw shapes that would always be the appropriate shapes in his mind for hills: heron heads, potatoes, bread rolls, fish. This medley of hills merged into mountain ranges on either side of Flat Valley. The mountains wrinkled their way from high peaks to the waters of Gorse Bay, like monster tuataras, shaggy prehistoric lizards with tails in the sea, heads and shoulders caped with snow. As the years went by he watched their tails nibbled off by bulldozers and the sea, and the sea responding to human interference.

When he grew up his reaction to the shoreline was not to dream, but like his mother, act. And he found that the shoreline was where he usually wanted to be. In small ways, and then on a larger scale, he constantly moved to preserve and restore what he loved, by re-initiating natural systems (ever frustrated by cars, pipes, boulders, groynes and livestock). He grew to resent cattle and sheep, which wandered unrestricted over the dunes of this casual countryside, eating native grasses to extinction and trampling fluid sand-shapes into lumpishness. He began to consider his parents' way of life as a sad struggle to produce useless, extravagant, inappropriate, destructive foods. He didn't like to hurt their feelings, so he made his visits short ones.

Orlando was a man of deep-running, possibly terminal frustrations. In his boyhood there were sandy beaches, swamps, clean waters, and fish in the sea around most of the long, long rim of the Sleeping Islands. That's what he loved, right to his middle. Wherever he went, he saw wharves being thrown up, stone walls and breakwaters erected at aggressive angles, rubble bulldozed into the sea, industrial waste seeping off the edge of the Islands, gross fishing techniques wreaking havoc in breeding and feeding grounds, raw sewage and crude chemicals pouring out of rigid pipes, and every responsible authority taking only one square kilometre of land or sea into account, saying 'She'll be right.' Everywhere people conceived of the earth and sea as a series of rectangular sheets of paper, to be shuffled, spread out and filed. One sheet could be burnt without the others even charring. This was the concept they privately lived by. Orlando was sad inside, and no wonder.

I had not been entirely wrong in my view of Orlando at eighteen, and yet I was far from right. I found it was true he had always been attractive to women. Over the years they had been drawn to him by the score. He had always, after his twenties, played the passive role in romance. Women pursued; he gave in with a good grace. It was generally understood that he was not to be forced into a culvert, but he grew uneasy about the chaos that seemed to surround him. I think his change of name had something to do with this; it was like cancelling an involuntary advertisement. It was not so much that he was sexy, anyway: it was more a case of being lovable. It was partly the woman of him that women loved, and still they wanted to peg him out and hold his title. He had a sleek rubbery shape, sheltered Eskimo eyes, and the physical density of a seal. Goodness knows, he did not look like a Valentino.

Orlando had never grasped the principle of faithfulness. When he warmed to a woman with her arms wide open it was not on his mind that other women in his life might be disturbed. Tenderness was in his nature, and he never made love to a woman without having love in his hands. At least he had grown out of making vows. And yet it went on happening. There was no end to the number of women with some beauty of spirit who reached out their hands to his body and then laid claim to his heart. He never told lies, and so they soon found out about one another, and then they sometimes tried to bury him under their load of grief. He didn't feel wholly responsible, though many a woman had tried to force guilt on to him like icing. He always handled their hurt with patient affection, so that his lovers became his friends again. As you know, it takes a special sort of man to manage this consistently.

At last he knew he mustn't carry on this way forever. When he had known Fern for half a year he made a private resolution. He would try for a while to be faithful. One by one he told his women friends that he had fallen properly in love, which was true enough, though not original; and that he planned to be faithful. Some were puzzled and indulgent; some were sceptical, intending to wait him out; some regarded it as a challenge; and some of them wailed and wanted him for themselves. He mopped up their tears and bound their self-inflicted wounds, and went on being friends until they felt friendly again.

It was less like making a decision than catching it; as sudden as catching a cold, but nicer. And when eventually he was free of his lovers, it was like being free of an ailment so chronic he hadn't known it was there. His heart and body were tired. At last he could rest them both while he waited for Fern to want him.

Every love is different, so it's fair to say he loved her in a way that was new to him. Her company was restful. He wanted to rest his back against her trunk, while her fronds shielded him from the hot sun of other women. He didn't feel the adrenalin flood of the hunter, nor the holy passion of the pilgrim, as he had often done in the past. He was getting older and had never been deprived. He would start by being her friend, and see what happened next. He knew he would lose something, and gain something, and was open-minded about the consequences. Naturally he didn't tell Fern about this decision. She might have found it heavy, although to him it was strangely quick, spontaneous, and light.

My resentment of him went below the belt. I wonder now whether I took one look at Orlando in his sandals and knew that my future fiancé Charles, with impeccable suit and crisp blond features, wasn't worth the anklebone of my mother's friend. In any case, it is easier now for me to see why he liked Fern. Her dogged efforts to achieve independence meant that at that time she simply stood outside the reach of his magnetism. She was safe to have as a friend. The very thought of another sexual entanglement, let alone commitment, gave her the horrors. If his invisible whiskers so much as brushed the fringe of her body space, she stepped at once into herself. He was exhausted by women who clung to him and admired her for standing firm.

I had thought him unreliable. He seemed to swing this way or that without warning; it was nothing for him to express opposite opinions on consecutive days. This never bothered Fern whose conversation also could be highly inconsistent. She understood that to test an idea you have to utter it, and have it taken seriously by someone sympathetic. I have only learned that now, as I write this account. Now I know that Orlando was only unreliable in just the way the sea is. Sometimes the tide is in, sometimes it's out; there's calm, there's storm, there's seaweed coming and going. But the sea is always, massively, the sea. He wasn't easily deterred, even when she disappeared. And so he found his way, of course, to Fish Beach. He brought a backlog of affection that was ready to burst its banks without her.

Over the next couple of months Orlando and Fern settled into a sort of routine. Hattie was glad to get rid of Fern in the afternoons when she walked along the beach to see Orlando, if he wasn't at sea. Out of habit, he set about propagating pingao and spinifex grasses from a bag he had brought from the north. He found a small local grass, spindly and flexible, and experimented with ways of multiplying that too. He tended seedlings of karo, taupata and ngaio, and divided the existing flax bushes, spreading them along the edge of the beach. She watched and helped and kept him company.

The days circulated; Fern circled her days. Each day and night was one revolution of a long, long turret shell suspended over Fish Beach and pointing east. The upper side was in the sun, the lower side in darkness. She had started as a baby, or before, on the tip where days were tiny, though they seemed enormous then. By now she had got the knack of it and liked the rhythm of swinging round the shell: morning, helping Hattie, afternoon with Orlando on the beach, evening shining into night. She twirled around acrobatically. At the end of her life she would come to the mouth and crawl inside, rifling around the guided spiral that led back to the safest, darkest point, the target of existence. Meanwhile she was only halfway along the shell.

The area was one of the most neglected and underpopulated in all the Sleeping Islands, which was why they were there, I suppose. Even so, the beach had been greatly damaged over the last century. The swamp had been drained and a rough road laid close to the shore. Fences were droopy and sheep wandered wherever they liked. Local people were disturbed because the tide came in further every year. Traffic was threatened in two places where the land had been cut away, making small cliffs dangerously close to the road. Old-timers remembered when their stretch of coast had billowing sandhills, relations of the ones a few kilometres to the north. They had taken the sand for granted.

In the middle of a long weekend Orlando announced a meeting of permanent residents, nearby farmers and holidaymakers from the combined area of Fish Beach and Teatown. In the dance-hall he showed slides (before and after) of a beach near Northcity which he had restored. The sand dunes had advanced up to fifteen metres during the two years he had been helping them to do so. The profile of the land had reverted from the vertical to gentle, melodious slopes. The pictures demonstrated exactly the process under way at Fish Beach, only in reverse.

As a cautionary tale he showed them marram dunes,

142

where the steep, stiff shape of that grass failed to adapt to our harsh winds and the sand had simply slid downhill, leaving tufts of tussock high and dry. He showed them dunes planted with spinifex, whose subtler shapes could curve with the changing gales, whose far-crawling fingers met the high-tide mark on driftwood and caught sand washed up among its fibres. He showed them the rare native pingao, flourishing on a distant beach away from marauding cattle: a red grass which grew to a peak with starfish pointers, perfectly designed for collecting a dune in its arms. As sand heaped up among its roots, the pingao constantly rose above its own creation, always king of a shifting, climbing castle. He showed them those bushes and trees which collaborate with sea breezes to become part of the very structure of the land.

And he showed them slides of driftwood: huge white logs washed up to the high-tide mark, rafts of smaller branches locked behind and into one another, swirls of twigs brimming where waves had dropped them on their way home. Most of the people present had no memory of driftwood on Fish Beach except in tiny quantities, and they would take their sacks and raid the beach for firewood after every storm. Orlando explained the function of driftwood on the beach: it meshed together to form the basis of dunes, it held windblown sand and tide-borne sand, and provided nutrients for the grasses. He showed them next what they knew was a possible future truth for them: bare boulders, water turbulently colliding with them, and not a grain of sand in sight.

Orlando turned on the lights and made a proposition.

'We are all worried about our beach: it's disappearing month by month into the sea. If we were a rich community we could pay an expert thirty thousand dollars to prepare a report on our beach. Then we could follow advice and dump three hundred thousand dollars' worth of boulders over the verge. That would be goodbye to the rest of the sand, for as you know, boulders might hold up the road for you, but waves would bounce violently away from the rocks and pump the last of the sand right out to sea.

'Well, we're not very rich. And we could do something cheaper, something modest and rudimentary. All we need is human labour and garden refuse.'

He asked them to stop taking driftwood from the beach and from the river mouth. He asked for dead trees and hedge cuttings in trailer loads, for the use of some tools, and the occasional day's labour. He asked them to mend their fences and keep their stock in their paddocks. He told them that the beach, what was left of it, might shortly seem untidy to their tidy eye: instead of bare sand, there'd be branches strewn around.

Fern had never seen Orlando in a didactic role before. He seemed almost apologetic about offering his special wisdom, won by years of observation and experimentation. He didn't ask for money. But before they could accept his gift, they had to come to grips with a beach management system that was so conservative that it seemed devilishly radical. There was heated argument. They didn't have a chairman and Orlando refrained from adopting that role. He waited and watched while they fought it out among themselves. In the end, as if they were doing him a favour, they agreed to give his scheme a trial.

Next day, Orlando and Fern went down to the beach. He stared at the outline of the land edge, and along the coast and out to sea, as he had a thousand times before.

'What are you looking at, or looking for?'

'I'm seeing the ghosts of the dunes. Can't you see them too?'

Fern knew only one ghost. Orlando was disappointed

that she couldn't see the way the mounds of farm land behind them were replicated in diminishing echoes out to sea, like ripples of churning light. Still, these sights were the curse of Orlando's life and he didn't really wish that vision on his friend. He had to see the ghosts in order to know where to build the foundations of the dunes again.

That day, the first load of pine tree prunings arrived and their work was about to begin. A big horse float pulled up on the road behind them. It was Doug Winchester who got out of the cab and let out his three grey Horses, noble and steady.

'Hello, Fern,' he said. 'I might have known we'd arrive at the same destination. I decided to go while the going was good. And here I am. It looked like an empty part of the map. I think I'll stay here a while.'

He put the Horses in Hattie's back paddock, and drove the hired float back to the nearest city. In a couple of days he was back.

Orlando had been roughly trimming back branches on the larger trees. Third Horse was a willing helper, and Doug brought his own extraordinary strength just when they needed it most. Together they laid trees not far from the base of the banks which had formed at the edge of the road. Limbs protruding interlocked with other trees, so they were rapidly immobilised. Smaller branches were laid behind the big logs until they seemed to make an empty basket framework, softening the right-angle at the base of the bank, a flat kit which would eventually fill with sand. At least, that was the general idea.

'This is a quick way,' said Orlando. 'The autumn storms will soon be coming. It would be excellent if the length of the beach was roughly lined before the equinox. We can do the fancy things later.'

Fern at first was inclined to heap the wood more steeply, on the principle that more is better. Orlando untangled some of her work. 'You can make things worse like that. It's too high,' he said.

'It's only up to my shin!' said Fern.

'But still it's a little cliff, a terrace, and the sea will want to shove it higher still, and bite the sand away from round its feet. The branches should be more like a school of fish or a flock of starlings: harmonising, and capable of any move except collision.' He drew diagrams on the sand and she got the point.

Another mistake she made was to line up all her branches in a queue, parallel to the straight road.

'It's OK to lay them parallel to the front of the waves, more or less. But that line, it should wobble a bit. As if you were scattering wood like wheat. And every grain wriggles into its own space, right?' She heaved and hauled and made an irregularly scalloped edge with bends and bays, and then there were curves on every plane.

Even as they worked, the branches sank into the sand. Orlando arranged for signs to be erected along the beach: 'Please do not remove any wood. We are rebuilding our beach.' He also sank a few measuring poles, marking the level of sand at the start of the operation. He was as familiar with human cynicism and forgetfulness and sabotage as he was with the movement of sand and water. Down one end, a barbecue area was built by a friendly farmer who also left a heap of offcuts with a big notice: 'Free barbecue wood. Cook your sausages here. But don't take driftwood.'

Fern had faith in Orlando, but still she was mystified at the speed of the sand buildup. Every time the tide came in it left a noticeable deposit around the edge of the branches, pouring in and staying as if it belonged there.

'Why didn't the tide do this before the branches were here?' she asked. 'I mean the sea always came to this point, or at least for the last year or so. So why did it take away sand before, and now it's giving it back?'

Orlando was patient, though the truth was obvious: it was there in the sand, the sea, the wood.

'When you go for a swim, the sand doesn't stay on your smooth shoulders. But it's caught in your hair, isn't it? Before we came to help, the beach was bald.'

Fern was wearing a ragged white petticoat, sturdy cotton with a coarse lace trim culled from Hattie's store, as a sun-dress. Orlando's eyes slid around her brown shoulders sheened with darker freckles. The skin between her collarbone and breasts was getting creased, as if her body were a heavy burden hanging from her neck. There was a sadness then, which she could have held in her two hands, making a hollow with one and a roof with the other. She let it fly away in the breeze.

Sometimes children pulled branches away from their carefully wrinkled wooden blanket, and built huts. Orlando didn't mind. They were making three-dimensional mandalas, and cunning shelters that cocked their limbs to the shapes of the stuff available. Their huts were scruffy and wonky and sincere, and placed human habitation in a fine perspective.

'I don't understand why driftwood stopped arriving here,' said Fern one day. 'It can't be just because of people taking it for firewood.'

'Well no,' said Orlando. 'It came down rivers. You know in the bush the way a stream will lure a tree into itself?'

'True.'

'The stream carries a load of light and space on its shoulders. The trees crowd over towards the light, and the one on the edge falls in. It has no other option. In the olden days it would have staggered down the river when the rains were heavy. But now that water is squashed into

147

so many pipes and culverts on the way, the trees are trapped inland and never reach the sea.'

The first of the autumn storms struck, and Orlando, Fern and Doug struggled inside it as they walked the beach. Fern was reminded of the dead landscape of burnt scrub up the valley from Kehua's place, for again dark ragged limbs stuck up grotesquely from the surface of the land, though here they emerged at motley angles and not in approximate parallels. And here too the grey tree corpses formed a scab, protecting land in the process of healing. Doug was thinking of a tempest of sperm competing in a wet rush through his mother's clenched womb to a rendezvous in a tunnel as fine as a hair with a speck that could receive only a single guest. Orlando had skin memories of the storm of his boyhood as the wind blasted sand particles into his face, ripping the air as willows had once done in the darkness. This time, no fences, no bull, just storm.

The rain came and went in gusts and showers, as if a hose were being waved around. Some clouds moved too quickly to drop their rain; the water blew into nothing. The wind forced new sand along pathways in the old sand. Flying grains were deflected by tiny obstacles, shivering to left and right and sticking as the gale sucked in its breath. Sand heaped up on branches like snow on a Vermont maple, great gobs of it, chunks of it held together by wetness. The beach was a small desert, puffing plumes of sand.

Branches were covered in front of their eyes, slopes were built up and then knifed away at the edges again. Loose wood rushed past them in the shallow water to reappear in some pocket a hundred metres to the north. They were cold, wet and happy.

When the storm abated two days later they went to inspect the damage. Fern was embarrassed on behalf of

148

Orlando when she saw the mess on the beach: the seaward edge of their artificial driftwood quilt was all messed up. Careful arrangements of branches had twisted away into spirals and peninsulas and frond shapes. But Orlando reassured her: the storm had merely shoved their work into sculptures of its own. The new dunes were greatly consolidated.

Nephrite Island and Stingray Island were circled by a sea current close to the shore, binding them together. A surge of sea went north on either side, like a river within the water, sometimes reversing, sometimes changing its bed, sometimes swerving to avoid an island or the jab of a breakwater, but always pulsing to unite the Sleeping Islands within its single system.

The heart that pushed the sea around the Islands was unknown, but moon movement and the earth's twirl played their part. The littoral current helped to dissipate the nation's industrial vomit. It also carried in suspension tons of sand from river mouths and glaciers and beaches, swirling round the Islands like an aura. Waves crossed over the current and channelled sand on and off the watery conveyor belt.

During the storm these waves had forced more and more sand among the branches so that baby sandhills were now solid entities of sand and wood. Nothing could shift them now, short of a bulldozer. But the very front edge of the sand heaps was now, in many places, a vertical face. They would have to repair the frontage with more meshing branches, while the equinoctial storms continued. Their move; the sea's move; their move; the sea's move. It was not like building a house; it was a dance, a dynamic physical conversation.

Fern was amazed at the power of Orlando, who had softened the knife-cut edge of the land and extended it up to six metres in a few months with raggletaggle methods and materials. Orlando was matter of fact, indeed cheerful at his very lack of power. He was just enabling the sea and the wind to do what they had done for millions of years, would still be doing if not for timber mills and cattle and culverts and barbecues.

eleven

          As winter began and continued there were more storms, some as wild as the first. After each one, Fern and Orlando and Doug walked the length of the beach and found where the sea had taken its tithe of sand, warning them of weak spots. It was a race against the weather then, to repair the unravelled edges and smoothe the right-angled toothmarks back to a seamless slope.

When there were major repairs involved, or when a new trailer load of prunings was delivered, Doug used Third Horse with a harness of ropes and pulleys. First Horse and Second Horse filled their habitual roles. Speed was not an issue on the beach, of course: they never had to haul anything too far since the branches dump was halfway along the beach, and a careful walking pace was ideal for the work. However, Doug did have a problem getting First Horse and Second Horse to move out of the way once a log was at its appropriate site. Somehow they worked it out together, although it took time; by the end of the winter, the two huge Horses backed and forwarded out of the way of Doug and Third Horse quite efficiently. The Horses were old and set in their ways. But they were really only one Horse; inevitably they learnt how to do this strange new job together. They were clumsy only when they were hurried or forced to overcome their prejudices.

At this time, by the way, Doug was staying in Hattie's cottage. It was ludicrous, of course, but there appeared to be no alternative. Fern took over a bed in Hattie's bed-room-cum-wardrobe. Doug lay diagonally over the four children's beds and didn't pretend he was comfortable. It was too cold to sleep outside, with snow-air blowing from the south. Orlando had even less room than Hattie. And anyway, any house in the settlement (since none of them was grand) would have been too small. Doug was nearly twice as tall as Hattie and certainly twice as broad. It was like having a horse in a cupboard. Anyhow that's how it was for a few months. Hattie didn't mind, but Fern did.

The weather was even more unpredictable at Fish Beach than in most parts of the Sleeping Island, so in between showers and storms there were warm times and still times. After one storm Orlando picked a long-legged pink starfish off the sand. Stiff in death, its uneven limbs curled snugly to some absent rock shelf. When alive, it would always lie low; sea currents traced its knobs and ridges. Its shape adapted inconspicuously, and clung without presenting a barrier. This gritty and sinuous creature outwitted the snaps of accidents and predators by sly regeneration from stumps, spurting almost any number of tails according to demand and even growing new starfish from its abandoned parts. The starfish became the model for a new shape, centred on a heavy log which had found a permanent place on the beach.

Among its half-buried branches Orlando rammed a pole with a rope attached. A light streamer tied to a stick found the line of the wind when planted in open sand. As long as the ribbon flowed in one direction, the rope was stretched at that angle in a slightly drooping line from centre to tip. Orlando, Doug and Fern spread branches in a tentacle whose target was the end of the rope. When the ribbon turned around, they began to build along the route of the new breeze. For two weeks they obeyed the winds' instructions. In that time, five distinct legs grew to individual lengths. The dominant wind had arranged that they build mostly to its particular angle, making the longest arm about four metres.

The shape was heaped to the centre and along its five spines. It was fixed in the centre, but elsewhere rested lightly upon the sand.

They threaded upright bamboo sticks through the ridges, holding the shape intact without attaching it to any base. It was free to cling, twist or swivel like its model, the starfish for which no breakage was a mutilation.

In subsequent storms its gristly legs turned and spread and coiled back towards its body, or stretched out even further. The delicate tips were broken too, and when the big starfish seemed more or less to have settled, Orlando marked its chosen points of extremity by planting five more sticks. He protected them further by tightly attaching a flax skirt to each.

The green stuff curtsied in a symmetrical, rustling eddy. Orlando's next development was to join the tips in a curved mesh of branches so that the form sucked only gently inwards from point to point; no longer a stringy, stretchy starfish but a compact, squat variety. Each line was firm, but loosely curved. The negative shapes that clung along each dimension, speeding and defining the movement of the air, were also part of the whole.

From tip to tip, the edge swooped mildly inwards towards the central pole, which stood much higher to allow for repairs, extensions, and records. Orlando had prepared the foundations of a hill as graceful as the Moving Mountain; but water, not fire, would build it. When storms threw sand among the branches of this sculpture, they didn't compensate by chewing off the front edge. It would stay there a long time, losing and growing limbs, and very hard to kill. This special labour was intense, demanding and finickity, being more of an art than a craft.

During the routine après-storm repairs, and especially while Doug and the Horses were working out the logistics of who put which foot where, Fern was sometimes in the way. Working alone at a distance, playing with kanuka sticks, she found that the wooden net she made could stand on its feet and be an eccentric fence. She had noticed the upright bamboo spines of the starfish prevented people destroying the form by clambering over it. With Orlando she chose a route for a guided pathway down from the road to the flat sand, angled towards the north-west. Fern spent a happy and frustrating afternoon with mallet and saw and binder twine. By dark she had built a fence one metre long and was proud of it.

This became her specialty, making fences. They were necessary to limit the damage done by people running straight to the sea over the dunes as if on a roller-coaster: this unsubtle route loosened plants and provoked instability. Fern's fences gave plentiful options, and they followed the contours of the growing dunes, which in turn were shaped by winds. These were not fierce fences, but loose and friendly. They hinted; they did not forbid.

There was no attempt at symmetry; the shape of each fence was determined by the branches chosen. Her favourite materials remained kanuka sticks and binder twine. Kanuka grows in a spindly fashion, acquiring its bulk by converging at canopy level with its neighbours; and so there were plenty of long, shaggy, narrow limbs around. Every branch had its quirks to be exploited in construction. Some were driven into the ground as stakes, others were inserted in criss-cross or parallels or wanderings as the fenceline curved to allow for a rock or a plant, or dipped to give access to the beach. Fern liked them to be primarily woven and used as little string as possible. It was like a three-dimensional jigsaw, in which the shapes of air were an integral part: it was growing, and like all organisms it would die one day. Every section would rot or be buried by windblown sand; growing trees would push it over and supplant it, or a dune would change shape and make that path obsolete.

When Orlando had a chance he planted out grasses and the occasional tree, and native ice plant on the dunes. They would help to hold the sand together and extend the sandhills of their own accord when spring growth started.

He was still committed to the occasional trip on the *Footloose*, though sometimes Doug would take his place; then the boss got extra value for his money and Orlando stayed back to work on the beach. One day in the spring, when Orlando was at sea and Doug doing a job for a farmer, Fern spent a couple of hours prowling around Hattie's property, just above the creek and beyond the orchard. It was dense with supple young willows in a frenzy of growth. She wanted to experiment with wooden weaving on a larger scale. Also she wanted a bedroom to herself. She took a tall step-ladder, ropes, secateurs and a saw to the willow patch, which was sending up new suckers daily and spreading towards the orchard. She told Hattie she was going to do some pruning, which was true as far as it went.

That day she trimmed back two young trees and tied their heads together. Weeks of practice with her fences had made her hands strong and her eye quick. When Orlando came home she could show him the rough outline of a tall hut among the willows. Luckily she was not a perfectionist. Even so, it took weeks before she finished the hut to the point where Doug could move in. She refused all offers of help; helpers made her feel defensive until she was sure of success. So much of the work

155

consisted of looking, thinking, trying, thinking again and changing a plan in the middle.

Finally, it was done: walls and roof of growing willows bent and tied to a central tree, trimmed to its trunk. Other green willow sticks were woven in and out of the uprights. At that point Fern permitted input from Hattie and the men. A big tarpaulin was tied over the top and walls. Doug and Orlando made a movable floor of chipboard on stone piles. It would have to be lifted frequently to keep new suckers under control. Once he was sure the place was waterproof, Doug ordered some silver builders' paper and some remnants of new carpet. When he had tacked them up as a double lining and added a secondhand door and door frame, the place was warm enough to sleep in. Because it would keep on growing, he would always have to pay attention to it. But at least he could straighten his spine and still not touch the roof except at the edges; he could stretch out fully on his home-made, super-long wooden bed; and he could sit and walk and even entertain in his new, personal hut. (Of course, it was dark.)

Orlando's work was hard work, but he liked it. He did get paid: with ready-cut firewood, fish, lamb, cabbages, apples, chocolate cakes and an old piano. The piano was delivered to the hall, as there was certainly no room in his shack. He borrowed what tools he could and tuned it, more or less, with a tuning fork made of number eight wire. Keys were missing here and there but he rattled out honkytonk polkas and folk tunes for Fern and Hattie to dance to, using the notes available.

Coyly, sometimes Hattie asked him for a dance. Then Fern felt caterpillars bristling through the arteries in her neck. Orlando refused to conform to Hattie's style and danced alone in his own way, leaving her to follow or not. He danced comedy without the slightest overlay of irony; he was a dolphin dancing without spectators. Fern

156

watched and felt her spikes dissolve and harden and threaten to dissolve again. She saw all the ugliness of Hattie, her bony big-chinned face, her thin grey hair with ashes of ginger combed in a cute wavy fringe, and hated that same durability which normally she envied and admired.

When Doug moved out, Hattie said Orlando's tin shack was not healthy and he should move in with her. Fern had no right to any opinion in the matter. When Orlando refused, Hattie pouted.

'You'll land up like that other man, carried off to hospital,' she warned.

Orlando lined his hut with dry bracken and the remains of Doug's roll of silver paper; it was warm and shiny, and somewhat smaller. Fern ventured to question him and he said, yes, Hattie was hinting at a liaison.

'But she's old enough to be your grandmother!'

'So? We're all grown-ups.'

'She wets her pants!' reminded Fern viciously.

'Nobody's perfect,' said Orlando. 'One day you and I may do the same.' He felt like being hard on her, and she had set it up. 'Are you jealous, then?'

'Certainly not!'

He pressed his advantage for once. 'Idiot. Hattie's a winner, that's all, and good luck to her. If you weren't here, I might stay with her, some of the time at least.'

'Would you!'

'I want to touch you. You don't even let me hold your hand. I need that; people can't live without a bit of that, Fern.'

'Yes, but, if you hold my hand, if my husband ever held my hand, it was just to hold me down and ram me.' It was hardly necessary to tell him this, let alone relevant.

'Well Hattie's not like that. She doesn't ram you. What makes you think that I would?'

'You're a man.'

True. Orlando bowed out of the conversation, if you could call it a conversation. In fact there was so much affection built up between them and so much mutual concentration, that if he had held her hand there would have been penetration, if only of love into love. Every line he thought of to promote his cause was straight from melodrama. He was an animal, and had never been ashamed of that. At that moment his frustration was so intense he'd have gone wandering again, except that he felt a commitment to the beach, which held him there up to his neck in sand.

Now she found herself trying to get his sympathy. 'I'm so ashamed, Orlando. I'm a nobody, a nothing, I do nothing. I've come all this way, I've turned my life upside down not once but twice – and where am I? Still just part of the scenery.' As soon as she spoke, she wanted to take it all back; it was rubbish. Perhaps he would believe her.

'If you won't let me make love to you, you'll go on believing that nonsense, and serve you right. What are we doing in this maggoty midden? Can't you use a little common sense?' He hated the sound of his voice. If he took a breath and tried a different approach he would only sound self-righteous. If he didn't, he would seem sullen. The only right act was to take her in his arms, yet that was against her will. Either way, he could mess things up for good.

He wanted to make love. Naturally. It was nearly twenty years since he'd had to say so and he was out of the habit. He'd saved up long enough, and it seemed that Fern was fond of him, and very much a sexual being. Certainly he had no competition. It's not surprising he was mystified by her strictness. It was absurd for her to talk about her husband. Since leaving him, she had had an affair and quite enjoyed herself.

158

The truth was that she longed to hold him and be held. But she valued him beyond any other man, and because of that she didn't dare. She was afraid that her remarkable left breast might harm him. It led her on; it was always nudging forward, straining to hop into his hands and settle there. It had never done anything she disapproved of or regretted. It had always helped her keep her balance. It had freed her from an enemy and a horrible job. Had she known, it was chock-full of God. And it was as lovely as a butterfly. For all this, it had knocked one man down and Fern was afraid it would hurt Orlando and drive him away. She tried to hold on to their friendship as it was, keeping heavenly possibilities at bay.

After this clash, Orlando and Fern would doubtless have made a futile attempt to withdraw from each other until one of them had a change of mind. But straight away outside events put their quarrel into perspective, so they stayed friends and didn't sulk.

I had better tell you that there had already been signs, during the winter, that Fish Beach was about to be invaded by the world whether they liked it or not. Several times they had heard and seen a helicopter hovering round the area of Old Woman Bluff, which was a couple of hours' walk up the coast. And what's more, a four-wheel-drive van had brought two men with theodolites and pegs; they had stayed working in the area till their job was done.

Now the day after Orlando had appealed to Fern and been rejected, a pageant of heavy machinery moved to the far end of their road, fanfared by its own frightful racket. The trucks and machines worked all the hours of daylight, extending the road along the coast northwards. Fish Beach became as rowdy as any big city undergoing mass demolition and resurrection. Some inhabitants left immediately. Others bought galvanised iron garages and set up instantly a dairy, a takeaway bar and a coffee shop, ignoring the county by-laws and making a quick dollar.

On day five of the operation a truck backed to the very edge of the beach, loaded with rubble. Fern watched in paralysed horror as the deck lifted, ready to dump its load on a fragile dune. Orlando, wielding long-handled secateurs, opened the truck door and hauled the driver out of his cab with one hand. The man was red-faced and Orlando pushed him against his own truck by the shoulders, snarling 'You drop that load on this beach and you're a dead man!' The driver, though not very bright, got the message. His boss was under instructions not to alienate the locals, and he found another place to dump.

They asked everyone they knew what was going on. The story was that a man from up north was going to build a holiday house on the Old Woman Bluff, where he would have a three-hundred-and-sixty-degree view of both islands and a great deal of sea. Orlando and Fern were quickly united in concern, curiosity, and suspicion. Try as they might, they couldn't imagine any individual in the whole of the Sleeping Islands rich enough to finance such an operation, who would choose to. The wealthy in general preferred the gentle, semitropical, luxurious far north of Stingray Island to the windy devastation of Gorse Bay.

'Mind you, money can buy anything,' said Fern. 'You could build in your climate. There's rain and sun provided free. They just need shelter and topsoil.' In their minds they contemplated the abrupt ridge of Old Woman Bluff rearing into the horizon; it was a bizarre choice of holiday site. They thought of a dozen kinder places where a millionaire could buy sea and solitude with half the effort.

Earth-movers and trucks of all sorts continued to rumble past their houses day and night, and through the noise of surf they heard explosions and engines in the distance. It was rare that a plane followed a route anywhere near Fish Beach, but one sunny morning a jet overshot their settlement, swooped in a circle, and turned back to land on Old Woman Bluff. Fern rushed out of Hattie's orchard and along the road to Orlando, who had just been swimming. 'How can they? That was some sort of jet!'

'I can't imagine,' said Orlando. They felt like cargo-worshippers. Other locals had been using the new road to peek (though this was not encouraged) and had reported a strange new airstrip in front of the building project. Orlando and Fern had kept their distance, since there was quite enough noise and dust without going looking for more. Fern made a connection in her mind with my last letter, which had arrived the day before; a connection she had been too naive to anticipate till then.

'Dear Mum, it's been a long time since you asked me to tell you more about Charles and my relationship with him. Well that very stuffy start to my letter warns you that I am about to try, and that it's not easy. I wish you hadn't challenged me; or perhaps I wish you'd done it long ago, when I was so very keen to marry him. I could avoid answering you, but once you wrote that down I had to answer myself. Coming in that first anxiously awaited letter, the question was loaded with emotional potency. I admit now that I have been thinking more about my marriage than I have about you – after my first week of amazement and relief and queries, which you have been answering one by one, thank you.

'Charles.

'I ordered a custom-built husband, in more ways than one. I knew what I wanted: solidity, predictability. I trusted patterning, so I looked for the parents of my future husband first and foremost. They had to be long married, and happily. And I know my judgment was good, for

Charles will probably go on forever being devoted and faithful, like his father. He was born to be married. He couldn't contemplate life in any other style. Which is an awesome responsibility for me to have shouldered, isn't it?

'From my point of view, his father was just right: handsome, nicely greying, rather plump, wealthy, set in a house full of stuffed country linen chairs and nice antiques, not showy but sound and well polished. He has worked in the same firm of lawyers ever since he graduated, oh so many years ago. Christmas and Easter at the Blue Lake bach. A trip to Fiji for every tenth wedding anniversary. He never forgets a birthday or a wedding anniversary, and nor would his son.

'Mrs Menzies was a mother I could model myself on. Not like you, you flashy little mouse, rushing pell mell from one hole to another. She does good works, is a part-time volunteer librarian at the geriatric hospital, she provides meat and three veg and pudding every night. I'm not putting her down: quite the reverse, in fact. She likes gardening and recently took up spinning. She's nice, warm, brisk: you know. They've had the same house since they married. If I imitated her, my marriage would last forever and that was the whole point.

'My only reservation was his Uncle Jules; but anyway, Jules is rich and powerful, and he has the ear of the rich and powerful too.

'With a blueprint like this and Charles as the site, what a solid marriage I would build! That's what I thought. The problem is, there's no life in it. There's nobody home! Somewhere inside himself, Charles has bolted in a panic. I thought it was just the new job; I was certain that success (he is successful) in the new situation would boost him, make him respect himself. Very quickly I found out I was wrong: his insecurity has a life of its own, quite unrelated to the outside world. You could give Charles a

Nobel Prize and he'd still be ravaged with self-doubt. I've always been careful with him – perhaps too careful. I've never felt I could make a joke about his job. A thousand times I've bitten off some crack about the Embassy and chewed it well and regurgitated it as wifely concern. He's respected well enough, I think, or he bluffs his way through. What seemed like an attractive boyish diffidence, and solemnity, now looks like a fatal hollowness. He is what he is. And why shouldn't he be? It's my problem, as I am the one who made a mistake about him, wanted him to be something particular for my sake. He's like his father, and yet not at all like his father.

'Mum, you taught me good manners and I've always used them with Charles . . . I must break off here to say this is awfully hard to write! Do you realise, it amounts to saying I'm worth more than he is? And all because he is not what I wanted him to be. Value judgments are the wrongest, the silliest thing to produce when you're describing another human being. I don't want to think like this! I want to respect him! If only he would respect himself. On the sly I have been visiting a counsellor (he was mystified and very hurt when I suggested we both go), mostly to try and rid myself of this attitude to him, which I find odious. I've had some sense talked to me. I've let my own feelings rip too, which has done me a power of good. But I'm no further ahead and I can only tell you the way I still feel now, although you will despise me for my lack of goodness and mercy and faith hope and charity, etc. That's almost a plea that you do despise me, because someone ought to and I can't; I despise Charles.

'OK. You wouldn't be ashamed of my actions, whatever you thought of my opinions, if you saw me alone with Charles. It was from you I learned, quite consciously, various tricks to bring people out, help them cope with their problems. I always suspected it was your way of keeping out of the limelight; but I was still impressed by how many people came to see you and went away feeling better, and clearer. Perhaps you don't even know the things you do, but you're brilliant at this, I tell you. You murmur small noises which somehow imply an intense, but not prying interest. You pick up cues I've missed completely (eavesdropping from my homework at the dining table, you realise) – and most miraculous, you do all this without using that jargon that sets my teeth on edge. See, you're not all bad! When you act the mouse, you do it on purpose, don't you? And still being you, I think.

'I was going to say, I am also real with Charles when I am doing my Fern-tricks; but it isn't the same at all. I'm serious, but far too urgent. I have a stake in this. I badly want to discover a trace of passion, or – well, anything apart from this abyss of self-doubt, which increasingly he fills up with urbane chat, slick witticisms, and alcohol. I can see that my hidden anxiety must leak into his and feed it, making him even surer that he is a failure, or whatever. Oh, what a trap!

'If not for General Merit, I might not have become aware of all this for years, for of course Charles still has great charm, and so would the life of a diplomat's wife, if, if, if. It's not what you're thinking. But then, I'm not doing you justice. You know all the subtleties.

'I don't expect Charles to be like the General: he's a sort of king, and one of a kind. I'm still bemused by his interest in me. I confess, at the moment I first met him, my whole self juddered. And since then, every time our eyes meet, or one of my elbows comes close to one of his, there is some nerve deep inside me which is stroked by lightning. I've had nine months to reflect on this now, and I'm not, I hope, going Mills and Boon on you. I acknowledge to my shame that this is my first experience of sexual arousal. That I've never had the littlest flicker of this feeling with

Charles. That in terms of simple (simple?!) sexual chemistry, I've made an appalling misjudgment out of sheer ignorance.

'Well, even if I hadn't been ignorant, perhaps I'd still have married Charles. It's not exactly comfortable, that lightning. It's a whisker away from a direct blast and being frizzled dead, and who needs that? Charles hasn't changed, not as much as me. I can see the rank arrogance behind my marriage. I've certainly changed the amount of effort I'm pouring into the relationship: I've plugged in a big fat hose and I'm pumping in love and attention. I'm patient, I'm understanding, blah blah blah and it's all completely self-defeating. After all, how can I hope to cure his problem, when his principal problem is me? All the same, he rather thrives on it. He likes me listening to him so nicely.

'But as soon as there's company, the relief is so great that I start to make faux pas (or passes). I'm cheeky, bigoted, crude, illogical, flippant and generally outrageous: the opposite of the devout wife, in short. I become myself again, but to excess, a trifle hysterical. He hates it. Ironically, other people don't. I've accidentally made rather a hit on the social scene here, in spite of my highly unpopular opinions. Clown from the boondocks. Charles is embarrassed by me, of course; he's puzzled too, and can you blame him? The process accelerates. I'm a train rushing downhill, no driver, out of control.

'I can only think of one way out. I've knocked off the pill. They tell me I could conceive after a month or two. It's a gamble but we are both so locked in a hopeless cycle that any change is better than no change at all, and this may be it. You are forbidden to say a word of reproach because my own conception was surely much less willed, much less auspicious than this, yet here I am, in a General sort of way fairly happy to be here. I am partly influenced in this move by the General, who has revealed new research on the horrific long-term effects of the pill even in people who have only taken it for a few years. So temper your response with that.

'Now some other news that will knock your ears off: General Merit, who can take his vacation anywhere in the world, is going to the Sleeping Islands shortly. He was a little vague, but he either has bought or is going to buy some land there to build a holiday home on! He's got a place in mind but he didn't say where. Uncle Jules is his contact over there. I have found out that Jules was also his agent in acquiring the greenstone club. There was an "exchange of gifts", the General giving Jules a pair of very old totem poles from a Middle RUSAn Indian tribe. I said, "How could you give away something that wasn't yours? And where did Jules get the money to buy the club in the first place?" But he seemed to believe that honour had been satisfied; it was not a sordid trading deal at all, but a matter of protocol between chiefs. What rubbish!

'Now listen. The General has promised to call on you. Yes, Mum, you! Partly because he likes the idea of Gorse Bay, in principle anyway. Partly because I would be so relieved to have his judgment (forgive me) on how you are and whether you need help of any kind.

'You couldn't be more surprised than me over this land deal, Mum. I never thought he'd choose the Sleeping Islands as a retreat. Particularly considering our Government's antinuclear policy. I thought, basically, our country would deeply offend him, repel him, disgust him. Don't you think it's strange he should be buying a place there, when you consider his job and his rank, and all the hectic RUSAn commotion about the unforgivable wickedness of the Sleeping Islands?

'Give my regards to Orlando (boobedoo). Love, Dot.'

This letter churned Fern up, and not only at the absurd

thought of a multitudinously starred RUSAn General visiting her in Hattie's cottage. It arrived in the middle of the crisis with Orlando, and the day before the jet plane. It was helpful to her in ways I could never have imagined.

She compared herself with Charles, who was said to be hollow. She sat on a hard kitchen chair and became conscious of her insides. There was a heart, certainly there was a heart. It was a cavity that pressed outwards towards her ribs, towards the colourful breast and towards her armpit. It was tough, rubbery, and sent tingles outwards. And she had lungs. Her breath didn't stop at her Adam's apple: she followed it down pipes into sacks which stretched and shrank, with a slight coolness at each inspiration. Her heart, her lungs, they were like moons, she was full of moons waxing and waning. Her moons were pumping and relaxing, so that what might seem like a temporary hollowness was, on the contrary, a fullness of air, of blood; the spaces had their business and their cargo. And she could feel the membrane of her diaphragm lifting and falling, and the full tubes of her intestines, wrapped into the space available, folded into U-turns and accommodating one another – no. If Dot despised Charles on account of his emptiness, it had no relevance to Orlando and herself.

Then the compliments about her clever listening: her daughter claimed that this was something she did brilliantly, as Orlando built beaches and played the honkytonk piano. She dared to think along with Dot that her idea of herself as a nobody was a fraudulent, virtuoso performance, designed to help others flourish. If so, she paid a price.

She put her right hand on her left breast and squished it around. Her neurotic dread of being touched by her best friend (and she admitted it was neurotic) came from this breast that could light up and fart a foul debilitating gas without warning. It was well designed to keep men at bay.

She loathed self-analysis, especially when it seemed to suggest some kind of change. These thoughts had done their job, so she put up a big stop sign: STOP. She would wait and see how things turned out.

It was important to warn Doug that if the General was coming, Jules might well come too as his associate and local lackey. To Fern it seemed appalling that by a fiendish coincidence father and son would probably meet and the son be devoured. But Doug was glad of a chance to front up and stop escaping in his mind. 'He could find me anywhere on earth, if he started trying. If I deal with it now, it's over.' Doug was also curious, of course, to judge his father for himself. With Hattie and Fern, he devised a plan that would give him the upper hand.

The General could come any day, or not for weeks. But it was reasonable to assume he might have arrived already, on that jet.

twelve

And so they prepared for his visit. Fern boiled the copper for a quick scrub of floorboards through the cottage. Mats were hung over the fence and the rhododendron bush and beaten. The kitchen never did look very tidy, because everything they needed had to be close at hand: teapot, saucepan, kettle, wash-basin, teatowel, plates, and so forth. But at least they could arrange things in clusters, instead of leaving them spread randomly over wooden bench and table, occupying every jot of the horizontal. Fern put a jar of manuka flowers on the table and built up the fire in the range ready to put in a cake.

Hattie had her bath while the cake was baking, and retired to her bedroom to dress, with much consultation. It was four in the afternoon, a probable hour for visiting. Fern dissuaded Hattie from her favourite fishtail evening dress in puce satin. She settled at last on a bottle-green crêpe with big shoulder-pads, pleated bodice, and skirt with broad stitched pleats. Then Fern got into the bath, topped up with a bucket of scalding water. It was soothing after her bustle of housework but she didn't intend to be there long. Hattie powdered and rouged and lipsticked herself a little more brightly than usual, and with her hair daintily fluffed up over her forehead was standing by the hip-bath for a little help with her garters when there was an imperative knock at the door.

Hattie left the kitchen door wide open and walked down the tiny corridor to receive the General, tall and glamorous, and his associate, Jules Menzies. They looked straight through the house at Fern, curled defensively in the hip-bath and gazing fixedly out the back window. Hattie's laugh tinkled with a flash of malice and she cried, 'Oh, fiddle de flea! Kind sirs, you are both very welcome. We shall take a turn in the garden while Fern gets dressed.' And then at long last, taking her time and Fern's as well, she closed the front door and guided them around her territory.

Obviously this included Doug's willow hut; it looked like a crude and woebegone tent with the tarpaulin roped down in six places and walls already sprouting again. As they approached, Hattie talked very loud and fast, thickly studding her chatter with 'General Merit' and 'Mr Menzies'. She started to lead them past the hut when the General asked her what it was for. They paused outside the door and Hattie said, 'It's a very unfortunate case, General Merit and Mr Menzies. Poor boy, poor boy. Such a handsome boy he was, Mr Menzies. He was kicked on the head by a horse.'

'May we see him?' asked the General.

'That's not a very good idea,' said Hattie. The General insisted and she whispered very loudly, 'Don't you frighten him, that's all. I'm warning you both, he mustn't be frightened, or look out!' She opened the door, and when their eyes got used to the dark, and their nostrils to the obnoxious stench, and their ears to the buzzing of blowflies, they could make out a huge, half-human form on its hands and knees rocking back and forth in a strong unstoppable rhythm, a mad, elephantine, catatonic, hypnotic, driven wobble. It was a mechanical body that had lost its centre of equilibrium and would soon fly into a thousand pieces; an unstable concoction of bone-screws and flesh-metal and muscle-springs, about to explode in the face of anyone who came too close.

'What's his name?' asked Jules, and Hattie told him.

'No!' croaked Jules, and Doug ceased his rocking for an instant and looked at him from one half-hooded eye, dribbling from sloppy lips. He grunted, and resumed his rocking with a menacing lurch towards the door, which Hattie quickly closed. She nodded sombrely and led them through the orchard, showing them the three great Horses in the paddock beyond.

'Which one did the damage?' asked Jules. 'Lethal brutes! They should be all put down.' He was very, very upset, and only just covering up.

They came back inside the cottage where Fern was washed, brushed, dressed and furious, her cake slightly burned on its cracked top. The bath still occupied the majority of floor space in the kitchen. She shook hands with the General over the hip-bath, and acknowledged Jules Menzies courteously. He was resplendent today in a cream silk suit, black shirt, and flesh-pink tie.

'Won't you sit down?' said Fern graciously, but there was no space. Her mind was full of my descriptions of the General's apartment and the General's holiday farmhouse, with their multiplicity of bathrooms and servants and the eternal cleanliness of pale grey carpets and peach suede armchairs; she was shamed by the tin container of water between them, contaminated with three days' secretions and sand and stickiness from not only her body but Hattie's as well. Then she somehow remembered that she was not empty, but full; that she was a good listener, and a wood weaver, and the person Orlando regarded as his best friend. So she said with aplomb, 'Would one of you kindly help me lift this bath outside? Then we can talk comfortably, and have some tea.'

The General nodded at Jules, who was obliged to take one of the handles, in spite of the cream trousers. As they went down the back steps a little slopped over his shoe. The container between them created an intimacy that was half sunny, half obscene. They tipped the water out by an apple tree, and returned the bath to its hook on the outside wall.

His last encounter with Fern, a year ago, had left Jules stunned. He remembered only the sight of her unzipping her jump suit, and the blazing breast before it blasted him to the floor. He held her in awe – and so he should; she was the only woman who had slapped his manipulating hand. She was a particularly unwelcome companion for him at this moment when he was reeling once again, having just seen with his own eyes a dream son degenerated into a bogeyman. For so long he had been yearning to meet Doug. He had been saving up the encounter for a treat, a reward for years of patience and discretion, and of course for his morally superior sperm. This was the worst blow of his life, and he had to pretend he had not been clubbed. They went into the cottage in silence.

They all sat around the table on kitchen chairs. The space between them was too narrow for comfort, considering they had to talk across half a planet and a culture gap like the Grand Canyon. Never mind, there was tea and a piece of cake. Fern quizzed the General about me, keenly listening for clues about our relationship. He presented his friendship as fatherly, although technically it should have been grandfatherly. He spoke of Charles, but this was just a convention. Meanwhile he was scrutinising her, of course. He laundered his observations when he reported back to me, but I deduced that he thought she was a slightly queer, ladylike person living in a hovel with a madwoman. He was thirty years older than Fern, but he would happily have put her into an old people's home.

Hattie flirted daringly with them both, the General humouring her and Jules patently irritated. Jules spoke of Department business, abstractedly. They were expanding

172

again, had taken over two more floors. Then with studied moderation, Jules probed for information about Doug.

'Oh, he just turned up with his Horses, out of the blue,' said Fern. 'Such a nice young man he was, and very handsome.' Jules winced. 'And then this awful kick on the head . . . He was in a coma for days and the doctors thought he would die.'

'It might have been for the best,' said the General, for once unaware of the subtext.

'But surely something can be done!' cried Jules despairingly. 'Surgery – drugs?'

'Oh, no,' said Hattie, with commitment. 'He's had the very best experts in the country to see him already. Mr this and Mr that.'

Fern hastily added, 'They flew him to Middlecity, you see. But nothing could be done. So they sent him home again. He's heavily drugged, of course. Otherwise we could never take care of him.'

'His brain isn't just bruised, you know,' said Hattie intrepidly. 'A whole chunk was sliced by the hoof and it just fell right off. Very sharp hooves these big horses have got.'

Fern changed the subject. 'What I want to know, General, is why you are here. What are you building up on the Old Woman Bluff? Is this your holiday retreat, or something more?'

'I guess our standards might be very different, but yes, it is my holiday retreat,' said the General. 'I'd be delighted to show you around. Shall I send a vehicle for you tomorrow? Ten o'clock. Then you can see for yourself.' He was pointedly excluding Hattie.

'May I bring my friend Orlando?' asked Fern.

'Can I come too?' asked Hattie.

'Certainly,' said the General to Fern. 'I'd like to meet Orlando.' And they left.

'That's not fair,' said Hattie.

'I quite agree,' said Fern. 'But you just come along anyway.' It wasn't often that Hattie needed encouragement.

They went to rescue Doug. He fell out the door in his haste to breathe fresh air. They took a lamp to his hut and carefully pulled out the heaps of dung and rotting vegetation which lay on sheets of plastic round the floor. But the smell was slow to go, and many flies opted to remain in the hut or returned after being lured into the dusk outside with the lantern. Hattie wired a glass to the top of a broom handle and filled the glass with methylated spirits. She stalked each fly individually, holding the glass of meths underneath until the fly fell senseless, drugged by fumes, to drown in the violet. Doug was just as disturbed at meeting his father as Jules had been to meet his son. Doug had put his whole self into the big scene, and now he went straight to sleep without a meal.

In the morning a jeep arrived with a soldier chauffeur. 'Orlando Puddleigh and Fern Willnott?'

'And Hattie Taylor,' said Fern firmly as they trooped down the path. Doug just had to miss out, of course.

The others got into the vehicle which took them over a brand new road up the coast. When they came to the base of the Old Woman Bluff they were on the barest of grey ground, where sparse growth had been singed off in the last scrub-fire. They pulled up in a parking area with an eye-prickling view of the north, west and east. It was almost at the top of the bluff, and they could see huge excavations and new buildings were well under way. Jules came out to meet them with hands outstretched.

'Welcome! Isn't the site superb? Isn't it a perfect place for a holiday home? So inspiring – so cleansing – so elevating, after the sordid metropolis.' He had a vested interest in their approval. He shook hands with Orlando as if they were old buddies.

'Well, yes,' said Fern. 'Doesn't he like gardens at all, or trees?'

'He'll never get a decent vegie garden, not up here,' said Hattie.

'It does require a certain vision to see the long-term possibilities.' Jules took them to a higher spot still. 'One priority is shelter. You can see the boundaries of the garden area by that hedge – look.'

They saw a hectare or so marked out around the building site by a hedge already a metre high. Hattie's spectacular success in the garden was based on leaf mould, encouraging chats (exhorticulture), and buckets of white-bait dug into trenches. She kept muttering, 'Well hex on my chooks, facks on the mux,' or something to that effect. Jules said he had decided to use local plants and they were very impressed with the growth rate of this bush. Fern saw with an inexplicable quiver of spite that it was no native but the Mean Spiky itself, current long-term pre-tender to the landscape. They noticed heaps of topsoil scattered around the property and hoses carrying water from underground tanks. Jules confirmed that water had been carried in by tanker, but he showed them a catch-ment system that used the face of the hill itself, capable of keeping all the tanks full.

The main building was set back in the sloping hill face, with a curving expanse of double glass, two storeys high, a hundred metres wide. They stepped into a foyer-cum-lounge grand enough for a luxury hotel. It was still bare, with concrete walls and floors. This was Sunday but dozens of builders and workmen and professionals were going about their jobs with a briskness not normally seen in the Sleeping Islands even on a Monday. Some of the voices heard were RUSAn, some local. The place was elec-tric with intentional behaviour. None of them had seen such purpose, such efficiency on a building site before; it was an expensive atmosphere.

Four men passed them with a computer system on a trolley. Jules led the visitors into an area which had been made comfortable with rugs and lightweight furniture of canvas and brightly painted pipes. The General came forward to meet them. He could play the gracious host in a coal mine, and he welcomed Hattie almost as warmly as the others. Orlando was not on his best behaviour; he was vastly uncomfortable here. General Merit offered them a choice of drinks and they took coffee, except for Hattie: she made him recite the entire range before she settled on vodka and Coca Cola, which sounded very RUSAn to her. She made a face but swallowed gamely. The General waved his hand towards the airstrip of segmented metal, and explained they were using a system like that of an aircraft carrier, making it possible for Air Force jets to land and take off from a short runway.

Orlando roused himself to ask questions. By the time he had finished, it was clear that the General and his friends and followers and staff could stay here for an unlimited length of time, with their every need provided and multiple luxuries too. A further walk around the hideaway showed in various stages of completion a swimming pool, a gymnasium, a small cinema, offices, a tiny hospital ward and operating theatre, a billiard room, and even a conservatory where tropical plants and others were thriving under artificial conditions. Hattie was very perplexed. 'But how? How?' was her gauche, persistent catch-cry. To silence her the General told her the truth.

'Money,' he said. 'Everything is possible. Even speed, even in the Sleeping Islands, is possible. You just have to spend enough money.'

They were already in a state of shock when the General said very calmly, 'We're looking at a resettlement programme for your area, by the way.'

'I don't want to live up here!' cried Hattie.

'That's not the idea,' said the General. 'It's not a final plan at this stage, so don't worry your head about it. For instance, the proposition has to be examined by the Department of Philosophy. But assuming they approve, I think you'll find yourselves living in much finer circumstances before too long.' He smiled benignly, shaking their hands as a clear signal of dismissal and uttering courtesy phrases.

They were driven back to Fish Beach in a depressed state and silent. They looked down the hill at the row of homes that most people in most parts of the world would regard as at least adequate, if not luxurious, and which the General chose to perceive as a slum and a nuisance. They looked at the beach with its fringe of embattled branches. At this stage of its rehabilitation it might seem bedraggled and disorderly to the uninitiated: the sand not white or gold alone, but shifting shades of dun, the vegetation not luxuriant palms but a stubborn remnant of scrub with hopeful new plantings of grasses and flax and taupata. It was a much loved and cared for beach, which the crowded world would envy and despise, given a chance.

All of them felt sure that any protest they could make would be shoved aside in the face of the power the General obviously wielded: a man who could get an operation like this organised and nearly completed in months by remote control, in a backwater of the Sleeping Islands, did have an awesome power. The scale of the work he had initiated from the other side of the planet would usually have taken ten years.

Fern wondered how to arouse national interest in the cause of the soon-to-be-displaced persons of Fish Beach. She couldn't see that many people would care. Orlando knew the beach would be reclaimed as a wharf area, and the sand deliberately abolished with boulders along the side of the road, harbours and beaches being mutually exclusive.

He knew exactly where the breakwater would be erected, and the wharf. If he could see ghosts, he could also see into the future by virtue of acid experience. Hattie tried to picture a new house in Oystercatcher and could only imagine her own cottage in its own garden by its own beach, where she had lived for so many decades. She felt sick. She wished on herself the curse of senility; if only she were babbling nonsense, wandering down the road in a pink nightdress, she could underestimate the General and blot him out of her mind.

Their bad moods lasted a couple of days. Then the General's jet took off again, and ritualistic hopes asserted themselves. Fern wrote to Hilary, asking for advice about mobilising public opinion. Orlando planted out a good strike of pingao. Hattie selected an arsenal of tools with which she planned to murder the General if ever he came to call again. She put a slasher by the front door, a mallet on the kitchen table, a pair of hedge clippers on the bench and a pair of pliers by the bed, just in case there should be time for refinements in this particular assassination. Doug came out of his hut and blinked in the sunlight. Planes came and went like buses.

You can imagine how mortified I was when the General brought back his opinion of my mother's way of life and her friends, variously deranged, decrepit, and anarchistic. And then this letter from her.

'Dear Dot, I hate your General. He is up himself, insensitive, a fascist, a selfish, hard-hearted, icy megalomaniac. That's the polite version. He is building a cross between a stately pleasure dome and Fort Knox on the Old Woman Bluff, or actually half in it; it's burrowed into her side. And just in case we disturb his exquisitely fragile peace of mind, he intends to resettle the inhabitants of Fish Beach along the model of the homelands of South Africa. We don't know yet where his Generalship intends to ship us; no doubt he's looking for a suitable salt mine. Why don't you ditch him and find yourself a Specific instead?

'Yours in a rage, Mum.'

When I told the General that Fern disliked the thought of being moved, he was mildly surprised and perhaps slightly offended. Beyond that, nothing. He assured me she'd feel differently once a real alternative was offered. She couldn't be living in a hovel by choice! He had a big mind, but not big enough to imagine that; or possibly it was too big to be bothered.

I asked him if on his next trip to the Sleeping Islands I might accompany him. This was against all protocol and he was cold when my wish slipped out. I immediately begged his pardon and retracted like mad. But he was already working out how he could arrange precisely that; not to please me, as a matter of fact, but for other reasons. His coolness did not stem from dissent, but because I had jumped the gun.

'Dear Mum, I hope you've calmed down a bit since your last letter. I'm sure it's not as bad as all that, and soon we can all talk it over. Yes, all! Yes, talk! Yes, soon! In another month or so the holiday home will be virtually completed. Furnishings from RUSA have already been despatched. The General is planning to take his first vacation there, probably of three weeks, the longest holiday he's had for years. Another plane will transport the cream of his art collection, which he feels will be safer there than anywhere in RUSA. (Isn't that a strange idea?) Anyway, he needs as always to make room here for new acquisitions. He doesn't like to have the same collection on display for more than a few months at a time.

'That's where I come in. As a Sleeping Islander myself, I am commissioned to help him arrange and document the First People collection, which has grown a little since I first saw it. I haven't argued against this incongruous suggestion for of course I am longing to see you and meet Hattie in her little house, and also dying of curiosity to see the hideout which he and you describe in such contradictory terms.

'In fact, everything and everybody you two describe in contradictory terms. For instance you did mention a boy called Doug (though not who he is, or where he came from), and you told me how you built him a funny hut. But you never said anything about his being intellectually handicapped. I don't like to press the General because he does hate chatter. But are you certain this boy is safe to have around? And why on earth isn't he in a home of some sort, or a hospital? It hardly seems your responsibility! I am bound to assume that the General and you are such radical opposites that it's downright painful for you to keep company. But which of you is telling the truth?

'That reminds me: I'll be so glad to get out of this place for a while! The first and second rounds of peace talks are over. Why "rounds" I don't know. I suppose it's like the square of a boxing "ring", and the opponents bounce back and forward at all angles, and the fans roar for blood, blood. Thank goodness with a bit of luck I'll be out of RUSA by the time they start. I never feel more grotesquely out of joint than when the talks are on. They make it all seem so unbearably complex, and all so sacred. As far as I can make out, RUSA has one thousand nuclear pumpkins and one thousand nuclear puddings, and her "enemies" have fifty nuclear strawberries and thirty nuclear peas. So RUSA says that since the Africans have all the nuclear strawberries in the world, therefore before RUSA can concede one piece of pumpkin she must put five hundred nuclear potatoes up among the stars. Then they can "safely" start talking about disarmament. Meanwhile they are "making the world safe". Excuse all the quotation marks, but even my fingers feel sarcastic, they can't believe I expect them to write such bosh. The RUSAn god is the only god, the god of the nuclear pumpkin and potato, and thou shalt have none other god but theirs. To think that once the stars and planets were named for gods! What can I do, what can I do? I've joined a peace group, much to Charles's horror. Daily he expects to be recalled to Middlecity and rebuked and his career dismantled, because of his wife's insubordination. And to the General, who is right at the heart of the problem (which has no heart), I express my views in every way I can devise at every opportunity. He is impermeable, and it is that which makes me despair, even more than the immaculate lunacy of the media. He is a loner. I have reason to believe that I am as close to him myself as anyone, and that is not close. If only I could reach him! I can't even tell whether he believes all these lies, or whether he blandly condones them. And I don't know which is more frightening.

'To change the subject (please, please), I've got a small subversive plan concerning his collection of Sleeping Island treasures. Once I arrive, I'm going to get in touch with the Sleeping Islands Art Gallery. I want them at the very least to know what's back in the country. And I can't do the job he wants without some expert help. Perhaps, moreover, he might be persuaded to give at least Hine back to the nation. In any case, I've a sense of relief that she will be nearer to where she belongs.

'So: see you in a few weeks, eh? Love, Dot.

'P.S. Not pregnant this month.'

thirteen

Six weeks later I was on a plane with the General, and not the sort of plane I was used to. It had a brisk military ambience. We were served drinks and food by Air Force personnel, and sat in reasonable comfort in a space that held about fourteen people. I had said an ambivalent goodbye to Charles. We were both glad to be parted for a few weeks but put on the face of bereavement. I suspected, and surely so did he, that the General had some private business to carry out with me. We all conspired to maintain the cover story.

It was the first piece of wickedness I had ever experimented with, and when I sat down in the aircraft my heart was pounding with excitement. He maintained perfect decorum, so that I began to doubt my own instincts. Then he sensed something, astute judge of human behaviour that he was (when it suited him); he smiled, looked thoughtfully at his own hand and mine and then at the back of the head in the seat in front of us, and so without a word he apologised for a lack of touching, and explained it. I could wait.

We stopped over in Hawaii and I didn't see him for twenty-four hours, even for dinner at the Holiday Inn. Then at last we were on our way to the Sleeping Islands.

We touched down at a time that felt like late night but was early morning, and landed miraculously on the Old Woman Bluff. He said he had shortened the name to Old Man Bluff; it was time-wasting to say the whole name, and somehow 'Old Woman' was vulgar. I felt he was taking a gross liberty. But now that I hoped – how I hoped – our relationship was about to deepen (and yes, I used those words to myself, although what I meant was it was about to get sexy in act instead of sexy in fantasy, and what I should have known was that our relationship could never be deeper than the curious accommodation we had reached) I was not so rude to him as I had been before. I caught myself being almost deferential. What nasty tricks life, or rather lust, plays on us: I was ashamed, but I couldn't help it. Wasn't that what he liked about me, my iconoclasm? Was it likely he would suddenly be too slighted to screw me, after bringing me halfway round the world to do just that? I suppose it demonstrates just how feeble my marriage was, when you see how submissive I became at the prospect of bedding the General. Or should that be, being bedded by? My mood was passive all right; on heat and grovelling, I would maim the English language and my own self-respect in order to get what I wanted.

All right, I have now punished myself sufficiently, so we can get on with the story. We arrived. The platinum General took a catnap and got down to business on this so-called holiday; I just flopped where they dropped me.

When I woke up, it was one of those macabre, disoriented moments; where am I, what time is it, which is north, what is my name, what have I done, where is the bathroom, should I eat breakfast or supper or lunch? Times and places zoomed around me and I held on tight to the bed, which I discovered had the ultimate mattress, adapting itself sympathetically to my every movement. Goodness knows what technology had produced it. I think my confusion was partly due to finding myself in perfect equilibrium.

So. I was on the Old Woman Bluff, or in it, tucked into her side. Some dregs of perversity made me determined to use the old name forever. I was upstairs in the world's most perfect bed, gazing through a wall of thick double glass that curved to the shape of the hill. I could see the ocean broadcast below and around me, clean, pulsing, as always the source of peace and wholeness. I sat propped on peach silk pillows, basking in a view which would surely mend my raggedness of spirit. A knock on the door signalled a breakfast tray: perfect timing from a discreet young RUSAn woman. The room itself was discreet, close to anonymous, but designed apparently for Woman. The girl and the kitten hung on one wall. White walls, thick white carpet, and the bed in flounces of lemon and apricot. Mirrors. Tall white drapes that opened or closed at the push of a button by the pillow. I felt like a newsmonger, making mental notes of every detail, as if preparing to report back to a committee. I was in my own country, but I never felt more a stranger, except for nearness of the sea.

I soaked for a long time in the bath next door, supplied with relaxing salts and oils and perfumes and shampoos, all very concentrated. The toilet was oddly designed, somehow, and I assumed it was a special model for conserving water. When I was dressed the phone rang and the General asked permission to come to my room. And there he was, his splendid self; the only difference was that of opportunity at last. He seemed no more relaxed, no less so. He offered a car so I could go and see Fern. I was wishing for discipline to be thrown out to the wekas and the possums, and he obliged to the exact degree required to fan my fires: he picked up my hand, bit the fleshy part of the thumb quite hard, then looked me in the eye and saluted. It was calculated and a little freaky.

Then I was off in the jeep to see Fern. For the first time we were both women, contemporaries, taking responsibility for ourselves. I didn't think Hattie was in the least

bit mad; she was simply designed to survive. And
Orlando, in an environment far more fitting than the
Department of Philosophy's Social Club staff social, I
liked; I was glad he was keeping my mother company. We
had a frisky afternoon, walking the beach, talking our
heads off, sizing one another up and reassuring ourselves.
All the time, of course, I was sharply conscious of the
evening drawing near.

The General and I had a meal which was probably
superb, in a dining room all to ourselves. I can't say
anything about the food but I do remember champagne.
But then there was always vintage champagne: the
General was no sybarite, and it saved him having to make
trivial decisions. I felt suddenly shy. My hesitating silences
he covered adeptly with anecdotes that could be spun out
indefinitely. I ate and drank, I suppose, and he made
pleasant noises with his mouth. After dessert and coffee
(I presume there was coffee) he put his hand on mine. It
was strong, shiny and dry, with liver spots round the
knuckles.

'Honey,' he said, like a movie star. 'I want very much
to ask you into my bedroom. If this is not what you
intended, please forgive me.'

I rose to the occasion. 'If I had had a single doubt, your
gentlemanly speech would have dispelled it.'

He took my elbow and we moved to the sound of a
silent minuet to his room, which was conveniently next to
mine. Even the shyness about who would use the bathroom first was smoothed over by his perfect manners. But
while we were being so politely explicit, I had another
point to establish. I was off the pill. Should I use a
diaphragm? Or would he, dot dot dot? Our formality was
extreme.

'Honey don't you bother about that. Everything is
taken care of.' In RUSA, this is a euphemism for saying

you have had a vasectomy. I was glad to be free of that messy business.

The big moment was upon me. My first man, apart from Charles! I didn't know the etiquette and took my cues from him. I felt that *Gone With the Wind* would be my safest guideline. He undressed me expertly, biting my shoulder, my chin, my arm – it seemed he was a biter. I can joke about it now but believe me, at the time I was incandescent with desire, which was complicated by a sense of immense privilege. I was scared to take any initiative because he was a General, and I found that he did prefer it that way.

To my surprise he left the jacket of his uniform on. I do like skin on skin, and while the fabric was very finely woven the ribbons and buttons gave me much discomfort. One piece of my flesh was pinched between a button and the jacket at a critical time, frankly taking the edge off pleasure. A medal he wore pressed hard into my breast, leaving an indentation that remained for half an hour. He caressed me methodically and productively, and when at last his cock arose and entered me it was like a missile. When the warhead was released he was staring fixedly at something behind my head, which later I discovered was a small, framed flag of RUSA.

At the time of his first insertion I wasn't conscious of anything more than what I've said already. He regarded every copulation as a serious business, more as if he were going about the affairs of state than indulging himself in a furtive love affair.

And so it happened every night after dinner, always with his jacket on, always with this air of dedication. Although he was a brilliant man I cannot say he brought much imagination to our lovemaking. Nevertheless, I was devoted to him, an acolyte, in an atmosphere I could never have dreamed in a million years. It was like the

Arabian Nights for me: engorged luxury, the art of idleness, erotic paraphernalia, and a hint of being every night on trial for my life. There were even guards, and a forbidden gunroom, and a room for computerised wargames complete with large table map of the world, where cities and military installations flashed and moving submarines and aeroplanes dotted their routes across the surface. I wasn't supposed to see that, but I snooped when a soldier-cleaner did the rounds.

What first attracted me to the General was his overwhelming power. In the capital of New RUSA, every Senator, Congressman, and diplomat deferred to him in manner, if not in words. The President himself, I had seen, treated him warily. (We'd had our turn at the White House.) His power seemed physical, or psychic, rather than constitutional. Nobody ever discussed the nature of his responsibilities in my presence and I had naughtily probed without success. It was just accepted, this power; he carried it around almost visibly, he breathed it in and out at will. Now that I was enclosed with him for several hours every night there was a tinge of fear to my idolatry.

My days were stimulating because I made them so. The General had shown me round the holiday complex which was now to all intents and purposes complete. There were living quarters for other people as well as ourselves and those who maintained equipment and grounds. More than forty could be accommodated, so that the General on his holidays could play host to a house party, and loneliness or boredom would never emerge. I did think he had carried planning too far, but that was an occupational hazard I dare say.

Apart from the extravagant facilities he had shown the others, there was now a creche, a library, an art gallery (of course), an aquarium and an aviary. Birds and fish were there in superb variety, two of each, as Noah had also arranged. These rooms were made for pleasure, but there were also laboratories, including one where plants were growing in water, sealed off from the atmosphere and using and re-using nutrients enclosed in glass containers: perpetual motion as expressed by horticulturalists. A laboratory assistant explained that this was the most economical method of food farming ever developed, and this room could produce enough to maintain health and energy in fifty people indefinitely. 'Now I know I'm in the Arabian Nights,' I said to myself.

It should have been heaven, inside the Old Woman Bluff with the General. There was everything the heart could desire, as they say. He spent all day in his office or the computer centre and preferred me out of sight until the evening. I had a library, swimming pool, conservatory, bar, and the ocean (through two layers of very thick glass). I had music, films, and furniture of luxury and taste. Yet from the start my urge was to go outside and walk through the single gap in that broad, spiky hedge which had grown explosively, pampered as it was with fertiliser and perpetual irrigation. I'd mostly refuse the inevitable offer of a vehicle and driver, and walk down the scraggy hillside which I could have despised. It was bare, scalded bones, it was scraped rock of sand solidified, nothing grew except frilly yellow lichen and a few tight, rolled-up or razor-edged grasses. The winds were always on the verge of pushing me back to the General or over the cliff into the sea. My feelings didn't quite make sense, and I explained them to myself as the joy of the child who walks towards her lost mother.

For of course at the bottom of the hill, a couple of hours' walk away, was Fish Beach and Fern, who still had to do things herself, like wash and cook and (when Hattie permitted) help in the garden. There was Orlando who was also doing things natural and difficult.

Moreover, lurking among the willows there was Doug, meekly frustrated at the need to keep out of sight while the the General was in occupation. We were allowed to meet, and he trusted me because he was a trusting person. I was able to tell him that Jules was expected shortly. Sometimes I opened the gate of the Horses' paddock and they proceeded in their capricious, compulsive formation straight to his hideout. Then I could see the power of his gentleness. Yes, I liked Doug. He was always calm, but naturally, under the circumstances, he was short of stimulation. So I'd trot after him among the willows, or sprawl in his hut (which now had a narrow, surreptitious window), and talk to him of life in RUSA. He had a gentling influence on me. It was like having an extra-special younger brother.

Once I'd dispensed with my obligations up the hill, what I wanted to do was help on the beach. At first they fussed. 'You're a visitor. You're on holiday.' Finally I persuaded them that I had been a visitor and on holiday for over a year, ever since I'd gone to RUSA.

'I belong here. I'm a Sleeping Islander. I'm fed up with holiday.'

So I was allowed to work on the beach, moving branches, mending paths, tying fences. My hands got rough and bits of torn brown skin stuck out all over my fingertips. Luckily the General did not like to be caressed. or doubtless he would have been annoyed. In the evening a jeep would come to collect me and I would return to the holiday complex for another dinner, another evening with my hero. We slept apart.

Naturally I had brought my tramping boots, but the General seemed anxious that I should spend no nights away from him. I read that as a sign of affection. Once he relented, and Orlando and Fern walked into the bush with me. We had two delicious days in the wet, dark, pungent green, following a well-marked route from hut to hut. When we emerged a jeep was waiting and drove us straight home. Although it was only afternoon tea time, the General rushed me to bed with an urgency that I found quite romantic.

My wish to invite some experts to see and catalogue his art collection met with an outright veto. I dropped the subject at once, in case he should also discover and forbid my contingency plan. I drew up full descriptions of his treasures, measured them carefully, and I photographed them from every angle. I made as thorough a record as I could of Hine and the prow, club, spear, bailer, and ear-pendant, and the small collection of cloaks which he had lately acquired through Jules. I did the same for all the paintings he had freighted to the Sleeping Islands. The General paid no attention to the process at any time. It confirmed my impression that he had no more interest in the individuality of his works of art than you would in the individual beauty of a banknote. Then I carried out, and not impulsively, my single act of defiance. I sent a copy of my catalogue, including all photos, to the Director of the Sleeping Islands Art Gallery. I described the site of the General's house as clearly as I could. I said the General had no wish for any outsider to view the collection. I wanted no reply to my letter, which was sent for her information only, and I kept no copy. I posted it from Hattie's address. I felt strangely easier when I saw the mail van take it in the right direction: away from Fish Beach, towards Oystercatcher and thence to Middlecity.

I decided which things went where. The paintings I placed in reception rooms and bedrooms, and in the library, because that was as close as I could get to their natural place: they were supposed, expected, to hang on walls where people coming and going and staying could have a good look at them. He'd brought a substantial fraction of his collection, leaning heavily towards the Impressionists; whose were the paintings he understood the best.

I stood back from the big, luminous 'Waterlilies' canvas which I'd hung at the far end of the foyer, the most worthy site I could find. They were comparatively close to the exit, the waterlilies, (and far too close to suit a conservationist) but nevertheless they looked trapped to me. Even the frame protruded from the wall and clenched the water tight, as if to say 'Got you!' Something flowing and flowering had been nailed down, or rather, nailed up. I thought I saw already how it would fade, dry, and shrivel, hidden in this barren fortress. The painting was dimly lit of course except for when people came to worship. I knew what was proper. But still I felt that casual eyes and bright lights would do it much less harm, deep harm, than keeping it in a concrete meat safe. The General was only protecting his investment, but after all, how many centuries did Monet expect it to last? Even in captivity, it reflected in so many lines and lights the joy of making, that joy of the moment which is so much more durable than the joy of having. Luckily I could work on the beach as an antidote to these uneasy feelings.

The General's gallery was a single square hall with a high roof, fitted with flexible light fittings and movable plugs that could be exchanged for hooks and other fastenings. The space was infinitely flexible. Pedestals, cases, platforms, and even false ceilings could be assembled out of lightweight units from an excellent storage system in an adjoining room. I found it ironic that the gallery should be so carefully designed, so satisfying and pleasant to work in, because I knew my display would not be pleasant or satisfying. I planned to show only the objects from the Sleeping Islands here, and it was impossible to make them look impressive or even correct in this ludicrous context (except, of course, for Hine-Mother-of-us-all). Still, I took pains.

I arranged them so that they all appeared to be on the verge of leaving. The spear, suspended from the ceiling as if about to be thrown, pointed its outrageous wooden tongue towards the door; its white ruffle of feathers fell backwards like a jet trail. To get into the gallery you had to confront the spear point at eye level, and manoeuvre past.

The prow of the war canoe was placed so that the huge body of the vessel would really have fitted behind it. I put the prow close to the door and left the length of the gallery empty behind it. Naturally, the bailer was in that imaginary canoe, near the back. I could picture the canoe there whole, and sometimes found myself wishing it was full of warriors about to leap on to this strange shore. In the gallery, I evaded the General's personal power. At times I found myself treating him in my mind not as a lover but as an enemy when I was surrounded by these potent things that were neither his nor mine.

It was easy placing Hine, who belonged wherever she was; she just squatted on the floor in the centre of the gallery. I wanted her to be able to make a quick getaway if the occasion arose. Seen from above, for she was only waist-high, she was more self-contained than I remembered, and there was a distinct implication of malevolence. I was not the object of this malevolence; I shared it.

The greenstone club I hung from the ceiling behind Hine's left shoulder, as if it had been flung back and was now on its downward stroke, killing an enemy of the stone god. It mulled the light in its centre. As I said before, the General now had four ancient cloaks to add a new dimension to his collection (a female dimension), all made of very fine flax and feathers in varied patterns. I was exasperated at him for getting these, after all I'd said. I hung them on a wall in fan formation. As for the whale-bone ornament, I didn't know where to put that. It didn't fit in with my concept of the exhibition in any way. When I raised the alternatives with the General, he said, 'Ornaments are for adorning beautiful women,' and gave it to me with a silver chain. He could surely see I didn't feel comfortable about owning it or wearing it. But I accepted, because at least this made it 'mine' to give away.

I could see the General deeply disliked the way I had organised the gallery. It made him very uncomfortable. He said nothing about it because fundamentally he couldn't be bothered.

Often I spent time in the gallery alone, just being. I loved to touch the canoe prow with my eyes, tailing a thread of carved wood as it twisted and joined to itself again in a regenerating pattern. Ridges turned into lacy hollows, a spider's line into its throughways, the shell of a snail into its own cavities. I tried in vain to stop the wood from shimmering but tongue tangled with fingers and became finger, finger hooked into a tail and became tail or tongue, claw became ear . . . I kept long watches by the canoe, but we never became familiar. Again and again I almost grasped the line and when I blinked, it had wriggled away. I never knew for sure where my eye was simply too slow and ignorant to fill in the missing pieces, and where the carver had brilliantly deceived me. The carving enticed, mystified and rejected me. It wanted no disciples. It was built to help its owners get on with the job and swiftly, not to gratify a casual prowler like myself. The carver of Hine, centuries earlier, shared the same tradition. No wonder her sorcery was enigmatic.

The rest of the holiday centre was cold in spirit; I found in the gallery an intimate sense of presence which was a comfort to me. Several time I had an unmistakable feeling that someone had walked in behind me, and I turned and was still alone. I supposed it was ghosts, or a ghost, and if so, I preferred their company to that of most of the humans in that complex. I thought I was divinely happy at this time, but I must have been tense, to find rest among ghosts.

I specially felt this damp, misty intimacy when I was near the sharp-edged greenstone club. It had impressed me strongly when I first saw it, because of its simplest of beauties. From the side it was kidney-shaped, with a handle at one end. It was slim, organic, jellied, and exactly right; that's the best word for it, for it was positively right, not negatively faultless. Before the first chisel stroke on the jade boulder, this club was waiting (as Hine was, exactly). Light now lived freely, moving in its flax-green core.

Don't think I'm being sentimental here. Because of course to be a club for close combat and be essentially right, clearly implies being used. This club must have killed again and again. That was what it was for. It sang a single, intrinsic note, the note of violent death.

Now I had an unexpected urge to steal it and fling it down the hill. On two separate occasions my hand spread out to take it, before I understood. When I had hung the club in the first place, I thought I felt it throbbing in my hands and I didn't find this hard to interpret, for I was using a noble object to decorate the holiday house of a foreigner. Greenstone is saturated with the spirit of all who have handled it, after all. We know that, although I have found it embarrassing to explain it to sophisticated people. The club had been unused for a long time. I had no enemy to use it on, or so I believed. Dangling on its cords it was always restless, swinging slightly as if it were trying to get out that door and away. Well, that had been my intention; the club and I were in harmony.

'I belong here,' I said to the General one evening.

'I know you do,' he said. 'That's one of your main attractions.'

'It's a funny little country,' I said.

'It has its special importance,' he said. I was pleased he appreciated that.

It was the longest holiday he had taken in fifteen years. I asked him why, hoping it was because of my delectable company. At no time had he said specifically how many days or weeks he intended us to stay. On the other hand, he was communicating with RUSA all day, every day, so it wasn't so much a holiday as a change of executive suite. He said he wanted to get used to the place, make sure everything was functioning as it should, and so on. I accepted that he concealed most of himself, his job and his intentions from me.

I began to get restless, mostly because of the uncertainty. I spoke of Charles; he'd be expecting me back. The General said he could do very well without me.

'Relationships are never as complex as you fear. He'll be thriving in your absence. You're not a particularly healthy companion for him, Dorothy. You're far too strong. You make him cringe, not on purpose, but you make him cringe.'

'But he'll be missing me!' He hadn't written once.

'Maybe so. But I happen to know his secretary is consoling him. Louise.'

I was shocked. 'That's not at all like Charles,' I protested.

'No, but it's certainly like Louise,' said the General. 'Don't worry, nobody else knows.'

'Then how do you?' (Good question.)

'She sent me a telex,' said the General. 'Now don't fret. He isn't lonely, I promise.'

This made me even more anxious to get back to him.

But it was impossible, psychologically and practically, to cross the General. It was a long way back to RUSA.

When I had been with him for nearly five weeks a certain tension was developing between us and even I was bound to perceive it. We had made love every single night, except for the one I'd spent in the bush. I had asked him several times to remove his jacket in bed without success. Unexpectedly one night he agreed, and made love to me like a celebration. His mood was noticeable, and that's saying a lot: I could tell he was almost triumphant.

'We can go back to RUSA quite soon now,' he said. He told me that Jules would arrive the next evening and we could leave a couple of days later.

I was never satisfied. When I went down to see Fern the next morning, I didn't feel happy any more. I didn't care if I never saw RUSA again. Admittedly, I did see it was my duty to return and sort things out with Charles.

I went to find Doug in the willows and told him that Jules would arrive on the Old Woman Bluff that very evening. 'Good,' he said. 'I must go up and speak to him.' All of us crowded into Hattie's kitchen while he talked it out. 'Look at me!' he said. 'I can never be imperceptible or indistinct, specially when I'm riding the three Horses.' That was certainly true. 'Wherever I go, I am obvious. Wherever I go, Jules Menzies can easily seek me out. I haven't enjoyed hiding myself away, and I'll never be good at it.' That was also true: he was inclined to burst the seams of any hiding place. 'If I go on like this, I'll be a prisoner of myself. It's time I wrote to Mum and Dad, for instance. I think it would be far more natural if I had a chat to Menzies, man to man.'

Orlando backed him up. 'It's often a good idea to change your mind.' Fern was the one who'd first implied that he should run away from Jules. But since that day in Pipetown she'd had her turn at lurking behind curtains, and she knew it made the soul go pale.

'He's part of me and I am part of him. And after all, what can he do to me?' asked Doug.

'Nothing,' said Hattie. 'It's far too late. You're much too big for him to cripple now. He'll have to let you be, for there you are!'

'I want him to respect me,' said Doug, and Orlando thought it was quite possible.

So Doug prepared First Horse and Second Horse and Third Horse for a journey, and the next day they set off in their usual unselfconscious, formal parade. They arrived on the Old Woman Bluff in the afternoon. I had stayed in to pack, and to observe the meeting of Jules and Doug, with some idiot thought of intervening if they came to blows.

I saw the grace of the Horses grounded in immense power. First Horse arched her neck and raised her hooves high in a backwards dance that celebrated obstinacy. Second Horse matched her in silky movements and in mountainous strength. Third Horse carried a man that was worthy of the animals. Watching them crest the hill and delicately pick their way to the guard by the hedge, I felt Horse as a being much older and shyer than humans, much burlier and daintier, and thoughtfully created. And Doug did not detract from their dignity.

He told his business to the guard who relayed it indoors on his walkie-talkie. Video cameras at the perimeter of the General's grounds had already announced the arrival of Doug and his mounts. Doug asked for Jules Menzies to meet him outside the hedge. The return message court-eously requested him to proceed to the front door. Doug refused; his Horses sheered away from the Mean Spiky hedge.

So Jules emerged from the desert palace and walked to meet his son. Doug stayed mounted and reached down to shake his hand. I hurried to be near them, for no good reason.

'How do you do, Jules Menzies? I'm Doug Winchester. I believe you are my sperm father.'

'Don't call me that, I beg you!' cried Jules with tears in his eyes. I had never imagined he was vulnerable. He had always been a showy figure; beside and below his heraldic son, he seemed a pale, verminous plagiarism, although he was the original model.

'I was curious to meet you. I have something to say to you. I acknowledge you as my sperm father, thanks to a biochemical technicality. Legally, you have no connection with me. And that's how I'd like it to be in reality. If our paths cross in the future we shall know each other, and who we are. But I take no responsibility for our relationship, and I hereby reject any which you might choose in the future to assume.'

His language was as grand as his Horse. He would have looked down on his sperm father even with feet on the ground. As it was, he chose to elevate himself still further, to put himself right out of reach with syntax.

Jules was as confused as he was disappointed. 'But I thought you were brain-damaged? I'm expecting two of the world's finest brain surgeons on the next plane from RUSA, tomorrow. But there's nothing wrong with you, is there? Or does your – condition – come and go?'

'It was a ruse to keep you at a distance. But now I find it more appropriate to confront you than to avoid you. Clearer, somehow.' Thank goodness for that! Otherwise he might have been kidnapped by brain surgeons.

Jules was very white. 'I'm so relieved. I'm so glad you're whole. In fact, you're splendid!'

Doug softly clicked to his Horse to move away, first leaning down to shake Jules' hand.

'If I can help you in any way – would you like a job –

or a trip – or a boat – or a farm – or an island?' Jules called after Doug as he walked away on his twelve long legs, on his waltz of a Horse, past the resort and the airstrip to go exploring, since he had come so far already. I found myself feeling sorry for Jules at this moment. It was a scene he had planned for, had lived for, without exaggeration. It had been played upside down and backwards, and then gone into the shredder.

Still, he was always resilient, was Jules. As his son rode out of earshot I could see him thinking, 'Oh well, that wasn't so bad. I can try again another day.' He patted his hair, which he had specially combed for this encounter. It was parted on the side. The main wave lay diagonally across his head, as firm and crisp as if it had been set in a butterfly-curler. I remembered Orlando expressing a prejudice against men with this sort of hairdo, saying they were not to be trusted. It wasn't the way it grew, for Doug's grows just the same way. It was the way it was restrained into obedient charm, whereas Doug lets his grow naturally, that is, criss-cross and ebullient.

fourteen

That night we were to have a farewell
dinner for Hattie and Orlando and Fern. I insisted on it.
Not that I had to do anything: I just said the word, and
the cook produced a sumptuous meal. The others were
picked up in the early evening and we went for a walk to
the top of the Old Woman Bluff. It was high summer by
now, and light till late in the evening. Conditions made
for perfect visibility. The General came too . . . I say that,
because even then I found myself as a matter of course
grouping my friends and family into 'us' as opposed to
'him'.

I was pleased to have achieved that degree of understanding. The whole fantastic exercise began to seem
worthwhile. I had loosened my link with the General,
having gratified my wicked wish to excess. I'd seen the
gulf between us, if only of nationality. I had gained a bit
of respect for Charles, who had broken out of character
the minute my back was turned. (And who could blame
him?) I believed he and I could pick up the threads and
darn our marriage together again.

We could see the tip of the Moving Mountain that day,
and imagine the long narrow sweep of land beyond it to
the north. Together they formed a hand, lightly grasping
at the ocean, emphasising the precarious hold of the
Sleeping Islands on the planet or the planet on the
Sleeping Islands. No doubt ships were pulling in and out
of Pipetown, loading liquid petroleum gas in bulk; any
day now a single match could ignite the city and people,

melt them down into one red-hot lumpy flow to the sea. That was the gamble of Pipetown, and always had been. Meanwhile Uncle Elliot lived there in silence, his brown bark loosening every year. When we turned we saw green bush, white-topped mountains, sea layered in shades of blue from palest aqua to indigo. Our very words for blue were shifting and mixing out there in the sea, curving around the horizon.

I felt the division between the General and us on that hilltop. He looked like the master of all he surveyed, a landlord or conqueror. Orlando was shut inside himself, possibly weeping over Jerusalem. Hattie seemed ready to fly off the edge like a hawk. Fern was sad about my leaving. I think she had postponed sadness for our separation until then. For a year she had been following the flame inside her, bursting out and burning all around her, and she had now come close to a resting place where it could smoulder less ferociously. It was only now, so late, that she felt ripped ragged down the middle, because I had gone and was going again to RUSA. At Fish Beach we had become great friends, my mother and I. The wind hit us in the eyes. I was doubly wretched, for I was leaving not only Fern but my other mother, the country I had grown up in, the bush, the beach, the hills, the air that was like no other.

We walked back to the holiday complex. Shortly I could stop being a troglodyte. Jules Menzies joined us in an elaborate dinner and a great deal of champagne. Hattie got silly on it very fast and flirted with Jules who tolerated her this time.

Not even the General had seen fit to import an orchestra. But after dinner Jules brought out a piano accordion, which held the greatest fascination for Hattie. Fern had had no idea that he played, and all of us were astonished (except the General, whom nothing could astonish).

Jules went up in my estimation because of the excessive vulgarity of his instrument. Fern could never see any good in Jules and called it sublimation, with spit in her voice. We moved to the gallery, of all places, because it had a shiny wooden floor, and he played 'Under the Bridges of Paris' and 'I'm Forever Blowing Bubbles' and other tunes, all in the key of E flat and very mechanically. Hattie danced exuberantly, tirelessly, first with Fern (who was dressed as a lady that night), then with the General, then with Orlando, and then with Jules himself, separated from him by the width of that pleated black skin with its two keyboards, multiple buttons and lavish mother-of-pearl. The General danced with me closely, protectively, almost tenderly, and I softened to him with incipient and premature nostalgia. It wasn't entirely uncouth, dancing in the gallery. I knew we were performing a ceremony of some significance, though I hadn't the faintest idea what it was.

We were all distracted by the gyrations of Hattie, who kept thrusting her stringy little breasts towards Jules's piano accordion as it inhaled and exhaled; she was perpetually on the point of being nipped in its folds, which was doubtless her ambition. Thus the most dramatic event of that dancing scene went almost unnoticed. Orlando asked Fern to dance and she whispered in a champagne flush, 'I have a breast which might turn blue and gun you down.'

Undeterred, he put one hand at her waist and spun her round and round Hine-mother-of-us-all, spiralling round and round and back again till convex became concave and vice versa, and Fern's love like a sleepy stingray lolling in the shallows floated its angel wings, whipped its barbed tail and sailed into deep water. When Jules stopped for a breather they stayed joined together, lightly, in case the second touch might be harder to make than the first.

When it was time for bed (Hattie being most reluctant to admit it) I felt my watch unhook and fall to the floor. I left it there. We moved through the building to the foyer, and my mouth said, 'I've dropped my watch. I'll go back and get it.' My legs walked back, my hands untied the cords around the sharp-edged club and tucked it into my pants under my dressy full skirt. My watch was picked up and put on my wrist. It was me who did these things, and yet it wasn't me at all.

Then I joined them in the foyer and choked over my goodbyes; they left. I fled to my room with the perfectly true excuse of emotion. The General didn't come in till after I'd hidden the weapon in a drawer. My impulse was still to throw it out the window, not to use it; but of course this was an air-conditioned vault and the windows were tightly sealed. The General brought two brandies and we sat down in the armchairs. Then he opened the most extraordinary, the most unexpected conversation of my lifetime. That is, I certainly hope I never have to sit through one like it again. He was unexcited, practical and serious, as if he were dealing with a household budget.

OK, I'll try and tell you how it was, and you try to imagine being me, listening to the General and struggling for the words to answer him.

'Dorothy, I am happy to tell you some good news: you are pregnant.'

'I can't be! You had a vasectomy, you said you did!'

'If you think back, you will remember I merely said that everything would be taken care of – and so it will. I couldn't think of a better mother for my child, under the circumstances, and he will lack for nothing. I assure you, I shall be a proud and responsible father. So it's true: everything is taken care of.'

'Except my feelings! I never intended to get pregnant! I'm on my way back to Charles! You've cheated me, you've cheated him! Anyway, how do you know – how could you possibly know at this stage?' I recalled the peculiar lavatory in my personal bathroom, and the laboratories, and decided not to press that point.

He took his time over well-considered statements. Perfectly reasonable and unflustered, he was certainly the right person for his particular job. 'I'm sorry, honey, that I was unable to give you the full story at the time. Believe me, I've had your welfare at heart, as you are about to discover. You are bound to be glad I brought you here when I tell you that shortly there is going to be a little trouble in the world. I'm sure you'll agree it's best if you stay here and start a new life. I don't think you realise how lucky you are.'

'What do you mean, a little trouble? There is always a little trouble in the world, and more than a little, so what's new?'

At that stage I was still staggering from his first blow, and I didn't want to hear another word. This made me nag and needle him till he told me more than enough – oh yes, more than enough! It was probably no more and no less than he had intended to reveal from the start.

'What's comparatively new is that we plan to use strategic nuclear weapons. You understand what that implies in military terms, don't you Dorothy. It means a nuclear war which is limited, tactical, and preventive.'

'Preventive? You can't be serious!'

'I'm always serious, Dorothy. What we're preventing is any opportunity for the United African States to utilise their own nuclear arsenal, which is already dangerously large. As you very well know, they have recently become a serious threat to world peace.'

'Only after RUSA started waving a big stick at them!'

'Be that as it may, their aggressive tendencies must be curtailed before they imperil the whole world.'

'Oh. You mean RUSA is the world, but Africa, that's not the world. Have I got it right? So you just want a small nuclear war, do you General?'

'Not so very small. Not too big and not too little. If a job's worth doing, it's worth doing well. We intend to nihilise every state which might be sympathetic, as well as the entire U.A.S.' An interesting thought struck him. 'It will be very instructive to see whether our desert areas recover more rapidly than the rain forests.'

'What do you mean, our desert areas?'

He looked at me in surprise. 'Sorry, that's not quite accurate. We've been experimenting with climate control over the last ten years or so, you see. It's been going pretty well, so I find myself thinking of parts of the desert as our creation.'

I poured myself a big brandy and tried to take it slowly. 'I still think your choice of enemy is arbitrary. What have they ever done to RUSA, those African states?'

The General looked mildly peeved. 'Just trained thousands of terrorists and exported them all over the world, that's all.'

'There's that world again. Your world.'

'Most of it, nowadays, that's true. And Africa as enemy was never an arbitrary choise; that's just silly, Dorothy. There were many candidates, I assure you. The African union was chosen after lengthy and heated dialectation. And I think it was a good choice. For one thing, the states were allegedly neutral in the old pre-RUSAn disputes.'

'But accepting aid from you! Some of them were more like allies – some for Old RUSA, some for New.'

'Now honey, once RUSA evolved, obviously some former associates had to be shed. Surely you can see that was inevitable?'

'I still say they didn't deserve the honour of becoming your number one enemy.'

'There were other factors. For instance, Africa is equidistant, more or less, from both Old and New RUSA. In a nuclear age, you understand, that is critical; Africa is not our neighbour. For practical and bureaucratic reasons, the creation of RUSA made the selection of a new antagonist imperative, or we could have generated internal dissension.'

'That's something that's never made sense to me. Why two sworn enemies should suddenly, out of the blue, unite to form the Supreme Power of RUSA. You were paranoid about each other, your two halves! I don't understand how it happened.'

'You don't have to understand, honey. It is enough to know that we submerged our differences in the cause of world peace.'

'Is it true there were nuclear weapons fired?'

His eye was stony. Then he seemed to recollect that I was to be the mother of his child and he condescended to explain.

'There could be a certain amount of truth in that, if you take the strictly chrono-historic view. The official record shows that there were two weapons-tests that went awry on opposite sides of the world, at the same time.'

'A simultaneous cataclysm,' I said crudely.

'Subsequent political developments substantiate the official records. The RUSAn approach to pre-RUSAn events is basically a commonsense one. We contextualise them: that is, we apply the post-RUSAn consciousness, and where appropriate we interpret them in the understanding that those two great nations were always one in spirit, with similar goals, histories, and methodologies. Only our ideologies were falsely perceived as non-harmonious but all those differences have been long resolved, chiefly by focusing on the practical. Yes. It was a demanding time for our leaders. Old RUSA and New RUSA (then using their divided names) each chose to direct a warhead at a key target in a comparatively underpopulated area, as a demonstration of intent and capability. It instantly became clear that our respective leaders were unwittingly signalling something quite different and surprising: namely, our essential oneness, our indivisible singularity, a fact which had been unrecognised until that historic moment. In a flash, we discovered that we were perfectly synchronised twins of equal strength, parallel halves of a single, immensely potent whole, reaching towards each other across Bering Strait . . .'

He was unusually thoughtful here. I found myself wondering whether he felt professionally cheated by the supersonic resolution of that clash by civil authorities. I may have been goading him when I said, 'Who won, then?'

He was fair. 'We were too evenly matched, I told you, to extend the confrontation without laying waste the world.'

'You mean, RUSA.'

'And after that, an alliance was inevitable. In a way, the official establishment of RUSA was a mere formality, a rationalisation.'

'So who won?'

'The popular view in each half of RUSA was that they were the victors. The constitutional arrangements satisfied both parties.'

'Fear played no part, of course.'

'No no! But you see, man needs enemies, Dorothy. The great nation is always a nation at war. All progress, expansion, growth of mind and industry – it all arises from the military mind. You so-called pacifists, you want it all ways. But the hard truth is that you cannot have peace perfect peace, my dear, and also have your refrigerators and video records and motor cars and the new physics, and if you can't see that, you're not as intelligent as I gave you credit for.'

'So Africa was elected the enemy. Because of geography.'

'Yes; and because it was the right size. These little wars are nothing but an endless irritation. Whenever we try to sort out a problem in some trifling nation, over and over again we find we cannot, categorically, win. It's always expensive and inconclusive, there's always bad publicity, and there's always resistance, this damn stubborn nationalistic pride – I tell you, it's epidemic. RUSA needs a war it can win. Which means a large war, the only sort which can be won. A young union of states like this African one is ideal because it will always be fractionated by national and tribal adhesions, making it so much easier to liberate as a whole. And indeed, it is perfectly placed on the globe. In cases of escalation, it is, at least, not close to the Sleeping Islands.'

'What's that got to do with the subject?'

'Simply that I think we'll be safe down here.'

I needed another language to answer him, and I didn't have one.

'I can see I have told you either too much or too little for you to comprehend. I'll go on. You're my wife, in a sense, and I'd like you to feel easy about my mission. We shouldn't have secrets from each other.' He glanced at the drawer in which I thought I had concealed the greenstone club. I should have known there were no hiding places here in the ultimate hiding place. 'These are affairs of state, but you will be fully protected from yourself until it's all over.'

'But there are peace talks on at this very moment! On your territory!'

'Precisely. There's never been a better moment to initiate an exchange. We hope the fact that those African leaders are in Washington will cause the U.A.S. to hesitate before retaliating. And their vacillation will be the key to our victory.' His argument was exquisitely symmetrical, and without rivets. There was no way for me to get inside it; I just had to admire it from the outside like a tourist.

His pauses were paragraph breaks, a blank before the next bullet. 'Nuclear war is inevitable. Everyone knows that in his heart of hearts. There has never been a weapon invented on earth that has not been used eventually. Since it is inevitable, we think it is preferable to have it sooner rather than later and to ensure that RUSA controls the focus. The sooner it happens, the sooner reconstruction can begin. When the plane leaves for RUSA tomorrow, you will stay here. I leave alone. I have to be there in person to set the exercise in motion.'

'You mean they can't do it without you?'

'For this particular operation I have been granted the privilege of ultimate decision. If I judge it is not an opportune moment (and I do have access to universal intelligence, of course), then I shall refrain from acting. They trust my judgment; they have good reason to. I'd like you to pay me the same compliment, but it's not essential.'

'What if the Africans concede all you want in the peace talks? What if they lie down and submit?'

The General looked as if he had taken a mouthful of burnt porridge. 'There is some danger of that at the moment. I've been pressing our representatives to take a softer line, so as to calm the U.A.S. and also to hand them the role of aggressive party. There is a little confusion at the moment but twenty-four hours should set it to rights.'

'You mean, no matter what stand they take, you're going to bomb them?'

'I told you, honey, we need this war. Economically, and spiritually. War is a natural and healthy condition of man.'

'But not of woman!'

'How dreary. Not that again. You know perfectly well what I mean by man, Dorothy. Am I always to be pestered by your semantic bagatelles?' He did look quite irritated, and waited for a moment to be sure that I was chastened.

'I have said that resistance is not anticipated. Nevertheless, we are prepared for that eventuality. It has been decided that for the benefit of all RUSA, it is best that I and other key members of the military and the government immediately evacuate once the operation has been inaugurated, and locate ourselves in certain other parts of the world, those parts which we divine will be least affected by any adverse consequences. This is not our only refuge, you understand. But I'm sure you will be gratified to meet my house guests when we return. I don't anticipate spending more than a few hours in RUSA before we come back here. I'm expecting the President to bring his good lady, and as you know she is a very charming person.' He was pleased to offer me this delightful titbit. I took a gulp of brandy.

'Is she a midwife?'

'Oh, Dorothy, we won't be here that long! Mind you, we have the capability. But our scientists estimate that in the worst possible scenario, it would be safe to emerge within a couple of months. That's in this country, of course. It will be very different in Africa. You used to call this God's Own Country – haven't I heard that phrase?'

'Yes. In the Pacific Ocean.'

'Well then. My point is made.'

I couldn't see it. 'So this holiday complex is nothing but a bomb shelter. I should have known, I should have known. My god, you're like a chain-smoker moving into the non-smokers' carriage on the train because it smells so much nicer.' An insult that fell short of pulverising him, but then I felt entirely feeble, as if all my bones had been pulled out.

'You must admit it's luxurious for a bomb shelter.'

'I cannot imagine why you chose the Sleeping Islands. Of all places! After all, we've banned all nuclear weapons from our lands and seas! We are totally, totally hostile to the very concept of nuclear weapons. You couldn't have picked a worse country in the whole world.'

The General smiled a most unusual smile. 'We have never opposed your stand on nuclear weapons. We appeared to, as a warning to other nations that might be similarly tempted. As a matter of fact it suits us very nicely. It means that in any exchange of hostilities, you, the Sleeping Islands, will be religiously spared by all parties. You have not a single RUSAn installation that could attract an African missile. We have bided our time; we saved you up for our sweetest intrusion. There is no safer retreat, geographically or politically, in the world.'

'Politically! You'll be torn limb from limb when the locals find out.'

'Why? What law have I violated? There are no nuclear weapons here. A few guns to deter scavengers, or avengers maybe. I own this piece of land. I have built me a nice, tight little house where I can holiday in style.' He poured himself another brandy and I watched him sniff it. He had gone on drinking, eating, screwing all these weeks with this on his agenda.

'I can't believe you could contemplate bringing a child into the world, after the holocaust!' I thought there was no answer to this.

'These are very emotive words, honey, and not at all accurate. Let us both acknowledge that in your delicate condition, you are liable to overreact. I advise you to take those hormonal changes into account when you reflect later on what I've been saying: you see my point, don't you? I'm trusting your good sense will prevail eventually. Now this word holocaust, for instance: let's examine that objectively. True, the enemy territory will, I hope, be devastated, which is no more than they deserve; and unfortunately the Middle East and parts of Europe and India are bound to get some fallout. After all, we are gambling, but the odds are heavily in our favour. No, it's not gambling: rather, it's a truly daring experiment, a gallant journey of exploration to the very edge of human endurance. Yes. It is even conceivable (but not in the least probable) that some parts of RUSA itself will be uninhabitable for a decade or two. If so, that is a sacrifice we must face up to. But here in the Sleeping Islands all we have to do is wait, in comfort and tranquillity, and life will continue as before.'

'Life, you say. It's not my idea of living. And what of the nuclear winter?'

'I promise you, there'll be nothing on that scale. Trust me, honey. I have good reason to believe that is just scientific propaganda, or in other words, mumbo-jumbo. There are so many gaps in our knowledge, Dorothy, so many hysterical theories about nuclear war. Every ill-informed prophet of doom has his following, and nobody listens to common sense any more. It will be marvellous to clear away all the mystique and the horror stories once and for all, to get a few facts under our belt at last.'

'Why did you curse me with your baby? Why me?' Now that I knew the man, this was an appalling question. I dreaded to learn what I might have in common with the General.

'You have the supreme advantage of being a native.'

'I'm not your friendly native guide at all. I'm of English and Scottish stock. We only came out here three generations ago. Native my foot.' (I believed this at the time. Now I'm not so sure. And anyway, we're all immigrants,

212

like the gorse. What matters is how we behave when we get here.)

'Excuse me. I mean you were born here, you talk and think like a Sleeping Islander, you know the customs, the edible plants, the animals, the laws – '

'Laws! What laws? There should be a law against you. You're a nuclear weapon yourself, that's what you are.' Oh dear. I wish I could show myself in a better light. I was operating at the level of a two-year-old in a paddy, just when I longed for magical eloquence. Beneath my inarticulate curses there was a wild drive to keep on living.

'Don't be childish, Dorothy. To go back to your question, I decided almost as soon as I met you that you would be the ideal woman for this venture. You're fit, healthy, intelligent, used to the outdoors, and quite – spirited. Of course you have your faults, I think we both know that. But on the other hand, most of the women I mix with would be quite useless in a situation like this.'

'A country cow. I see.' I cursed my vanity, my monumental gormlessness. But there was more at stake than wounded pride. He didn't waste time telling me I was charming, witty and pretty.

'When you get used to the idea, you'll realise that given the particular circumstances we shall make an excellent couple. Between us, we have everything we need to live through the trying times and emerge triumphant.'

'Until you die, fifty years ahead of me.'

'I'll die happy knowing I have left at least one son to enjoy my heritage.'

I found my tongue and a few clichés. 'Your heritage? It will be a crumbled mausoleum, derelict in a desert of your own making. You'll be another Pharaoh, yes, buried with all your treasures and your widow and child – but dead, General, in a ruined world, under a mountain of ice.'

He rose, not at all offended. He smiled indulgently. 'I can see you would rather bypass our usual diversions tonight while you absorb all this new information. Believe me, honey, it has been difficult for me to keep silent on the matter. I am greatly relieved to have shared my thoughts with you at last. I know you'll get used to the prospect. After all, you are an intelligent woman. Goodnight, my dear.' And he left the room.

fifteen

A few hours later I changed into sturdier clothes, took the greenstone club and got ready to carry out a new plan: to kill the General in his sleep. First, to draw courage, I looked out the window at moonlight on the sea. The world was a bubble, the sea and sky an iridescent film slithering over the surface. The General was able and willing and planning to prick it. I weighed the club in my hand and practised assassination. Then I found my door was locked and I wept on the bed in anger and frustration.

Yes, I did weep, honestly. But there were two of me and one was weeping with relief.

For in a red-violet sort of way, I wanted the General to live, to do his deed wearing my colours, to come back to the palace and rule the world with me his empress. I wanted my share of the boldest act in the history of the world, I wanted to light up and overhang, to burn and cool and freeze a continent, I wanted to subdue and exterminate nations, I wanted possession of the General and so possession of time itself. I wanted to command fertility and barrenness, I wanted to cease judging and be certain, I wanted to be the General by bearing his son, by doting on him, by furling myself in his flag. I lay on the bed, appalled and happy, flaming with happiness and fear.

My passion for the General had always turned me into a child. With him and because of him I had been only a feeble voice for the right I believed I believed in. Not feeble in sound: I'd screamed and shouted and stamped

215

my foot, knowing and secretly wallowing in my impotence. Whenever I cried out on behalf of humanity, my voice was jagged and prickly. Could I have done better? I doubt it. I think I wanted in equal parts to be the General and to be Hine. Neither was possible, so all I produced was noise, which baffled the beat of my heart.

It was three in the morning. A blue-grey figure clad in a blanket appeared, shaking with dry convulsions, begging me wordlessly for something, perhaps the club. I knew she must be Kehua, and that it must have been she who had kept me company in the gallery and helped me steal the weapon. I offered it to her but she could not hold it because she was only a ghost. I could do nothing to help her.

Early next morning, Fern and Orlando and Hattie set out for the Old Woman Bluff. Each of them pretended it was just for a last, unsolicited farewell to me, but each was privately smitten by ill-defined anxiety. Doug hadn't come home that night, by the way; I suppose he had a lot to think about after his meeting with Jules. The three of them were relieved to see the small jet still on the airstrip of interlocking metal plates.

When they came to the Mean Spiky hedge and expected to walk through the gap unchallenged a soldier prevented them. They asked to see Dorothy and were told it was not possible. Their anxiety at once became alarm. They hovered outside the hedge, at a loss for any positive move to make but convinced they should not go away. Kehua joined them, greatly distressed, unable to express herself now except by piteous khaki looks and a hand outstretched towards my window. Fern was worried specifically that if Kehua let go of the Old Woman Bluff, she would also lose hold of me. And how could she hold the bluff when she was on the bluff herself?

One section of the air-proof glass frontage slid sideways

and the General strode out, followed by an aide with suitcase and briefcase. He saw the group at the gateway. He opened the gate, and stood between two Mean Spikies to confer with them and gracefully to bar their way.

They had a leisurely conversation, a superficially amiable chat.

'Dorothy overdid it last night, folks, I'm afraid,' said the General. 'She woke up with a do-it-yourself headache. My doctor gave her an injection of pethidine which sent her straight back to sleep, and we've put her on board the plane already.'

They stalled for time. Orlando drew out more details of my hangover and offered a variety of alternative cures. Fern discussed the previous evening's menu in laborious detail. And Hattie paid the General many pretty compliments on his appearance and deportment. Because they had seen a curtain twitch, and me waving and mouthing through the glass.

Kehua knew far more than all of them, even me. She certainly knew where the General was going, and what he had done to me, and what he was going to do to the world in two days' time. So she did what seemed best to her at the time. She was not equipped to hold material objects, although she naively persisted in trying, right to the end. However she could mobilise them by her will. (She chiefly consisted of will.) Nobody could touch the Mean Spiky bush (which we subsequently renamed the Benevolent Spiky) without being stabbed deeply, and suffering wounds which without exception inflamed and filled with pus. It was quite different from green gorse, for instance, which will leave its prickles under your skin almost like a calling card, and there they stay until you dig them out, because you are bored, perhaps, but not because they hurt you. Gorse was a vegetable kitten compared with the angry dragon of this Mean Spiky hedge, which Jules had

had planted around the General's refuge to keep out wind and unwanted humans.

Kehua willed the plants to intensify their growing, to bend and lock behind the General, to knit like a scar in front of his legs. Once entwined, there was no disentangling the branches. Before he noticed this sly ambush, Kehua adroitly bent other growing branches round his chest and groin. He tried to grasp the neck of a branch between thorns but the plant is so constructed that this is impossible: there is no access to any stalk not guarded by long spikes with venomous tips.

The General yelled to his assistant who was still on the inside of the hedge. The aide went back for long-handled secateurs, although it was already too late to rescue his boss. Even the hope of retrieving his body seemed now a flimsy one, for he was deeply embedded in a ball of thorns which were pricking his skin, even through his uniform. He was visible only in scraps, so thoroughly was he covered.

When the aide returned and clipped gingerly at the outside twigs, the General began to scream. The secateurs jammed and the hedge grew so rashly that the soldier had to abandon his tool and leap back out of the way. We had to pull back too as the hedge grew taller, wider, and denser by the minute. The General was under a hill of subtly shifting spears and skewers, leaning on him, leaning into him. He tried to keep absolutely still and his self-control was phenomenal; naturally this did not prevent the thorns from growing inwards as well as outwards. The two bushes rooted on either side of the General regarded his body as a soft interference.

Like Alaska and Cukotskij Poluostrov, like Fern and Orlando, they were two segments which must pierce the rift between them, must stretch out and touch thorns until they interlocked and grew into the very body of the other, which was, after all, so like their own. The General was a hollow to be filled by the bushes; flesh was no barrier; eyes and mouth were easy points of entry; bones could also be penetrated. His high-pitched continuous scream disturbed the plants until they crippled his voice-box, and after that their growth was less frenzied, more sympathetic.

Fern and Orlando were much sobered and would have rescued the General if they could. Hattie was leaping up and down with glee. And I flapped the curtain and hammered with silent fists on the glass of my cage, until Fern attended to me at last.

She undid her buttons and pointed her left breast. It burned icy blue and the others stood back. Where she aimed, the glass melted and dripped in waxen shapes to the ground. I was on the upper floor, but I had read many schoolgirl adventure stories where Brenda slips out of the dorm for a midnight feast, so I knew what to do. I ripped the silk sheets in half, joined their ends, and tied the stuff to the bed leg. Then I tucked the club into my bodice and shinned down to the ground. I was still locked in by the hedge, but Fern scorched a passageway and I ran through, and Kehua healed it up again, and we were running the length of the bluff as fast as we could go, except for Kehua, who vanished.

There were men standing by the plane ready to leave for RUSA, and we waved to them as if we were out on a carefree jaunt. One I knew well and I said to him, 'The General's tangled up for a couple of hours, so the trip's delayed. May we borrow this four-wheel-drive for a little joy-ride?'

'You have to have a driver,' he said. 'Where are you going?'

I flapped my hand and reluctantly he summoned a youth to drive us. We piled in and headed along the hilltop towards the spit and Whale Peninsula and the place with no name. It was misty, and the mist became a fine rain.

We quickly reached the edge of the kanuka forest. As if this were our final destination, I invited the driver to come out and see the view, which he did, although I have no doubt he was heartily sick of views, views, views, being a native of New York. Then his radio started to crackle. Fern pulled out the vehicle keys and hurled them way down the hill into a clump of coprosma. Orlando stabbed the back wheels with his pocket knife, then we ran hectically into the kanuka, following a hidden gully down, down towards the causeway over the estuary and away from the soldier's futile pistol shots. I held the club with one hand, grabbing flax and branches with the other. When I had dropped it for the second time, Orlando and I made a quick ribbon of flax torn and tied, and hung it round my neck.

We skidded down the slope, following hoof marks. Cattle had long been negotiating the easiest route through this forest. They had eaten and trampled most of the undergrowth, leaving a clear way through the tall skinny shaggy nimble tree trunks that kept changing places in a sociable zigzag bone dance. Small bushes were misty with rain and showered warm dampness as we pushed through. I just stumbled from one foothold to the next, but Fern knew this hillside off by heart: kanuka, kanuka, hebe, fern, fern, bracken, daisy, kanuka, fern, flax, kawakawa . . . I didn't know where we were going or why, let alone how. We were not thoughtful, hesitating beings, we were cattle stampeding or godwits migrating. We were expelled from the bluff in horror and fear, and also we were being sucked ahead by some unknown attraction.

We clambered through tree ferns and swamp at the

base of the hill and down to the gravel road. Nearly there! Or anyway, nearly somewhere. Turning the corner we could see the house of Kehua, and the estuary marbled in bronze, grey, and navy blue, mangroves a solid colony round the rim as if they had been there forever. The sky was a riot of curls and drama as the rain blew away for a while. We all stopped. The magnet was not in that direction. Orlando said, 'Wait.' We saw someone moving inside the Ewers' house.

'The old pa,' said Fern. 'That's where she'll be: Kehua.' We backtracked and climbed a stiff hill; simple now, it was pasture with patches of scrub that were easy to dodge. We were all going to the same place fast, for whatever reason.

Down the ridge of the hill almost to the level of the mudflats, where a couple of thousand black swans ankle-deep in snails and crabs were pickily eating the roots of eel grass; and straight up the first rise of Whale Peninsula. Down again and through the ditch made by Kehua's ancestors, neglected now and half-filled with scrub. Up a steep slope, hanging on to bracken and the trunks of nikau palms. And there, huddled in a grove of dappled kohe-kohe trees, was Kehua. Right beside her were the three great Horses, and Doug.

Hattie flung herself on the ground and panted. We all had to sit down or lie down, but she was really far too old to go running up and down hills. Moreover, her pink lisle stockings were ruined. When I look back and think about this expedition, it is all so queer. At no stage did we behave logically. It was more as if a hurricane had picked us up and blown us willy-nilly to this meeting place. All the way, we felt as if we were running for our very lives. Well, I can tell you, I was glad to get there.

Kehua raised huge echoing eyes in a foggy face and said to Fern, 'I've let go. But look – it's still there. I want to let go and I thought I had let go, and it's still there. What's gone wrong?'

Fern said, quite irrelevantly, 'The plane hasn't taken off yet.'

Kehua's eyes fixed on the greenstone club, hanging heavily around my neck. I took it off. 'If I had really let go,' she said, 'I wouldn't still be here, would I? I've been holding on so long, I don't know how to do it.' She seemed to think it was an urgent problem. But we had to flounder around and let the solution come of its own accord.

Hattie said, 'Anyway, the General's dead by now. Surely he's dead. Of course he's dead, so what's the worry?' She knew that the General had locked me up and lied about me, that's all.

'I don't know about that,' I said. 'He has lived through three wars already.' I thought of the hideous scars beneath his jacket.

'You wouldn't expect a war to kill him!' said Kehua. 'Of course he's dead. Don't be so silly. But I won't be finished till I let the Old Woman Bluff go. That is the third part of my job, and now it's time. Give me the club.'

She had a strange blind spot about her physical capabilities, that lady; she had never quite lost the habit of having a body. The weapon slipped through her hands again, of course, so I had to do what she wanted to do herself: test it for size and shape in the cleft at the back of her skull. It fitted perfectly, sending out a resounding boom of stone on bone as it did. I was about to take it out of the cavity when Kehua restrained me with a gesture. I let it nestle in her skull. Once I twiddled it involuntarily, as if it were an acupuncture needle. The light that was shaped like her body glowed lilac and her face was petrified, just for a second. Then the light faded to its shade, and I lowered the greenstone club.

After that, I did what my hands had been itching to do

ever since the club came back to the Sleeping Islands. I stood at the lip of the Peninsula above the bluff like the face of a sperm whale, and flung the sharp-edged club into the sea.

Then Kehua leapt, launched herself from the same point of the cliff, and her blue shadow sank into the water, hovering there like a stingray briefly, then diving; and the half-light of her was quenched in the water.

Kehua's leap made sense. It was what she had been pining to do for a hundred and fifty years, and it was also her immediate, urgent duty. But I was horrified when Doug's three Horses followed. They moved stolidly to the edge of the lip of Whale Peninsula, and one by one walked into the air: First Horse tail first and head raised high; Second Horse following with hooves whipping, mane lifting; Third Horse with Doug on her back, stepping deliberately after them. Their leap was mythical, and I half expected them to sprout white wings and fly away. The water was shallow, as always, even though the tide was in. I doubt if it was more than one metre deep, and yet the Horses vanished utterly. Not a whinny, not an ear, not a flick of tail whitening a wave. The sea jelled over them as if they had never been, and accidentally I couldn't help crying.

I thought I would never forget Doug's doubtful face as he went down with his Horses. And yet very soon I had forgotten Doug, forgotten the General, forgotten myself in the anarchy of the senses which erupted. There is no single word for our experience, no word which would give you a quick way of understanding it. Perhaps it's better that way. After all, none of us has managed to interpret it. You'll have to go through it with me, as it happened, and it did happen, whether we understood it or not.

First we noticed a queer stillness, as if the airwaves were about to turn, like a tide. Trees stopped moving. A seagull fell out of the air. The very rain, which was light and cloudy, seemed to pause where it was, and not fall. Then there was darkness, although it was day; a thick, full, active darkness.

Mainly it is that darkness which I remember in nightmares and flashbacks. It crawled around me, climbed over me, blundered into my mouth and nose. I was in its way. It was heavily wired with painful impulses that raced back and forth on their circuits, like sunlight skidding up and down a glossy cobweb. When they hit me, the scene was lit for a split second and I was connected randomly with another person of flesh or shadow.

In those flashes of dark vividness, I half-knew many things. A woman of scraped green ice, of tiny twisted water-threads that melted as warmth approached her. Rocks frothing, graphs jagging. A thicket of blackened gorse, tall gorse with thin trunks, a forest of tangled carbon. A tattooed warrior with his skirt twisting in a quick wild move held a baby tightly to his chest and gouged out its eyeball with his fingers. He held the eye high above his face and then he swallowed it with gusto, fine threads of blood clinging to his chin. Over and over again I participated in the same scenes. Warrior swallowing baby's eye; bodies in combat, phosphorescent sweat; spearing, clubbing, gouging; blood vessels trailing from wet lips; muskets shattering morning bodies; carved and feathered spears pressing on skin and plunging through; tomahawks crunching, adzes thudding. Kehua alone among heaped bodies, Kehua alone and about to wail, Kehua's skull opened by a greenstone club, cloven with one competent blow, her spirit streaming lilac towards the sea, and then arrested, grey-blue, rolling back to the scene of devastation slowly like a fog coming off the water.

Understand, it was not a state in which we were taking a moral position. On the contrary, we were part of all parts of this world. Let us say, so that I can make my point, that I experienced Kehua's death fifty times, although it could have been ten or a thousand. As part of that one action, I was a bystander thirty times. I was the victim ten times, and ten times I was the killer. We were in it, right inside it, ripping out our own eyeballs, cleaving our own skulls, shuddering with the static of dislocated emotion.

Sounds as well as sights came in these same erratic surges. They were mostly disconnected from events, audible strobes never perfectly synchronised. A plane took off. Mangroves thrummed like the automatic bass of a distant rock record. One tragic noise kept recurring, acute as a whale song: the sands of the spit were in convulsions, sliding and reheaping, exposing buried bones and making new ones, setting harmonics free to resonate in their sky-high storm. But mostly it was screams and battle cries and a roaring from below the earth as palpable shadows crammed tightly on to that one peninsula, and rushed and killed and died and made an airless, doorless stairwell which hauled us down and down and down into clattering chaos.

It was evening, as far as we could tell, when the din in our heads decayed and our corpuscles began to calm. It was as if we had all shared a single epileptic fit. The air was still opaque, but now the obscurity was due to dust and approaching night. The atmosphere was heavily coloured by the setting sun. Perhaps there had been a great fire or an earthquake but we could see too little to know.

We huddled together for comfort, all wondering whether the world we had eaten that afternoon was permanently with us, bumping against us, breathing our breath. It wasn't possible to turn that thought away.

I was starting to notice coldness in my limbs when a noise close by made me jump. Naturally; we were all very jumpy. I clutched Fern and a grunting animal came over the bank from the sea. When its head appeared, hair all askew with a lizard perched nervously amongst it, it was Doug's head. That was just one more miracle of that preposterous day. He hopped and crawled to my side.

'Whew, what a day!' he said. 'Here I am back from the dead.' He scratched his head and discovered the lizard, which must have dropped out of a bush. He was a still person as a rule, still enough for the lizard to remain on his head, reconnoitring. 'Where have I been? I don't know. I never meant to go after Kehua. It was none of my business what she did. But the Horses! I'm not used to them contradicting me. First Horse usually picks a sensible path. I don't know why she wanted to follow Kehua.'

'She wanted to be alone for once?' suggested Orlando.

'Anyway, first thing I knew I was under the water; I was made very tiny and wet and long, you see.'

'I don't see any such thing,' said Hattie; she had seen too much already that afternoon.

Doug was quiet. Then he said, 'All the same, I was made tiny and wet and long, like water. Then I was pouring through a tunnel made of scraped water; it was all very fast, much too fast. I said to myself, "Hang on! I'm a young man, I'm not ready for this." Everything slowed down slowly and reversed, and then I found my body had been forced under a bush at the bottom of the cliff, jammed behind that old whale fossil.'

'Old whale fossil!' said Hattie. 'It stands to reason, if it's a fossil, it's got to be old.'

'I don't know about that,' said Fern. 'It's all relative.'

'What have you done to your ankle?' I asked. It was all swollen. I tested it and he winced; there were no broken bones.

'Just wrecked it, that's all,' said Doug. 'But what a

racket! Didn't you hear a terrible racket? I must have passed out. And the nightmares I had!' On purpose, Doug was behaving like a normal person, and it was infectious, as he hoped.

The thing to do was to find shelter for the night. All of us were exhausted. Doug was in pain and unable to put weight on his left leg. Whale Peninsula had seemed only a little promontory by day, but now it was crowded with frightful memories, and the darkness was real; moreover, there was no Horse to carry the injured colossus. The journey down the neck of the peninsula was long and stumbling. On the beach at the base we rested, while Orlando went to check the tide.

Not only was the tide out but the channel had shrunk to nothing. It was virtually dry. This was odd, but convenient, for it meant we could take a very short cut across to the place with no name where there would surely be warmth and food. Truly, I don't think we'd have made it round the long way, not that night. So we stumbled and limped over sand and stones and shells to the road, taking it step by step as visibility was almost nil.

The road was a shambles of rocks, cracks, and bits of fallen pine. There were no lights anywhere. We knocked at five cottages before we reached the house that had been Kehua's. Nobody was home. The Ewers' car was not in the garage. We knocked and shouted, but there was no response. Fern found a broken window we helped her through and she opened the door. The lights weren't working. She lit some candles, knowing where to lay hands on them. She tried the phone but it was out of order.

By the light of the candles we could see that the house had shifted on its foundations. The ceiling was cracked and the back door wouldn't open. There was no cold water on tap; we used a minimum of hot water, as the tank would soon run dry without its electric pump. Fern knew how to create a bit of comfort. She lit the log stove in the basement room where by common consent we remained, and she put a kettle on to boil. There were mattresses piled in one corner which we spread around. Hattie was asleep before the kettle boiled, snuggled under a quilt. I put a firm bandage (made from a pillow case) on Doug's ankle, and Orlando made tea. Fern opened tins of asparagus and baked beans and heated them on the fire. She toasted some frozen bread slices, and even poured us all a small glass of brandy.

'It's an emergency,' she said convincingly. 'Even the Ewers have to do their bit for Civil Defence.'

We drank to our hosts in high good humour, and ate tinned peaches and ice cream for dessert. It was our second consecutive celebration dinner.

Doug went straight to sleep. Orlando and I washed the dishes. He and Fern lay down on separate mattresses, close enough to hold hands. I lay awake.

Perhaps the General was wrong. In the next few weeks my pregnancy would assert itself, or disintegrate into a phantom. It would be best to base a decision on the assumption that his information was correct.

That was logical, I thought. I was proud of bringing that much logic to bear on the subject, but that was the limit of my capacity for clear thinking. I sweated and threw off the blankets, in a panic over what he had done to me and at my own softheadedness. He had forced this new life not only on me but on the baby – not that it was a baby, it was a coagulation of cells, a gob of mucus. And how eagerly I had walked into his fortress, how like a groupie! It was all my fault, it was all his fault — well, it didn't matter whose, because there in the faultline lodged the butting, eager seed of a new person and what would I do, what would I do, what would I do?

Every way was barred by logic. Return to New RUSA and present the child of a monster to this (almost) impeccable family man, my ex-husband. Abort the foetus and live with guilt, loss, and grief – for already I found myself using phrases like 'my baby' and booting them out of my mind, because my baby did not exist. Give birth, offer the child for adoption to a queue of barren couples, not warning them of the villainous father. Keep the baby and raise it alone with the strong risk that it would arouse in me rage and disgust, misdirected from their legitimate target, and hover around that child in a surgical search for congenital wickedness. I had a strong respect for genetics, as clearly the General had too when he selected me cold-bloodedly for his mate.

As I tried to think my way through the barriers I kept crying, not for myself or my child (our child) but for the General. The General, my General! He was dead, and how could I be purely glad about that? The unfairness, the loneliness, the waste, the cavern in the world and in my life now that he was dead! If you wanted a person to lean on, they don't come any taller or stronger than the General; I had leaned on him, in spite of myself, and now I was very low.

sixteen

We were all sharply awake before dawn, and even in the first half-light we could see how dangerous it had been to spend a night in the house, let alone to use water and light the stove. The upstairs wooden deck was dangling from one corner. Hattie found a small transistor and we listened to a news bulletin.

'A search-and-rescue team is on its way to north-west Gorse Bay, following yesterday's earthquakes and landslide. The helicopter team hopes to rescue six people who are reported missing. Residents of a small settlement were safely evacuated before roads were damaged. One of the missing persons is understood to be a distinguished RUSAn visitor, General Alexander Merit, who was trapped at his holiday home when it was destroyed. All the General's staff and house guests escaped before the worst of the earthquakes, except for Mrs Dorothy Menzies whose husband Charles Menzies, is attached to the Sleeping Islands Embassy in Washington . . . '

The sun was rising, and we abandoned the idea of breakfast to move outside, which seemed altogether the safest thing to do. It was one of those mornings made of apricot ice cream and blue-black ink, and lightly glazed with milk. None of us had seen this place in the light, from this angle, except Fern. We were trying, confusedly, to get our bearings when she said, 'It's gone! It's just not there any more! She did let go, she certainly did let go! The Old Woman Bluff, it was over there, see? That huge hill: it's disappeared, just disappeared!' She tried to explain, she drew diagrams in the air to show where the grey-green bluff had stood, repository for all shadows in the area. 'It's completely disappeared!' she kept saying.

That wasn't strictly accurate. It still was somewhere, but in a different form. It must have collapsed mostly to the seaward side, sliding back in to the very nest it had hatched from so many million years ago. There were great boulders tumbled all over the estuary and heaped up on the far side. And strangest of all changes, we could now see directly across the water into the ocean: the estuary had acquired a second exit and entry channel. In fact, since the causeway had also collapsed, it was no longer a mere lungful of sea puffing into the land, but part of the uninterrupted ocean joining Gorse Bay to the Tasman Sea.

The kanuka hill, the spit and Whale Peninsula now formed an island. In consequence of the upheaval it was no longer possible to walk back to Fish Beach the way we had come.

Fern was fascinated by the breach in the hills: she couldn't stop looking, and making half-finished squawks of amazement. Trying to get a closer look, we crossed the road and went through gorse to the mangroves, and climbed a tall rock. Fern said, 'The Bluff was the positive version, and now we can see the negative.' Land and sea were like a jigsaw puzzle, except that one piece (the sea) had no ending. Though not large, mangroves were well established around the far side of the estuary. They would affect the new environment and be affected by it. They marked an edge, or limit. Orlando thought the Ewers' house might well fall into the sea in a month or a year, but then again, it might not.

Now it was fully light and the clouds were clearing off. We heard helicopters. We saw one flying towards Fish Beach, if Fish Beach still existed; it dropped out of sight behind the low hills. Hattie was agitated about her house, her orchard, her hungry animals. A second helicopter was coming our way.

It landed cautiously. First out was a news team from the Sleeping Islands Broadcasting Corporation with video gear and tape recorders. And floating down behind them, the unmistakable one-off figure of our Prime Minister. For the news team, discovering us (as if we too were a new topographical feature) was at first their coup of the week and rapidly became the coup of their careers. For me, it was the opportunity I ought to have been strenuously seeking since the moment I escaped from the fort; I should have crawled all night over broken bottles to see this man, instead of neurotically dithering over a hypothetical embryo. Here he was, warm hands out to welcome ours, the famous brain doing press-ups behind that elastic face.

I had to tell him about the General: the ice-cold fact inflated with one whoosh to its real size, as big as the world. My great fear was that General Merit had lied about his absolute and exclusive responsibility, and that if he failed to arrive in RUSA another general would slide smoothly into his seat and start the war without him. Where to begin? Not with Kehua or the breast that melted glass. I spoke only to the Prime Minister, a man whose goodness had not yet been much bruised in office. I spoke into him. I watched him hearing, matching my lurid story to the bland and balmy version he must have heard from Jules Menzies, evaluating me as a witness, fitting my information into his knowledge of the current state of world affairs and making a crisp, self-sufficient decision.

As the only evidence which could be easily verified, I referred to the packet I had sent to the Sleeping Islands Art Gallery, and I blessed the second-rate camera which had caused me to photograph the General's works of art not only in their indoor settings but also in full sunlight.

232

I knew I'd included many details of the buildings and its surroundings. I'd placed Hine outside the front door and snapped her from many angles and from a variety of distances. I hoped that the photos would show the scale of the General's establishment, some of the hardware, and unmistakably the location.

For the Prime Minister this was a bagatelle, but the reporter reacted strongly. Africa was a long way away. But somewhere in that heap of rocks, right there, were 'priceless art treasures', smashed and abandoned, and worst of all, squandered. Monet and Renoir aroused their passion. They didn't begin to grasp the significance of Hine-Mother-of-us-all, so I told them how many million dollars she was worth to the General now that the early artefacts of the First People were in fashion. When I saw how my catalogue gave me credibility with the media, I felt quite positive about the loss of the paintings; perhaps that was what they were for.

The Prime Minister shook my hand again and thanked me with a disciplined passion that seemed to hold me upright at the moment I found that I did require support. He confirmed the death of the General. He said that a peace group had been aware of Merit's presence in the country, and that he had shared their intuitive anxiety. The helicopter left at once for Middlecity, leaving the air wriggling with the man's vitality.

As I had been speaking in front of the cameras an awareness had come to me, quite incidentally: I had turned my back on Charles, not unkindly but inevitably. The cost of loyalty would have been infinite. I took it for granted that my straightforward delivery of the facts was appropriate. Our Prime Minister was only concerned with the substance, but I knew Charles would be saddened by my style. Where were my reservations, my nods to the opposition, the courtesy of guest to host? He would see this public interview as an exaggerated form of my party behaviour, without even the excuse of a few cocktails. Oh, certainly he would consider it his duty to accept me back and make apologies on my behalf. But quite unexpectedly I knew I'd rather not. I wished him well, but I'd rather not.

The reporters had radioed the search-and-rescue helicopter which arrived shortly. There was so much more fuss and talk talk talk that eventually I felt like screaming. But we were carried to Fish Beach at last and I lay down on one of Hattie's beds while the others rushed about.

After a couple of hours Fern came into the darkened room with a cup of tea. 'It's all been a bit much, hasn't it?' she said. I simply overflowed on to her shoulder. I guess she thought it was all over, but for me it was beginning again. When I tried to tell her, I choked, I couldn't say the words. Thank goodness at last she guessed. 'Are you pregnant, Dot?'

'I'm pregnant! The General made me pregnant deliberately, he did it on purpose!'

She tipped out the cold tea and made some fresh. I sipped it, and she helped me say everything. All the terrible options, the ifs and buts, the jagged maze I was hobbling around in. At last Fern said, 'It doesn't seem like a problem that can be solved in one sitting.'

'But I've got to, I've got to! I can't bear it any more, not a minute more, I can't bear it!'

'You've got at least four weeks' grace, as I see it. And if we keep on talking it over, you'll certainly know what you want by then.' I couldn't believe it. 'You'll have to believe it, Dot, or you could make a bad mistake.'

That night the problem was still intractable but a little bit tamer. And over the next two weeks we all discussed it over and over again. It was still my problem but it was also, marvellously, ours.

For instance, Hattie picked up the carving knife and snarled through her teeth, 'I'd like to kill that man!' I laughed, the first time for a fortnight. But I had to admit it was easily half my fault. And who did I want to annihilate, after all?

Orlando said, 'Remember, this bundle of cells is tiny, tiny, compared with the lives you have saved.' (I know, I thought; but it's me.)

'You feel guilty at the idea of having an abortion,' said Fern. She was right, and yet I couldn't imagine where this guilt had come from, just when I needed it least. I had supported two of my friends through the process and the issue of guilt had not touched me. I held those friends firmly in my mind and their good, sensible choices. 'What do you fear the most? Be as unreasonable as you like,' said Fern.

I knew at once. I feared a child who would murder the world because it was his destiny, a destiny conferred by me.

Hattie fell about laughing. 'Pox upon box, fox on my cocks! What a silly creature you are!' She could hardly talk for laughing. I felt pretty insulted, and gave her arm a good shake. 'You think you can map out its life! You're no better than the General. Every baby's different, you never know what's going to pop out of you next! I've had lazy ones and busy ones, brainy ones and dumb ones. I've had a professor and a city councillor, pretty ones and ugly ones, miners and fishermen and waitresses. I've had them honest and I've had crooks, I've had Lily who's lost three children and a husband and she's still smiling. I've had Fred who had a nervous breakdown because he got a cold sore. I've had Danny who steals by computer and Benny who's given away a fortune. There's some I wouldn't trust with a Girl Guide biscuit, I've had a hermit and I've had a nun, and I'll tell you one thing, I never had one that was

235

perfect.' She lay back in her chair wiping her eyes, over-come by another paroxysm of laughter.

I deserved that, for I knew I wasn't being rational. I had only to look at Doug to know that a small man can father a great son, and an innocent child be born from a spooky, ego-ridden conception.

'That's the worst of it in a way. I'm just a vehicle. Something's taken me over. Not the General, this little lump of dots dividing and dividing inside me. I've been colonised.'

'No no no no,' said Hattie, 'It's just another person. People are mostly all right. You just have to make enough room for them. There's usually enough room.' The skin of Hattie's belly had stretched to make room for a thirtieth child, and other children had moved over in beds, while Hattie stayed mysteriously intact around all those hitch-hikers. I felt a twinge of hope; having a baby was a big deal, but not too big, maybe.

Another day, Orlando was sorting out his thoughts aloud with me as an audience. 'You said you wanted the General because of his evil . . . Now wickedness is made by people, at a certain time and place, for a certain time and place. It's not like a weed; it needs cultivating.'

'Are you sure?' I asked.

'No, I'm just thinking he wasn't born wicked. He made himself wicked with the encouragement of millions of people. He was wicked for them, on their behalf. That's why you wanted him: you helped to make him.'

'I think I did,' I said, remembering all those cocktail parties.

'So he is part of you. The baby – '

' – foetus – '

' – sorry, foetus, is part of you as well.'

He stopped to think; I tested the idea. 'If this is true, it would be better for you to digest the General than to

236

purge him. If you have digested him you can't be damaged, whether you have an abortion or whether you have a baby. But feeling as you do now, I think you'd be unhappy either way.'

A little bit touchy, I said, 'How do you know about such things?'

He didn't know at all; he was just trying out a thought. For whatever reason, after that thought I felt better. The growing child had been a stick-figure implanted by the General: all angular and two-dimensional, like dots on a computer screen, or something made of steel cross-stitch. Now I could distinguish bubbles frothing inside my womb, roundness pearling damply over roundness.

After a few more days, in fact, I realised that somewhere deep below the levels of common sense I was expecting to keep this baby, and to live at Fish Beach. Nervously I expressed this seditious hunch. Everyone seemed privately satisfied. Doug squeezed my hand and limped outside. Hattie burrowed through her drawers and pulled out a most astonishing variety of baby garments and maternity clothes. Fern stressed solemnly that I didn't have to stand by this decision absolutely. Orlando paced and looked out the window, trying to be non-committal. But they couldn't fool me: I knew they were pleased. That helped to make the decision real, and final.

While I was brooding (so to speak) over my pregnancy, the others were busy. Thank goodness, Hattie's house had suffered little damage. Boulders had rained on Fish Beach and Teatown. One piece of stone as big as her rhododendron bush had come to rest by Hattie's cottage, smashing only eight chrysanthemums, one window and a climbing rose. Orlando's yard was full of smaller debris, bullets of rock and clay; his fence was a crazy tangle of splinters and wire but his hut was only dented. Not all the residents were so lucky; several of the lower houses were flooded.

The fall of the bluff had sent the sea lurching up and over the road. It looked as if the water had blown and sucked itself higher and lower than it had for many years. After all, when a hill falls over, even an ocean takes a while to readjust. Huge tides were the means it used, and they helped disperse the rubble. Doug's hut was far too near the creek to survive an assault like this; it was wrecked in a way that he luckily regarded as comic. Fern was almost pleased, though it meant that four of us had to live in Hattie's house. She had grown dissatisfied with Doug's hut, you see, and when there was time she helped him build a new one.

The sight of flooded paddocks and damaged roads was only too familiar to Orlando. Fences were strung with branches and seaweed, washed over by the sea, and most had been bent or pushed over. Debris large and small littered the sand. Almost every sand form had changed shape, and the beach seemed to be developing an entirely new curve to the north. Great lumps of rock had created a reef and even a couple of islands.

Orlando was ecstatic. Without that year of beach building, the sand would have vanished utterly, given such a shaking and a scouring. Instead, the beach (though vastly rearranged) had held its own; the new islands would help protect it in the future. He expanded and burst into crazy dances over the sand.

That didn't mean there was no work to do. Damage had to be repaired before autumn set in, and he and Fern were out there every day. Doug helped when he wasn't fishing or doing farm work. He missed his Horses, but after the first few weeks that didn't make him sad. As he said, they had earned their death. Work on the beach was harder without them, and sometimes we used a tractor. When local people compared their beach with the havoc up and down the coast, they were grateful.

There were many repercussions from the collapse of the Old Woman Bluff. Within a few days a boat arrived with the Director of the Sleeping Islands Art Gallery and her helpers. She had been bowled over by my original letter, and then hamstrung when I urged her not to reply: it was very uncomfortable for her. Now she blamed herself for the world's bereavement. She and her staff combed through the rubble, the new lowlands, searching for any least scrap of the lost works of art. As we helped them look, we became familiar with the new terrain whose raw, bald outline we began to understand. It wasn't easy walking on this long low hill, all boulders and bits of torn Spiky bush and clutter of concrete and steel and wood. Around the new channel mangroves were building scar tissue.

All that was found was the head of the spear (broken), and bits of framing. They sighed and sighed and had to go away with an empty boat.

Once the roads were open, sightseers and scavengers came by the carload. We had first pick of the flotsam and jetsam. Lots of it could have been useful for rebuilding the beach, if only strangers would leave it alone. We began accumulating building materials: beams of wood, and amazingly, sections of glass. It was a new glass, a type of plastic really, designed in RUSA expressly for bomb shelters. Ironically, it hadn't survived unbroken; but when it split, it split into neat modules. Sizable chunks had floated here, only slightly roughened by their journey.

Doug and Fern started a new hut behind the orchard on high ground. It's still not finished, although Doug took up residence there before my baby was born. Fern was inspired, she said, by the fall of the bluff. It's tall, this hut, of course: it rears up quite abruptly. It isn't dark like the willow hut, but alive with light coming through these slightly curved strips of heavy, transparent plastic. Irrational in design, seeming to follow the lead of afterthoughts, it is nevertheless calming to look at and to visit, which I often do. Fern is using willow work to line the hut so that eventually, inside, wherever there isn't a window or a door there'll be a section of basketry.

Her building work is only intermittent, as she and Orlando are frequently called away as consultants while the Department of Philosophy dismantles and rearranges itself, dropping old limbs and growing new ones. Jules Menzies has long ago gone to New RUSA, his true home, resigning from that high position about which Cabinet was already having second thoughts. Invited by the Prime Minister to express their views, Fern and Orlando advised him to allow the Department to break into units of those people with a commitment to any single project that they could justify in terms of the nation's development. It was rather a large idea; you could sum it up roughly as: 'If people strongly believe that an activity is worthwhile, and you see no harm in it, let them do it, in their own way.'

After years of having their ideas homogenised and neutralised, years of peripheral involvement with important activities, the civil servants were not short of dream projects and hobby-horses. Some resigned when challenged to put them into practice, but many are thriving, and learning, and doing valuable things, some of them practical and some highly esoteric. It takes time. Like pieces of wood on the beach, they are finding their own place, their own pivot, their own associates and their own function.

Remembering she had a house, Fern sold it to the tenants; all of us have eaten better since she got rid of it. She's invited Hilary and Jessie to come and visit Fish Beach, and she sent the Ewers a cheque.

seventeen

When I was about three months pregnant,
Fern said, 'This house is too crowded. I think I'll go and
stay with Orlando, if he'll have me.' I looked at her closely
and she went pink – not easy through a suntan. She put
on her turquoise hat, took one of the small mattresses and
knocked on Orlando's door.

'Well now,' he said. 'This is nice. Do come in.' She
squeezed past him. 'So let's have a look at this breast, shall
we?' he said like a doctor, and took off her dress. There
it was, glimmering today in tender green and orange
stripes. 'So it bothers you, does it, Mrs Willnott? I can see
it's a trifle larger than the other, so it must always be one
step ahead of you. Has it ever led you anywhere you didn't
want to go?'

'Not exactly. It tends to take me places where I didn't
plan to go. But I'm usually glad when I get there.'

'I must say I've followed my cock into many strange
women. Nevertheless, we belong together. Isn't that true
of you and your breast?'

She hesitated. 'No. It tricks me.'

'Perhaps it finds you just too slow. I'm inclined to think
this breast is simply wide awake and the rest of you half
asleep.'

Fern did feel sluggish as well as out of whack. 'Couldn't
I be right and you be wrong, for once?' she said.

Orlando said, 'If I'm right, the cure would be to wake
up the rest of you. Oh look, it's like a pumpkin. Are you
saving it for harvest festival?' He also had a courgette

fattening. Her special breast had a nipple today like a purple convolvulus after its flower collapses and the blue leaches away, leaving only a pale pink mouth that perfectly gathered the fullness of her breat into itself.

'If I were an agoraphobic bee,' said Orlando, 'I would try it this way.' And he was a bee, a white bee small as an ant, drilling into her breast with his tiny wings. He buzzed every scrap of her body, inside every finger and toenail and tooth. He circled and corkscrewed into the tips of her ears, her tongue, her tonsils, her eye, liver and heart. And as the bee went by, her cells woke up and waved and tickled his feet, and fainted. When he came out, he was burly Orlando again. He was breathless, because it's heavy work, rowing through chocolate with only a set of see-through wings for oars. He rolled over her then like an incoming tide, sunlight boiling in the ripples, and entered. Their coupling was nothing grand or fancy, speaking technically; for Fern, a swift and far and reckless ride over a rocking sea, reaching a place of comfort where her very hair lifted of its own accord like a soft hibiscus flapping its petals, not to fly away but to settle once and for all, not in a place but a person.

'I think that's done the trick, don't you?' said Orlando.

She was awake all over now, and what she had found in his body was a home.

By morning the colours of her breast had thinned, because Orlando the bee had churned them up and spread them through her body. Indeed, today in certain lights, if you squint and look sideways, you can sometimes see a multicoloured prickle of light on her arm or cheek or foot. But she told Orlando her breast felt strange with a different sort of strangeness, full and freckly. After a week the cause became apparent. Out of her nipple sprang a tiny fern, hardly visible, as delicate and deliberate as cobweb, of a luminous and mobile green. She shows it often to the sun, or else it fades to orange-white. This time she's not complaining. If Orlando tried to equalise her body once again, who knows what the consequences would be? When she is buried will be time enough to be feeding a community of ferns. Meanwhile, the fern is a sign that her days of burning and stunning are over. This is a different phase.

Fern is quite unreasonably happy. After all, it was quite by chance Orlando chose her as an experiment, to see if he could cure a habit. He deprives her of the only reward she ever had in marriage, that of anticipating a man's needs, for he never is grateful for that. He expects to make his own coffee and to do his own washing. If he is bored or angry he doesn't want to be stimulated or soothed; he wants to go on feeling bored or angry till he's finished and the mood dissipates of its own accord, bringing insights along the way. It wasn't long before she found a way of living with Orlando: it's just like living with a friend. And when he touches her, old gorse splinters squeeze out of her skin, and her skin is smiling.

After a series of explosions in my own body a baby was born. I named her Pax and we call her Pax or Paxie or Pixie or Piccolo or Popcorn or Paximonious, depending on the weather. As it turns out, even a fully objective, certified baby-examiner would be bound to declare her outstanding in terms of quaintness, charm, intelligence, creativity, wisdom, innocence and altruism. I know she's only six months old as yet, but already her total lack of wickedness is plain. Sometimes I am hostile to her, not because the devil is in her but because she drops her rattle from the high chair for the nineteenth time and expects me to pick it up. Whereupon four assertive people materialise, all competing for the privilege of protecting her from a cruel mother. We both make the most of that. When she was first born, I kept looking at Paxie and thinking, this is not justice. Hine should have punished me by sending me a child with goat's eyes or rat's feet; that's how much I blamed myself. Thank heaven the blame did not translate to Pax; but then, I'm obliged to love her or lose her, with that posse of vigilantes ready to tear her away if I don't.

I used to think of Doug as 'Little Brother', but he has eagerly assumed a father's role. He'd been so emphatic at sixteen that he'd live with men, or else (punishing himself in place of his father) in chastity. Now he's calling this year the year Dot, and says he's dotty over me and Pax. Neither false father nor sperm father, he is a father in the sense that Hine and Hattie are mothers. He carries the baby round in a sort of back pack, so Hattie calls us Dot and Carry One. And since we've started having night-time rendezvous he says he's always on the Dot. I'm not obsessed with Doug the way I was with the General; I like him more, and we have a lot more fun. I've seen how vain it is to look in every bird's nest for the perfect person, and I'm getting along where I am, with the people who happen to be here. There are other worlds, but this is the one I'm living in and I'm fond of it, especially on days like today when waves are knitting sunshine, and the General's dead, and Doug is looking forward to a ride. One thing I do insist on is that that blessed lizard is nowhere on his person when I come to the hut. I inspect his hair and shake his clothes and shoes outside the door, and I look in his mouth as well.

It's autumn again. Last week we had a tempest. In storms, if the moon is full, we still get debris from the Old Woman Bluff that was, although the majority goes north and east with the major current. The strangest thing rolled up on the beach last week. It was a massive lump of those old bushes we call the Benevolent Spikies. They don't grow round here of their own accord, and these had

244

been dead a long time, locked in an impenetrable bundle. We were all inspecting the beach at the time, and all of us felt, well, queer. An excitement emanated from that tumour of thorns.

Hattie stated categorically, 'That's the General!' and Doug agreed: she'd taken the words right out of his mouth.

'But no!' cried Fern. 'It's Hine-mother-of-us-all! I know it is!' and Orlando was talking too, trying to say the same thing.

As for me and Paxie, we would have recognised them both, at any time. 'They're both in there,' I said. Certainly there was room for two. 'She must have rolled out the door and straight into the General's bushes.'

Orlando went to get the tractor while we argued where to put the thing. Fern was renting the four-roomed cottage next to Hattie's and that's where she and Orlando were living. She thought that Hine should go on their front lawn; if the General had to come too, so be it. But Hattie wanted the great wooden knot in her orchard, saying the General should be near his daughter. Doug thought it was a national monument and should be on public land, but Fern said the locals wouldn't understand. I think I just wanted to be rid of it. By the time Orlando came back with tractor and ropes, we were all in a snarl.

'You're just being selfish!'

'No one appreciates the significance!'

'It's a horrible-looking thing anyway!'

'Well be like that, see if I care.'

'It's not the blinking General, it's Hine!'

'I remember that seed-pod, that's the very seed-pod!'

'It should be sent to Middlecity and the Museum.'

'Art Gallery!'

'Museum!'

'I saw it first. Finders keepers!'

'Put it outside the hall then.'
'Outside? It'll get ruined outside.'
'It should be buried in the cemetery.'
'In the rubbish tip.'
'It's worth a fortune.'
'I know her like my own mother.'
'It's a work of art. Creative basket work.'
'A wooden horse, you mean.'
'She's everybody's mother, not just yours.'
'Don't talk to me about mothers!'

When Orlando arrived at this interesting scene, he looped ropes around the bundle and tied it to the back of the tractor. It would drag along the ground, being far too large and heavy to fit on a trailer. He decided undemocratically that this bristling cocoon should be taken a long way away from Fish Beach, and we were too ashamed even to ask him where he was going.

He drove the tractor and its burden to the low rocky hill that had been, for a while, the Old Woman Bluff. At the crest of a spur he cut the ropes, which were hopelessly tangled in thorns by then, and gave the dead thicket a push with the tractor. Its own weight took it over a bank where it came to rest, having stubbed its toe on a small boulder. Orlando inspected the site; the Benevolent Spikies had stopped in front of a cleft below the bank, almost a rough and ready cave. Orlando brought the tractor cautiously down the hill and nudged the accretion of wood and stone and bone gently backwards, until it was firmly jammed at the back of the niche.

So there they stay, those two, Hine and the General, sheltered from some of the weather, locked in dialogue or silence.We celebrated their uncomfortable union that night at our Saturday dance in the hall, and Hattie wants us to declare the day a Fish Beach Annual Day of – something, she's not sure what, so far: Remembrance,

Coronation, or Fertility. If Hine wasn't in that bundle, I would probably have taken an axe to the General by now and done myself an injury, for those thorns retain their venom even when they're dead and dry. They protect him from me, and me from me. You see, the others are all contented, even serene in their way. I'm the only one who felt I had to choose an enemy. My declarations of war are mostly Dot to Dot, and they reverberate inside me. I hate hating myself, and I want to stop soon.

Digest him, Orlando said. Hattie's got an old Book of Common Prayer, and it's my intention to read the burial service over the General. I happen to know that he was a practising Christian, I mean Episcopalian. It's not just that I feel an obligation, although that does run deep. It's also because I want him pacified, despatched, just in case Hine can't keep him in order. I don't want him walking the earth, as Kehua had to. It's not going to be easy, saying all those words. Certainly I can give hearty thanks that it has pleased God to deliver this our brother out of the miseries of this sinful world, and willingly I shall commit the General's body to the ground in sure and certain hope of the resurrection to eternal life. If that's what he wants, he's welcome; you probably get what you expect after death, because you expect what you can cope with. And if I launch him on the way to his sort of heaven, perhaps I'll also free myself. But I'm supposed to beseech the Anglican God (who I hope is on good terms with the Episcopalian one) shortly to accomplish the number of His elect and to hasten His kingdom, and I think I might skip that bit, because it seems suspiciously like giving the General the last word.

It would be a terrible waste if Hine were also accidentally quietened. I think that would take a lot more than the overflow from someone else's burial service. Well, she's waiting there, a stone nut inside her wooden kernel. She'll come out when she pleases. Maybe a long long time after all her children have left home: maybe tomorrow.